We heard a chilling hiss and turned to find something big scuttling along the rocky path behind us. It was a feral lamia. The creature, at least one and a half times the length of my own body, was crouched on four thin limbs with large splayed hands, each elongated finger ending in a sharp, deadly talon. Long, greasy hair hung down onto the scaled back and across the face, too. What I could see of its features told me that the situation couldn't be worse. This was not the bloated face of a lamia witch that had recently fed, making it sluggish and less aggressive. No, it was gaunt, cadaverous, its heavily lidded eyes wide open and showing a ravenous hunger.

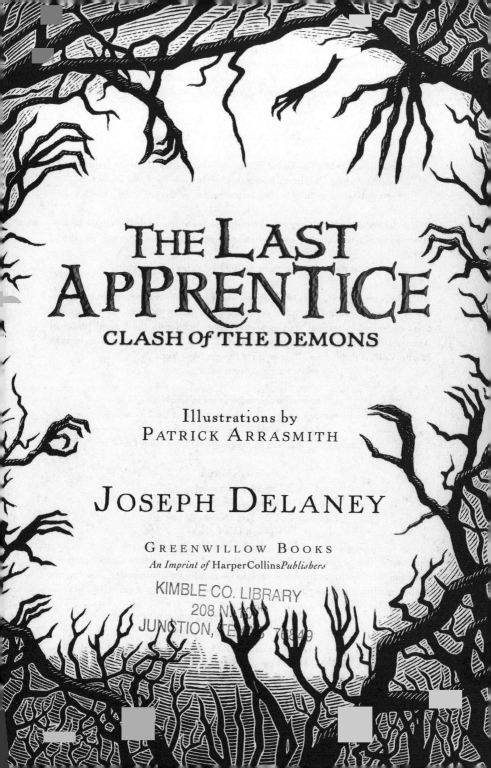

THE LAST APPRENTICE

CLASH of THE DEMONS

Illustrations by
PATRICK ARRASMITH

JOSEPH DELANEY

GREENWILLOW BOOKS
An Imprint of HarperCollins*Publishers*

The Last Apprentice: Clash of the Demons
Copyright © 2009 by Joseph Delaney

First published in 2009 in Great Britain by The Bodley Head, an imprint of Random House Children's Books, under the title *The Spook's Sacrifice*. First published in 2009 in the United States by Greenwillow Books.

The right of Joseph Delaney to be identified as the author of this work has been asserted by him in accordance with the Copyright, Designs and Patents Act, 1988.

Illustrations copyright © 2009 by Patrick Arrasmith

The text of this book is set in Cochin.
Book design by Chad W. Beckerman and Paul Zakris.

Library of Congress Cataloging-in-Publication Data

Delaney, Joseph.
[Spook's sacrifice]
Clash of the demons / by Joseph Delaney.
p. cm. — (The last apprentice ; bk. 6)
"Greenwillow Books."
Originally published under title: The Spook's sacrifice.
Summary: Tom is reunited with his mother and must return to Greece to face a new and terrible threat from the dark forces, and a momentous decision must be made, causing a serious rift between Tom and the Spook that threatens to separate them forever.
ISBN 978-0-06-134462-6 (trade bdg.) — ISBN 978-0-06-134463-3 (lib. bdg.)
ISBN 978-0-06-134464-0 (pbk.)
[1. Apprentices—Fiction. 2. Supernatural—Fiction. 3. Greece—Fiction.] I. Title.
PZ7.D373183Cl 2009   [Fic]—dc22   2009006188

10 11 12 13 14 LP/RRDH 10 9 8 7 6 5 4 3 2 1

First Greenwillow paperback edition, 2010.

FOR MARIE

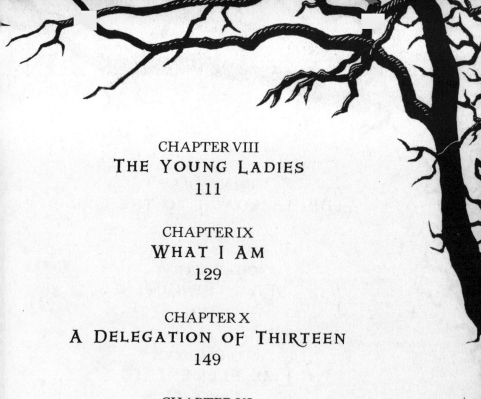

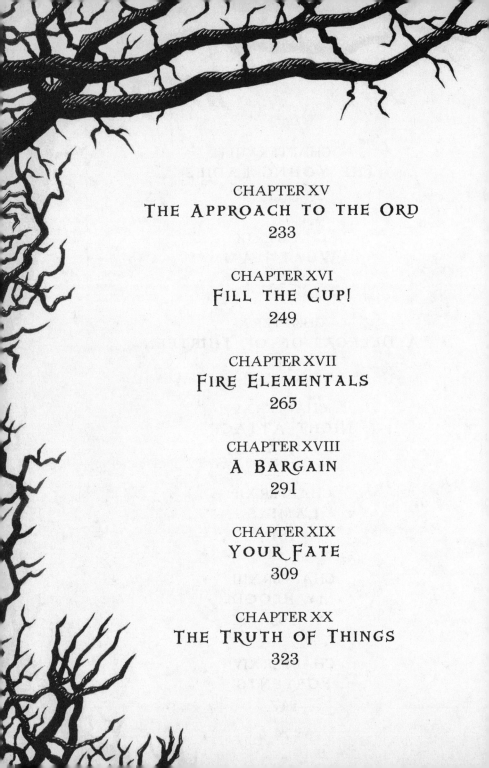

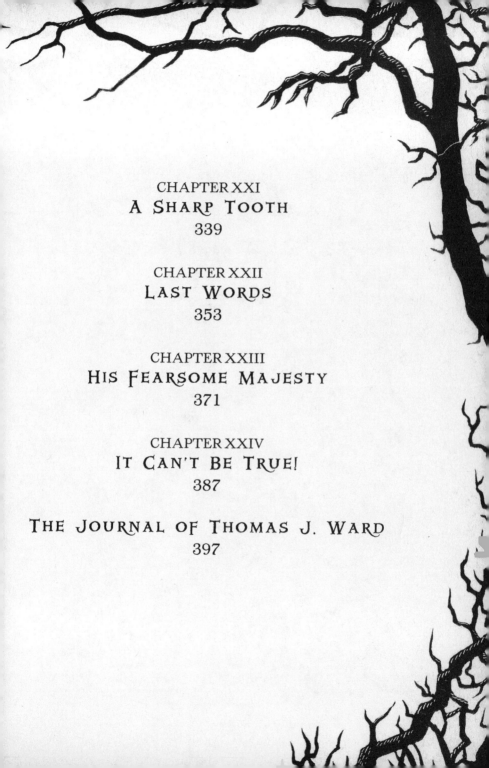

CLASH Of THE DEMONS

CHAPTER I
THE MAENAD ASSASSIN

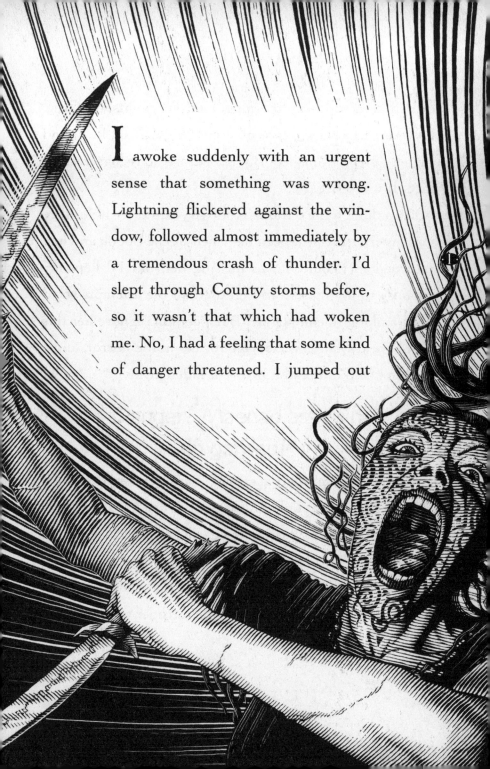

I awoke suddenly with an urgent sense that something was wrong. Lightning flickered against the window, followed almost immediately by a tremendous crash of thunder. I'd slept through County storms before, so it wasn't that which had woken me. No, I had a feeling that some kind of danger threatened. I jumped out of bed, and suddenly the mirror on my nightstand grew brighter. I had a glimpse of someone reflected in it, and then it quickly vanished. But not before I'd recognized the face. It was Alice.

Even though she'd trained for two years as a witch, Alice was my friend. She'd been banished by the Spook and had returned to Pendle. I was missing her, but I'd kept my promise to my master and ignored all the attempts she'd been making to contact me. But I couldn't ignore her this time. She'd written a message for me in the mirror, and I couldn't help but read it before it faded away.

Danger! Maenad assassin in garden!

What was a maenad assassin? I'd never heard of such a thing. And how could an assassin of *any* kind reach me when it had to cross the Spook's garden—a garden guarded by his powerful boggart? If anyone breached the boundary, that boggart would let out a roar that could be heard for miles and then it would tear the intruder to pieces.

And how could Alice know about the danger anyway? She was miles away, in Pendle. Still, I wasn't about to ignore her warning. My master, John Gregory, had gone off to deal with a troublesome ghost, and I was alone in the house. I had nothing with me that I could use in self-defense. My staff and bag were down in the kitchen, so I had to get them.

Don't panic, I told myself. *Take your time and stay calm.*

I dressed quickly and pulled on my boots. As thunder boomed overhead once more, I eased open my bedroom door and stepped out cautiously onto the dark landing. There I paused and listened. All was silent. I felt sure that nobody had entered the house yet, so I began to tiptoe down the stairs as quietly as I could. I crept through the hallway and into the kitchen.

I put my silver chain in my breeches pocket and, taking up my staff, opened the back door and stepped out. Where was the boggart? Why wasn't it defending the house and garden against the intruder? Rain was driving into my face as I waited, carefully searching the lawn and trees beyond for any sign of movement. I allowed my eyes to adjust to the dark, but I could see very little. Even so, I headed for the trees in the western garden.

I'd taken no more than a dozen paces when there was a blood-curdling yell from my left and I heard the pounding of feet. Someone was running across the lawn, directly toward me. I readied my staff, pressing the recess so that, with a click, the retractable blade sprang from the end.

Lightning flashed again, and I saw what threatened. It was a tall, thin woman brandishing a long, murderous blade in her left hand. Her hair was tied back, her gaunt face twisted in hatred and painted with some dark pigment. She wore a long dress, which was soaked with rain, and rather than shoes, her feet were bound with strips of leather. So this is a maenad, I thought to myself.

I took up a defensive position, holding my staff diagonally, the way I'd been taught. My heart was beating fast, but I had to stay calm and take the first opportunity to strike.

Her blade suddenly arced downward, missing my right shoulder by inches, and I whirled away, trying to keep some distance between myself and my opponent. I needed room in order to swing my staff. The grass was saturated with rain, and as the maenad came at me again, I slipped and lost my balance. I almost toppled over backward but managed to drop down onto one knee. Just in time I brought up my staff to block a thrust that would have pene-trated deep into my shoulder. I struck again, hitting the maenad's wrist hard, and the knife went spinning to the ground. Lightning flashed overhead, and I saw the fury in her face as, weaponless, she attacked again. She was shouting at me now, mad with rage—the harsh guttural sounds contained the odd word that I recognized as Greek. This time I stepped to one side, avoided her outstretched hands with their long, sharp nails, and gave her a tremendous thwack to the side of her head. She went down on her knees, and I could have easily driven the point of my blade through her chest.

Instead I transferred my staff to my right hand, reached into my pocket, and coiled the silver chain around my left wrist. A silver chain is useful against any servant of the dark—but would it bind a maenad assassin? I asked myself.

I concentrated hard, and the moment she came to her feet, she was illuminated by a particularly vivid flash of lightning. Couldn't have been better! I had a perfect view of my target and released the chain with a *crack*! It soared upward to form a perfect spiral, then dropped around her body, bringing her down on the grass.

I circled her warily. The chain bound her arms and legs and had tightened around her jaw, but she was still able to speak and hurled a torrent of words at me, not one of which I understood. Was it Greek? I thought so—but it was a strange dialect.

It seemed the chain had worked, though, so wasting no time, I seized her by her left foot and began to drag her across the wet grass toward the house. The Spook would want to question her—if he could understand what she was saying. My Greek was at least as good as his, and she made little sense to me.

Against one side of the house was a wooden lean-to

where we kept logs for the fire, so I dragged her in there out of the rain. Next I took a lantern down from the shelf in the corner and lit it so that I could get a better look at my captive. As I held it above her head, she spat at me, the pink viscous glob landing on my breeches. I could smell her now—a mixture of stale sweat and wine. And there was something else, too. A faint stench of rotting meat. When she opened her mouth again, I could see what looked like pieces of flesh between her teeth.

Her lips were purple, as was her tongue—signs that she'd been drinking red wine. Her face was streaked with an intricate pattern of whorls and spirals. It looked like reddish mud, but the rain hadn't managed to wash it off. She spat at me again, so I stepped back and hung the lantern on one of the ceiling hooks.

There was a stool in the corner, which I placed against the wall, sitting well out of spitting range. It was at least another hour until dawn, so I leaned back and closed my eyes, listening to the rain drumming on the roof of the lean-to. I was tired and could afford to doze. The silver chain had bound the maenad tightly, and she'd no hope of setting herself free.

I couldn't have been asleep for more than a few minutes when a loud noise woke me. I sat up with a jerk. There was a roaring, rushing, whooshing sound, which was getting nearer by the second. Something was coming toward the lean-to, and I suddenly realized what it was.

The boggart! It was rushing to attack!

I hardly had time to get to my feet before the lantern went out and I was blown onto my back, the impact driving the breath from my body. While I gasped for air, I could hear logs being hurled against the wall, but the loudest sound of all was that of the maenad screaming. The noise went on in the darkness for a long time; then, but for the pattering of heavy rain, there was silence. The boggart had done its work and gone.

I was afraid to light the lantern again. Afraid to look at the maenad. But I did it anyway. She was quite dead and very pale, drained of blood by the boggart. There were lacerations to her throat and shoulders; her dress was in tatters. On her face was a look of terror. There was nothing to be done. What had happened was unprecedented. Once she was my bound captive, the boggart shouldn't have so much as touched her. And where had it been when it should have been defending the garden?

Shaken by the experience, I left the maenad's body where it was and went back into the house. I thought about trying to contact Alice with the mirror. I owed her my life, and I wanted to thank her. I almost weakened, but I'd made a promise to the Spook. So, after struggling with my conscience for a while, I simply had a wash, changed my clothes, and waited for the Spook to return.

He came back just before noon. I explained what had happened, and we went out to look at the dead assassin.

"Well, lad, this raises a fair few questions, doesn't it?" my master said, scratching at his beard. He looked seriously worried and I couldn't blame him. What had happened made me feel very uneasy, too.

"I've always felt confident that my house here at

Chipenden was safe and secure," he continued, "but this makes you think. Puts doubts in your mind. I'll sleep less easily in my bed from now on. Just how did this maenad manage to get across the garden undetected by the boggart? Nothing's ever gotten past it before."

I nodded in agreement.

"And there's another worrying thing, lad. Why did it attack and kill her later, when you had her bound with your chain? It knows not to behave like that."

Again I nodded.

"There's something else I need to know — how did *you* know she'd gotten into the garden? It was thundering and raining hard. You couldn't possibly have heard her. By rights, she should have entered the house and killed you in your bed. So what gave you warning?" asked the Spook, raising his eyebrows.

I'd stopped nodding and was now gazing at my feet, feeling my master's glare burning into me. So I cleared my throat and explained exactly what had happened.

"I know I promised you I wouldn't use the mirror to talk

to Alice," I finished, "but it happened too quickly for me to do anything about it. She's tried to contact me before, but I've always obeyed you and looked away—until now. It was a good thing I did read her message this time, though," I said a little angrily, "otherwise I'd be dead!"

The Spook stayed very calm. "Well, her warning saved your life, yes," he admitted. "But you know how I feel about you using a mirror and talking to that little witch."

I bristled at his words. Perhaps he noticed, because he let the matter drop. "Do you know what a maenad assassin is, lad?"

I shook my head. "One thing I do know—when she attacked, she was almost insane with fury!"

The Spook nodded. "Maenads rarely venture from their homeland, Greece. They're a tribe of women who inhabit the wilderness there, living off the land, eating anything from wild berries to animals they find wandering across their path. They worship a bloodthirsty goddess called the Ordeen and draw their power from a mixture of wine and raw flesh, working themselves up into a killing frenzy until they are ready for fresh victims. Mostly they feed upon the dead, but they're not averse to devouring the living. This one had anointed her face to make her appear more ferocious, probably with a mixture of wine and human fat, and wax to hold the two together. No doubt she'd killed someone recently.

"It's a good job you managed to knock her down and bind her, lad. Maenads have exceptional strength. They've been known to tear their victims to pieces using just their bare hands! Generations of them have lived like that, and as a result they've regressed so that now they're barely human. They are close to being savage animals, but they still have a low cunning."

"But why would she sail all the way here to the County?"

"To kill you, lad—that's plain enough. But why you should pose a threat to them in Greece, I can't imagine. Your mam's there fighting the dark, though, so no doubt this attack has something to do with her."

Afterward the Spook helped me unwrap my silver chain from the body of the maenad and we dragged her into the eastern garden. We dug a narrow pit for her, deeper than its length and breadth, me doing most of the work as usual. Then we eased her into that dark shaft head-first. She wasn't a witch, but the Spook never took any chances with servants of the dark—especially those we didn't know too much about. One night when the moon was full, dead or not, she might try to scratch her way to the surface. She wouldn't realize that she was heading in the opposite direction.

That done, the Spook sent me down to the village to find the local stonemason and blacksmith. By late evening they'd fashioned the stones and bars over her grave. It hadn't taken my master long to deduce the answer to his two other questions. He'd found two small wooden bloodstained troughs right at the edge of the garden. Most likely they'd been full of blood before the boggart had drunk its fill.

"My guess, lad, is that there was something mixed into the blood. Maybe it made the boggart sleep or confused it. That's why it didn't detect the maenad entering the garden and later killed her when it shouldn't have. Pity she died.

We could have questioned her and found out why she'd come and who'd sent her."

"Could the Fiend be behind it?" I asked. "Could he have sent her to kill me?"

The Fiend, also known as the Devil, had been loose in the world since the previous August. He'd been summoned by the three Pendle witch clans—the Malkins, Deanes, and Mouldheels. Now the clans were at war with one another—some witches in thrall to the Fiend, others his bitter enemies. I'd encountered him three times since then, but although each encounter had left me shaken to my very bones, I knew it was unlikely the Devil would try to kill me by his own hand, because he'd been hobbled.

Just as a horse can be hobbled, having its legs tied together so it can't wander too far, the Fiend had been hobbled by someone in the past, his power limited. If he chose to kill me himself, he would rule the world for only a hundred years, a span that he would consider far too short. So, according to the rules of the hobble, he had one choice: get one of his own children to kill me, or try to win me to his side. If he could manage to convert me to the Dark, he'd rule the world until its very end. That's what he'd tried to do the last time we met. Of course, if I died by some other hand—that of the maenad, for example—then the Fiend might slowly come to dominate the world anyway. So had he sent her?

The Spook was looking thoughtful. "The Fiend? It's a possibility, lad. We must be on our guard. You were lucky to survive that attack."

I almost reminded him that it was the intervention of Alice rather than luck but thought better of it. It had been a hard night, and nothing would be gained by annoying him.

The following night I found it hard to sleep, and after a while I got out of bed, lit my candle and started to reread Mam's letter, which I'd received in the spring.

Dear Tom,

The struggle against the dark in my own land has been long and hard and is approaching a crisis. However, we two have much to discuss, and I do have further things to reveal and a request to make. I need something from you. That and your help. Were there any way at all to avoid this, I would not ask it of you. But these are words that must be said face-to-face, not in a letter, and so I intend to return home for a short visit on the eve of midsummer.

I have written to Jack to inform him of my arrival, so I look forward to seeing you at the farm at the appointed time. Work hard at your lessons, son, and be optimistic, no matter how dark the future seems. Your strength is greater than you realize.

Love,

Mam

In less than a week it would be midsummer, and the Spook and I would be traveling south to visit my brother Jack's farm and meet Mam. I had missed her and couldn't wait to see her. But I was also anxious to find out what she wanted from me.

CHAPTER II
THE SPOOK'S BESTIARY

THE following morning it was lessons as usual. I was in the third year of my apprenticeship to my master and was studying how to fight the dark: in the first year I'd learned about boggarts, in the second, witches; now my topic was "the history of the dark."

· 19 ·

"Well, lad, prepare to take notes," commanded the Spook.

I opened my notebook, dipped my pen into the bottle of ink, and waited for him to begin the lesson. I was sitting on the bench in the western garden. It was a sunny summer's morning and there wasn't a single cloud in the wide blue sky. Directly in front of us were the fells, dotted with sheep, while all around we heard birdsong and the pleasant drowsy hum of insects.

"As I've already told you, lad, the dark manifests itself in different ways at different times and different places," said the Spook, beginning to pace up and down in front of the bench. "But, as we know to our cost, the most formidable aspect of the dark in the County and in the wider world beyond is the Fiend."

My heart lurched and I had a lump in my throat as I remembered our last encounter. The Fiend had revealed a terrible secret to me. He had claimed that Alice was also his daughter—the Devil's daughter. It was difficult to imagine, but what if it was true? Alice was my closest friend and had saved my life on more than one occasion. If what the Fiend had told me really *were* true, it would mean that the Spook had been right to banish her. We could never be together again. The thought of it was almost impossible to bear.

"But although the Fiend is our biggest concern," continued the Spook, "there are other denizens of the dark who, with assistance from witches, mages, or other meddling humans, also are able to pass through portals into our world. Numbered among them are the Old Gods such as Golgoth, whom you'll remember we dealt with on Anglezarke Moor."

I nodded. That had been a close-run thing and had nearly cost me my life.

"We must be grateful that he's sleeping once more," said my master, "but others are very much awake. Take your mam's homeland, Greece. As I told you yesterday, a fierce female deity called the Ordeen, who is worshipped by the maenads, has caused bloodshed there on a vast scale since time immemorial. No doubt she's at the heart of all that your mam's trying to contend with.

"There's not a lot I know about the Ordeen. But apparently she arrives with her followers, who kill everything that moves for miles around. And the maenads, who are usually scattered across Greece, gather in large numbers to await her arrival. They're like vultures ready to feast upon the flesh of the dead and the dying. For them it's a harvest, a time of plenty, the reward they receive for their worship of the Ordeen and her followers. No doubt your mam will have lots more to tell us—there are blank pages in my bestiary that need to be filled."

The Spook's bestiary, one of the biggest and most interesting books in his library, was full of all manner of terrible creatures. But there were gaps where information was scarce, and he updated it whenever he could.

"I do know, however, that unlike the other Old Gods, the Ordeen doesn't need human assistance to pass through a portal into this world. Even the Fiend needed the help of the Pendle witches. But it seems that she can pass through her portal at will—and also return when she pleases."

"The followers who arrive with her through the portal—what are they like?" I asked.

"They are denizens of the dark, demons and elementals.

The demons mostly have the appearance of men or women but possess terrible strength and are very cruel. In addition there are the vaengir—flying lamia witches. So many have now joined her that only a few remain elsewhere. They live alone, or in pairs like your mam's sisters. Imagine what it must be like when the Ordeen arrives—a host of those creatures swooping down from the sky to rend and tear the flesh of their victims! It doesn't bear thinking about, lad!"

It certainly didn't. Mam's two sisters were flying lamias. They'd fought on our side during the battle on Pendle Hill, wreaking havoc on the three witch clans who opposed us.

"Aye, it's a dangerous place, Greece. Your mam has much to contend with. . . . There are also feral lamia witches, the ones who scuttle about on four limbs. They're very common in Greece, especially in the mountains. After this lesson's over I suggest you go up to the library, look them up in my bestiary, revise your knowledge of them, and enter a summary of what you find in your notebook."

"You mentioned that elementals live with the Ordeen as well? What kind are they?" I asked.

"Fire elementals, something we don't have in the County, lad. But I'll tell you what I know about them on another day. For now we'd better continue your study of the Old Tongue, which is much harder to learn than Latin or Greek."

The Spook was right. The rest of the lesson was so difficult it made my head hurt. It was very important that I learn the Old Tongue, though: It was commonly used by the Old Gods and their disciples, also in grimoires, books of dark magic used by necromancers.

I was relieved when the lesson came to a close and I was able to go up to my master's library. I really enjoyed my visits there. It was the Spook's pride and joy, and he'd inherited it, along with the house, from his own master, Henry Horrocks. Some of the books had belonged to previous spooks and went back many generations; some had been written by John Gregory himself. They chronicled a lifetime of knowledge acquired practicing his trade and fighting the Dark.

The Spook always worried that something might happen to his library. When Alice was staying with us, her job had been to make extra copies of the books, writing them out by hand. Mr. Gregory believed that one of his main duties was to preserve that library for future spooks, adding to the fund of knowledge whenever possible.

There were racks of shelves containing thousands of books, but I headed straight for the bestiary. It was a list of all sorts of creatures, from boggarts and demons to elementals and witches, along with personal accounts and sketches where the Spook described how he'd dealt with the dark. I flicked through the pages until I came to Lamia Witches.

The first Lamia was a powerful enchantress of great beauty. She loved Zeus, the leader of the Old Gods, who was already married to the goddess Hera. Unwisely, Lamia then bore Zeus's children. On discovering this, in a jealous rage, Hera slew all but one of these unfortunate infants. Driven insane by grief, Lamia began to kill children wherever she found them, so that streams and rivers ran red with their blood and the air trembled with the cries of distraught parents. At last the gods punished her by shifting her shape so that her lower body was sinuous and scaled like that of a serpent.

Thus changed, she now turned her attentions to young men. She would call to them in a forest glade, only her beautiful head and shoulders visible above the lush green grass. Once she had lured him close, she wrapped her lower body around her victim tightly, squeezing the breath from his helpless body as her mouth fastened upon his neck until the very last drop of blood was drained.

Lamia later had a lover called Chaemog, a spider thing that dwelt in the deepest caverns of the earth. She bore him triplets, all female, and these were the first lamia witches. On their thirteenth birthday they quarreled with their mother and, after a terrible fight, tore off all her limbs and ripped her body into pieces. They fed every bit of her, including her heart, to a herd of wild boar.

The book then went on to describe the different types of lamia witch—what they looked like, how they behaved, and most importantly for a spook, how to deal with them. I knew quite a lot about lamia witches already. The Spook had lived for years with a domestic lamia witch called Meg and had kept her feral sister, Marcia, locked in a pit in the cellar of his Anglezarke house. They had both returned to Greece, but during my time at Anglezarke I'd learned a lot about them.

I continued to read, making brief notes as I did so. It was a very useful revision. There was a reference to the flying lamias, called vaengir, which the Spook had mentioned earlier. My thoughts turned to Mam. Even as a young child I'd known that she was different. She had a slight accent, which marked her out as someone who'd not been born in the County. She shunned direct sunlight and during the day often had the kitchen curtains closed.

Over time my knowledge of Mam had grown. I'd learned how Dad had come to rescue her in Greece. And then later she'd told me that I was special, a seventh son of a seventh son, and her gift to the County, a weapon to be used against the Dark. But the final pieces of the puzzle were still missing. What exactly *was* Mam?

Mam's sisters were vaengir, flying feral lamias who, as the Spook had just explained, were only rarely found beyond the Ordeen's portal. They were now in Malkin Tower, guarding her trunks, which contained money, potions, and books. It seemed to me that Mam must also be a lamia. Probably vaengir, too. That seemed most likely.

It was another mystery I needed to solve, though I couldn't just ask her outright. It seemed to me that Mam had to tell me herself. And I might find out the answer very soon.

Late in the afternoon, given a few hours off by the Spook, I went for a stroll on the fells. I climbed high onto Parlick Pike, watched the shadows of clouds slowly drifting across the valley below and listened to the lapwings' distinctive *peewit* calls.

How I missed Alice! We'd spent many a happy hour strolling up here with the County spread out below. Walking alone just wasn't the same. I was impatient now for the week to pass so the Spook and I could set off for Jack's farm. I was really looking forward to seeing Mam and finding out what she wanted from me.

CHAPTER III
A Changeling?

ON the morning we were due to set off, I walked down into Chipenden village to pick up the Spook's weekly provisions from the baker, the green-grocer, and the butcher—after all, we would only be away a few days. At the last shop I told the proprietor, a large red-bearded man, that if any-one came on spook's business and

rang the bell at the withy trees, it would have to wait.

As I walked back through the village, my sack was lighter than usual because of the food shortages. To the south of the County the war was still raging, and the reports were bad. Our forces were retreating, and so much food was being taken to feed the army that the poorest people were close to starvation. I noted that in Chipenden conditions had deteriorated further. There were more hungry faces, and some houses had been abandoned, the families traveling north in the hope of a better life.

The Spook and I set off at a good pace, but even though I was carrying my staff and both our bags as usual, I didn't mind at all. I just couldn't wait to see Mam. After a while, though, as the morning began to warm up, the Spook slowed down. I kept getting ahead and having to wait for him to catch up. He began to get rather irritated with me.

"Slow down, lad! Slow down!" he complained. "My old bones are struggling to keep up. We've set off a day early— your mam won't arrive until midsummer's eve anyway!"

Late in the evening of the second day, even before we reached the summit of Hangman's Hill, I saw smoke rising into the sky from the direction of the farm. For a moment fear clutched at my heart. I remembered the raid carried out by the Pendle witches last year; they'd burned our barn to the ground before ransacking the house and abducting Ellie, Jack, and little Mary.

But as we began our descent through the trees toward the north pasture, what I saw was more a cause for wonder than fear. There were campfires to the south of the farm, a dozen or more, and smells of wood smoke and cooking were in the air. Who were those people camping in Jack's fields? I knew he wouldn't welcome strangers on his farm, so I wondered if it had something to do with Mam.

But I'd little time to think about that, because I sensed at once that she was home already. Faint brown smoke was rising from the chimney into the blue sky, and I felt the warmth of her presence. Somehow I just knew that she was back!

"Mam's here now—I'm sure of it!" I told the Spook,

my eyes glistening with tears. I'd missed her so much and couldn't wait to see her again.

"Aye, lad, maybe you're right. You go down and say hello. You'll have a lot to talk about and be wanting some privacy. I'll wait up here."

I smiled, nodded, and ran down the wooded slope toward the new barn. But before I could reach the farmyard, my brother Jack came round the corner into my path. The last time I'd seen him, he'd been seriously ill after being beaten to within an inch of his life by the witches who had raided the farm and stolen Mam's trunks. Now he was tanned by the sun and looked strong and healthy again, his eyebrows bushier than ever. He gripped me in a bear hug and almost squeezed the breath from my body.

"Good to see you, Tom!" he exclaimed, holding me at arm's length and smiling broadly.

"It's great to see you fit and well, Jack," I told him.

"And no little thanks to you. Ellie told me everything. I'd be six feet under now if it wasn't for you."

Together with Alice, I'd helped to rescue Jack and his family from Malkin Tower.

"Mam's back already, isn't she?" I asked excitedly.

Jack nodded, but the smile slipped from his face. There was a certain uneasiness, a hint of uncertainty and sadness in his expression.

"Yes, she's back, Tom, and she's really looking forward to seeing you again, but I have to warn you that she's changed—"

"Changed? What do you mean, changed?"

"At first I hardly recognized her. She has a wildness about her—especially her eyes. And she looks younger, as if she's cast off the years. I know that doesn't seem possible, but it's true. . . ."

Although I didn't say anything to Jack, I knew that this might well be the case. Human rules of aging didn't apply to lamia witches. As the Spook's bestiary had explained, there are two forms for a lamia, and they slowly change from one to the other. Mam was possibly slowly shapeshifting her way back to her feral state. It was a disturbing and scary possibility. Not something I wanted to think about too much.

"Tom—you know all about these things because of your line of work. Could she be a changeling?" Jack asked anxiously, his face suddenly full of fear and doubt. "Anything could have happened while she's been in Greece. Maybe she's been captured by goblin folk and replaced with one of their own?"

"No, Jack. Of course not," I reassured him. "There's no such thing as goblin folk. It's just a superstition. So don't you worry about that. I'm sure it's just the warm Greek weather agreeing with her. I'll go and see her, and we'll talk later. Where's James?"

"James is busy. He's making more money with the forge than I am with the farm at the moment. But I'm sure he'll find time for his youngest brother."

James was living here now and helping Jack out with the chores, but by trade he was a blacksmith. It sounded like his new business was shaping up to be a real success.

"Who are all those people camping in the south

meadow?" I asked, remembering the fires I'd seen as we'd descended Hangman's Hill.

Jack scowled at me and shook his head angrily. "You'd better ask Mam that question!" he retorted. "But I tell you, they have no right to be here. No right at all! Witches from Pendle, they are. And to think they're camping in *my* field after all that happened last year."

Witches? If indeed they were, I could hardly blame him for being angry. The Pendle witches had put Jack and his family through hell last year. With that in mind, why would Mam allow them so close to the farm?

I shrugged at Jack and set off across the farmyard. Just behind the barn, facing the rear of the house, I saw a new building—and James, working at his forge within, his back to me. Just outside in the yard, a farmer was holding the reins of a horse waiting to be shod. I almost called across to James, but I couldn't wait to see Mam.

As I approached the house, I was surprised to see Mam's climbing rosebush in flower. Last time I'd been here it had looked dead; the blackened and withered stems had been ripped from the wall when the Fiend attacked the house in his attempt to kill me. Now there were new green shoots climbing up the stones and a few roses were in bloom, gleaming a bright County red in the sunshine.

I paused at the back door and rapped lightly on the wood. I'd been born and brought up in this farmhouse, but it was now no longer my home and it was polite to knock.

"Come in, son," Mam called, and at the sound of her voice my eyes watered and a lump filled my throat. How I'd missed her! I stepped into the kitchen, and we were suddenly face-to-face.

She was perched on a stool, stirring the big pot of lamb stew that simmered over the fire. As usual, the curtains were drawn to keep out the sunlight, but even in the gloom, when she got to her feet and took a step toward me, I could see what Jack had meant when he said she'd changed.

Her smile was warm, but her face was a little gaunt, her cheekbones more prominent than before. Her black hair was no longer streaked with gray, and she really did look younger than when I'd last seen her, eighteen months earlier. But in her eyes I saw a wildness, an anxious, haunted look.

"Ah, son . . . ," she said, and she put her arms around me and pulled me close. Her warmth enfolded me, and I sobbed deep in my throat.

Holding me at arm's length, she shook her head. "Sit yourself down, son, and be strong. It's good to be together again, but we've lots to say to each other, and we both need clear heads."

I nodded and sat down facing her across the hearth, waiting to hear what she had to say. I desperately wanted to ask her about Alice and whether she might be the Fiend's daughter, but Mam's business had to come first. It must be important to bring her all the way back to the County for this meeting.

"How have you been, Tom? And how's your master?"

"Fine, Mam. Fine. We're both fit and well. How about you? How did you get on in Greece?"

"It's been hard, son. . . ."

Mam caught her breath, and I saw the emotion in her face. For a moment I thought she was too upset to speak, but then she took a deep breath and her manner became matter-of-fact.

"I'll come directly to the point. I've already visited Malkin Tower in Pendle and collected the bags of money that were in the trunks I gave you. Originally I meant them for you, to help your own cause here in the County, but things have taken a turn for the worse in my own land. Things are critical. I desperately need that money now to finance what must be done to avert a terrible disaster. Are you happy to surrender it back into my keeping?"

"Of course, Mam! It's yours anyway. Just do what you think best. Is it to help your struggle against the Ordeen?"

"It is, son. It is. Did your master tell you what we face back in Greece?"

"He doesn't know much about the Ordeen. He was hoping that you'd fill in the gaps in our knowledge. He's waiting up on Hangman's Hill to allow us some private time together, but he wants to talk to you later."

"Well, I can do that for him at least—though I fear that when we've talked, things may not be so easy between us. Your master is a good man with high principles. He won't be able to condone what I plan to do. But we'll have to see. Perhaps he'll realize that it really is for the best. Which brings me to the second thing I'd like to ask you. I need *you*, son. I need you to return to Greece with me and help me to fight the dark there. Others will help, too, but you have a special strength that might really make a difference and turn things in our favor. If I could avoid this, I would, but I have to ask. Will you come back to my homeland with me?"

I was astonished. My duty was to the County, and Mam's wish had always been for me to become a spook's apprentice. But if she needed help elsewhere, how could I refuse?

"Of course I'll go, Mam. But will Mr. Gregory be coming, too? Or will I have to stop being his apprentice for a while?"

"I sincerely hope he'll journey with us, son. But that must be for him to decide. I simply can't predict how he'll react."

"What are you planning?" I asked. "What do you need the money for?"

"All will be revealed in good time," Mam told me, and I knew now was not the time to press her further.

"Mam, there's one other thing I have to ask you," I said. "It's about Alice. . . ."

I saw the expression on Mam's face change. One moment it had been stern and businesslike. Now it suddenly softened, and sadness filled her eyes. Even before I asked the question, I feared the worst.

"The Fiend told me that Alice is his daughter. He's lying, isn't he, Mam? Surely it can't be true, can it?"

Mam looked at me, and I saw her eyes brim with tears. "This time he isn't lying, son. It hurts me to say it because I know how much you care about Alice. But it's true. She *is* one of the Devil's daughters."

My heart sank.

"That doesn't mean she's doomed to belong to the dark, son. There's a chance of redemption for us all. A chance to be saved. Alice has that opportunity, too."

"How long have you known?" I asked quietly. Her confirmation hadn't shocked me. I think that, deep down, I'd known it was true.

"Since the moment I first saw her, son, when you brought her here to the farm."

"You knew then, Mam? And yet you kept it from me?"

She nodded.

"But there were things you said. Things that don't make any sense now—that Alice and I were the future and hope of the County and that my master would need us both at his side. Why did you say that?"

Mam got to her feet again, put her hands on my shoulders, and looked straight into my eyes, her expression firm but kind. "What I said then, I still stand by. Alice cares a lot for you, and it's that affection that's kept her safe from the clutches of the dark this far."

"Alice contacted me just a few days ago. Warned me

that a maenad assassin was in the Spook's garden. But for her, I'd be dead now."

I saw the alarm in Mam's face, the fear in her eyes. "A maenad? I knew they were aware of the new threat I pose. . . ." she muttered, straightening. "But I hadn't expected them to know about you and send one of their number across the sea to the County. Darkness clouds my foresight. Things I would once have known are obscured, and it's happening at the worst time possible." She looked really worried.

"Although the maenad came from Greece, Mam, I could hardly understand a single word she said."

"There are many dialects in that land. But her killing frenzy wouldn't have helped. Talking to a maenad is difficult because they're creatures of emotion rather than intellect. They listen only to their own inner voice. But never underestimate them. They're a powerful group because they exist in great numbers.

"Anyway, we must be grateful to Alice for saving your life. Once she accepts that her birth doesn't necessarily mean she is destined to become a malevolent witch, Alice may prove a formidable adversary for her own father. Together the two of you might just manage to finally defeat him."

"Together? Mr. Gregory will never agree to that."

"I fear you may be right, son. And neither will he find it easy to accept what I plan to do. . . ." Once again she stopped short of telling me about her intentions. Why was she holding back?

"There are campfires in the southern meadow," I said, staring hard into Mam's face. "Jack says they're witches from Pendle. That can't be true, can it, Mam?"

"Aye, Tom. It's true. We need them, son. We need their help."

"Witches, Mam? We've made an alliance with *witches*?" The enormity of what Mam had done began to sink in. I dreaded to think what the Spook's reaction would be.

"I know you'll find it hard because of what your master's taught you," Mam said, laying a hand on my shoulder, "but we can't win without them. It's as simple as that.

And we have to win, we really do. We have to defeat the Ordeen. We cannot afford to lose. If we do, not only the County, but the whole world will be at risk. You go and bring your master down to see me. Then keep out of the way while I try to talk him round."

I did as Mam asked — went up to Hangman's Hill and told the Spook that she wanted to speak to him. I revealed no more than that, but perhaps my master read something in my face, for as he walked down toward the farm he looked far from happy.

Leaving him in the kitchen with Mam, I headed toward a small rise where I could look down upon the campfires of the witches in the southern pasture. The smell of cooking wafted to me on the breeze — rabbit stew. Folk in the County were short of food, and rabbits had been hunted so much that their populations were depleted and they were now hard to find. But no doubt our visitors from Pendle had their own dark methods.

I thought back over my own dealings with witches and

shuddered with horror. I remembered being trapped in a pit while Bony Lizzie sharpened her knives as she prepared to cut the bones from my living body. Then there was that awful moment when Mab Mouldheel had held a knife to little Mary's throat, clearly prepared to kill her had I not surrendered the keys to Mam's trunks.

Malevolent witches were ruthless creatures of the dark who killed innocents to use their blood or bones in their magical rituals. So the Ordeen must be terrible indeed if Mam was prepared to forge an alliance with such evil beings. But could I blame her? I too had been forced to compromise by fighting alongside Grimalkin to defeat Morwena and a host of water witches.

My thoughts were interrupted by the sound of the back door slamming, and then I saw the Spook striding across the yard, his face like thunder. I ran to him, but he scowled and turned north before I reached his side.

"Follow me, lad—we need to talk!" he snapped over his shoulder as he set off toward Hangman's Hill. After crossing the north pasture, he paused at the border of Jack's farm and turned to face me.

"What's wrong?" I asked, by now thoroughly alarmed. I was sure that the discussion with Mam had gone badly.

"What's wrong? Everything, lad. Just about everything! You know my feelings about using the dark. It just can't be done. You can't make alliances with witches and suchlike and hope to avoid being contaminated and drawn toward the dark yourself. Above all, lad, *you* can't risk it. That's exactly what the Fiend wants, as I've told you often enough. So you've got an important decision to make. Think it over very carefully—"

"Think what over?"

"What your mam's proposing. Going to Greece, joining forces with witches and . . . well . . . I'll let her tell you herself. I can't do it—the words would choke in my throat. I'm going straight back to Chipenden now. If you're not back within three days, I'll know that you're following your mam's wishes. In that case your apprenticeship with me is over!"

"Please!" I called, following him across the boundary.

"Don't go. Can't we talk about it?"

"Talk? What is there to talk about? Your mam's made an alliance with the Pendle witches. It's as plain as the nose on your face. So think on, lad, and make your choice. I've already made mine!"

So saying, he turned, climbed over the fence, and set off up the hill without a backward glance. I watched him disappear among the trees, hardly able to believe what he'd just said. He was ending my apprenticeship? How could he do that after all we'd been through together? I felt shocked, hurt, and angry. I didn't deserve that.

I went down the hill and crossed the yard, heading straight for the kitchen again. I needed to talk to Mam and try to sort things out.

CHAPTER IV
DECISIONS

"**Y**OUR master took it very badly," Mam said when I went in. "Even worse than I'd expected."

"He's gone back to Chipenden, Mam. He said that if I wasn't back there in three days, then it would be the end of my apprenticeship."

Mam sighed. "I was afraid of that. But you got on quite well with Bill

Arkwright, I believe."

"Who told you that, Mam?"

"People tell me things all the time, son. Either that or I find them out for myself. Let's just say I know what happened. You got off to a bad start, but things sorted themselves out and he trained you well. If John Gregory won't continue as your master," Mam went on, "then you'll have to make do with Bill Arkwright. I need him, too. I've already sent for him. I hope he'll agree to join us and come to Greece. He should arrive sometime tomorrow to talk it through."

"What do you want *him* to do in Greece, Mam?"

"He's a good spook, but above all he used to be in the army. We're facing a tremendous battle, and I'll need Arkwright's strength, fearlessness, and military tactics. I've told him it's vital that he come with us. He'll be able to strike a bigger blow against the dark there than he could in sixty years of service to the County."

It would be good to work with Arkwright again, I thought. He'd toughened me up a lot during the months

I'd spent with him north of Caster; maybe I could continue the physical side of my training. If it hadn't been for what he'd taught me, that maenad assassin would probably have killed me. On the other hand, I was really going to miss working with John Gregory. He was my real master and also my friend. It was sad to think that I'd never be his apprentice again. The house at Chipenden had become my home. Bill Arkwright, for all his qualities, couldn't replace that.

"Can't you tell me more about your enemy, the Ordeen, Mam? What makes her so dangerous that you need to defeat her in battle?" I asked. "What's the threat we face that we need help from so many people?"

Mam bowed her head for a moment as though reluctant to speak, but then she looked me in the eye and seemed to find her resolve. "The Ordeen has a terrible thirst for blood, son. And when she visits our world, those who accompany her through the portal in her great citadel, the Ord—demons, fire elementals, and vaengir— are similarly thirsty. Thousands of innocent people are slaughtered—men, women, and even children. She's growing in power, and each visit she makes to our world is more devastating."

"She sounds even worse than the Fiend."

"No, son, the Fiend is far more powerful, but he doesn't flaunt his strength. His aim is a slow accumulation of power, gradually increasing the evil that makes the world a darker and more dangerous place as he tightens his grip upon it. His plans are long-term—eventual total dominion.

"By contrast, the Ordeen has no long-term plans other than to drink her fill of blood and instill terror into everyone she comes in contact with. Many victims simply die of fear and are easy pickings for the maenads that swarm in her wake. She's a powerful servant of the dark—nothing compared to the Fiend, but we can't hope to confront him yet. For now we must concentrate on the immediate threat before us and destroy the Ordeen before she widens the range of her portal."

"What do you mean, Mam?"

"The Ordeen has been visiting Greece for thousands of

years; she materializes only on the plain before Meteora, where thousands of monks have their homes. Her visits take place every seven years, and each of these is more devastating than the previous one. The monks use prayers to defend their monasteries and try to bind the Ordeen within the confines of the plain. But gradually she's grown in power, while their effectiveness has declined. And now that the Fiend is in the world, she can count him as her ally, and the dark is much more powerful. Under the direction of the Fiend, more and more flying lamias have joined her. This time, it seems certain the Ordeen will use them to slaughter the unprotected monks in their monasteries high in the rocks. That done, the prayers that have helped to keep her in check will be no more. She'll be able to go forth and devastate other lands."

"They've been able to contain her just with prayers? Prayers really do work then, Mam?"

"Aye, whoever offers them up, if they are uttered selflessly and with a pure heart, the light is strengthened. So, although in decline because of the dark's growing power, the monks at Meteora are a great force for good. That's why we must strike now, before they're overwhelmed. Prayers alone are no longer any match for the Ordeen and the Fiend combined."

"So that is where we'll be traveling to—her citadel near Meteora?"

"Yes. The Ord, her citadel, always materializes through a fiery portal south of Meteora, near a small walled town called Kalambaka. Every seven years, give or take a week. We must stop her this time, once and for all. If we fail, next time she'll be so powerful that nowhere will be safe. But it's the County that will be most at risk. I am the Ordeen's old enemy. If I fail to destroy her, then she'll obliterate the County in revenge. The Fiend will tell her that my seven sons—all that I hold dear—are in the County, and she will eradicate it. Her murderous followers will hunt down and kill every living person. That is why we must defeat her at all costs."

At supper, Mam sat at the head of the table. We tucked into her delicious lamb stew, and she seemed happier, less troubled, despite all that we would soon face in Greece. I remember it well, because it was the last time all of us — Mam, Jack, James, Ellie, little Mary, and I — ever sat around the same table together.

I'd spoken to Ellie and James earlier. My brother had seemed content enough, but Ellie was a little reserved, no doubt because of the witches camped out in the south meadow. Now, at supper, I could feel a tension in the air — much of it seeming to radiate from Jack.

Jack said grace before the meal, and we all, except for Mam, answered "Amen." She simply waited patiently, staring down at the tablecloth.

"It's lovely to be back with you all," she said when we'd finished our prayers. "It's sad that your poor dad can't be with us too, but we should remember the happy times."

Dad had died during the winter of the first year of my apprenticeship. He'd suffered from congestion of the lungs, and even Mam's skills as a healer had been unable to save him. She'd taken it hard.

"I wish that my other sons could have visited, too," Mam

continued sadly, "but they have lives of their own to lead now, with their own problems. They're in our thoughts and I'm sure we're in theirs. . . ."

Despite those sad absences, Mam chatted away cheerily, but the tension in the room was growing, and I could see that Jack and Ellie were uneasy. At one point, through the open window, we heard what sounded like chanting from the direction of the southern meadow. It was the Pendle witches. Mam ignored them and carried on talking, but poor Ellie shuddered and looked close to tears. Jack laid a hand on her shoulder and stood up to close the window.

James tried to lighten the atmosphere by telling me about his plans for the brewery he hoped to start the following year. But it remained a tense, uncomfortable meal. Eventually we got through it, and it was time for bed.

It was strange to spend the night in my old room again. I went and sat in the wicker chair and stared out through the window across the farmyard and hayfields, beyond the north pasture toward Hangman's Hill. The moon was bright, lighting everything to silver, and I tried to pretend that I was back in the days before I'd ever become the Spook's apprentice. I brought all my memory and imagination to bear, and for a few moments managed to convince myself that Dad was still alive and Mam had never left for Greece, that she was still helping with the farm chores and working as the local healer and midwife.

But I couldn't block out the truth. What was done was done, and things could never be the same again. I climbed into bed with a strong sense of loss and grief that brought a lump to my throat. It was a long time before I managed to fall asleep.

Bill Arkwright arrived late the next morning. His huge black wolfhound, Claw, bounded across the yard toward me; her half-grown puppies, Blood and Bone, scampered along at her heels.

I patted her while the pups circled us excitedly. Arkwright was carrying his huge staff with its big, sharp blade. He walked with a swagger, and his closely shaven head glowed in the sun. He looked a lot friendlier than the first time I'd met him, and his face lit up with a warm smile.

"Well, Master Ward, it's good to see you again," he said. But something in my expression made his smile fade. "I can tell from your face that something bad has happened," he continued, shaking his head. "Am I right?"

"Yes, Mr. Arkwright. My mam's made an alliance with some of the Pendle witches. She's had to, because she needs their help to fight the dark in her homeland. She wants me, you, and Mr. Gregory to go with her back to Greece to fight the Ordeen. My master was furious when he found out about the alliance and stormed back to Chipenden. He said that if I didn't follow him, I could no longer be his apprentice. I feel torn between them, Mr. Arkwright."

"I'm not surprised, Master Ward. But I can understand Mr. Gregory's reaction. What your mam's asking goes against everything he believes in."

"Well, I've had to choose between what Mam wants and what Mr. Gregory wants," I told Arkwright. "It wasn't easy, but my first loyalty must always be to her. She gave me life, and I was her seventh son. So she has to decide what's best for me."

"You've had a very difficult choice to make, but I think you're right, Master Ward. As for myself, I've a decision to make, too, it seems. I'm going to listen to what your mam says with an open mind. I must confess that it's a challenge—it would certainly be exciting to travel to such a faraway land. So, for now, I'll not say yes and I'll not say no. I'll wait to hear more from your mam's own lips. An alliance with servants of the dark, you say? Well, sometimes we have to compromise in order to survive. Neither of us would be here now if it wasn't for the witch assassin, Grimalkin."

That was true enough. She'd fought alongside me in the marsh, and together we'd defeated Morwena and a host of water witches. Without her I'd have been killed. Servant of the dark or not, the alliance with Grimalkin had been worthwhile. It seemed clear that Bill Arkwright didn't have the same scruples as my master.

❂ ❂ ❂

We found Mam talking to James behind the barn. When she saw us, she took her leave of my brother and came to greet our visitor. "This is Bill Arkwright, Mam," I told her. "He's come to hear what you have to say."

"Pleased to meet you, Mrs. Ward," Arkwright said, giving a little bow. "I'm intrigued by what your son has told me and would like to know more."

Mam turned to face me and gave me a warm smile. "I'd like to talk to Mr. Arkwright in private for a few moments, son. Why don't you take a walk to the south meadow where the campfires are. There's someone there who'd like a word with you."

"What? One of the witches?" I asked, puzzled.

"Why don't you go and find out?"

I wondered why she couldn't just discuss things with Arkwright while I was there, but I nodded and left them to talk.

The campfires were scattered across the big field next to land belonging to our neighbor, Mr. Wilkinson—half a dozen of them, with two or three witches around each fire.

Who could want to talk to me? I wondered. As I walked across, I could see food cooking, and once again there was a tantalizing aroma of stewed rabbit.

It was then that I heard footsteps behind me and turned quickly, my mouth opening in surprise. Facing me was a girl of about my own height. She was wearing pointy shoes, and her black dress was tied at the waist with a piece of string.

Alice.

CHAPTER V
ALICE DEANE

"**M**ISSED you, Tom Ward," Alice said, tears threatening to fall. "Ain't been the same without you."

She came toward me and we hugged tightly. I heard her sob and felt her shoulders trembling. As we pulled apart, I was suddenly filled with guilt. Although I was now delighted to see her, I'd spent long

 · 65 ·

weeks obeying the Spook and turning away each time she'd tried to contact me.

"Thanks for using the mirror to warn me about the maenad, Alice. She would have killed me but for you."

"I was scared you wouldn't listen, Tom. I've tried to contact you before, but you always turned away."

"I was just doing what the Spook told me."

"But couldn't you have used it one more time after I warned you? Just to let me know that you were all right? Worried sick, I was. Your mam told me she was meeting you here when she contacted me with a mirror and asked me to join her. So I had to assume you were all right."

I felt a little ashamed but tried to explain. "I can't use a mirror, Alice. I've promised the Spook I won't."

"But that's changed now, ain't it? You don't need to worry about Old Gregory any longer, do you? Going to Greece, I am, with you and your mam. We'll be together again at last. And I'm glad he decided not to come with us. Won't have him looking over our shoulder, will we?"

"Don't talk about the Spook like that!" I snapped angrily.

"He's worried about me. Worried that I'll be compromised and drawn toward the dark. That the Fiend will win me over to his side. That's why he won't let me have any contact with you, Alice. He's trying to protect me. Anyway," I continued, "how do you know he's not coming? Were you spying on us?"

"Oh, Tom, when will you learn that there's not much I don't know?"

"So you *were* spying."

"No, actually. Didn't need to. It wasn't hard to work out what was going on when we all saw him storming back to Chipenden."

For a moment, despite my hot words, the thought struck me that if the Spook stayed home in Chipenden, then there really was nothing to stop me from being with Alice. But I felt another strong pang of guilt and dismissed the idea instantly.

"Look, it'll be good on this journey, Tom. Your mam thinks differently than Old Gregory. She doesn't mind us being together, and she still stands by what she said last year. That together we can defeat the Fiend—"

"Your own father, Alice!" I interrupted. "I found out your dark secret. The Fiend is your own father, isn't he?"

Alice gasped and her eyes widened in surprise. "How can you know that?"

"He told me himself!"

She looked shocked. "Well, ain't no use denying it. But it weren't my secret, Tom. I didn't know until he visited me the night before Old Gregory sent me away. Terrified, I was, to be face-to-face with Old Nick, and it was even worse when he told me I was his daughter! Can you imagine what that was like? Thought I belonged to him. That I was on my way to Hell. Going to burn there for all eternity. I felt so weak in his presence that I had to do anything he told me. But as soon as I was back in Pendle, your mam contacted me using a mirror. Told me I was a lot stronger than I thought. Gave me new confidence, she did. I've come to terms with it, Tom. So I'm going to fight him. What else can I do but try?"

A mixture of thoughts and emotions churned within me. Mam and Alice had been in contact using mirrors in the past. Clearly it was still going on. And that made me very uneasy.

"I still can't believe that Mam's made an alliance with witches!" I said, gesturing at the campfires around us.

"But all of them witches are sworn enemies of the Fiend. Twenty or more of 'em are coming with us. They know it was a big mistake to bring him through the portal, 'cos now he's trying to make 'em all do his bidding. So they're fighting back. Destroy the Ordeen and it's a big blow against the Fiend. Some from each of the main clans are coming with us. Your mam's organizing everything. It's just exactly as she wants it. Glad to be here again, I am, Tom, away from Pendle."

Only last year the Malkins had abducted Jack and his family, Mam's own flesh and blood, but now here she was, commanding the Malkins and the other Pendle witches, forming an alliance with them to help bring victory. It was hard to take in. And then there was Alice—what had she been up to back in Pendle? Had she moved closer to the dark again?

"What was it like back there?" I asked. "Where did you stay?"

"Mostly with Agnes Sowerbutts. Tried to keep away from the others, but it ain't been easy."

Agnes was her aunt—a Deane who lived on the far edge of the clan village and kept herself to herself. She used a mirror to see what was going on in the world but was a healer and certainly not a malevolent witch; bad as Pendle was, Alice had stayed at the best possible place. But what did she mean by "the others"?

"Who else did you see?"

"Mab Mouldheel and her two sisters."

"What did *they* want?"

Mab, although no more than fifteen or so, was the leader of the Mouldheel clan. She was one of the most powerful scryers in the whole of the Pendle district, able to use a mirror to see clear visions of the future. She was also malevolent and often used human blood.

"They knew about the journey to Greece and what we were going to do because Mab scryed it. They wanted to come, too."

"But Mab played a big part in bringing the Fiend through the portal, Alice. Why would she want to destroy one of his servants?"

"They realize they done wrong and want to put it right. Don't you remember how Mab was reluctant to join with the other two clans? Soft on you, she was, and only did it because you betrayed her and drove her from Malkin Tower."

That was true enough. I'd tricked her into releasing Mam's two sisters, feral lamias, from the trunks. In revenge she'd led her clan into an alliance with the Deanes and Malkins to raise the Fiend.

"So what happened, Alice? Are they here? Are they going to travel with us?"

"Your mam told me to contact Mab again and ask her to come. Ain't arrived yet, but they'll be here soon enough."

"Apart from Mam, do any of the witches know who your father is?"

Alice shook her head and looked about her furtively. "I've told nobody," she whispered. "As far as they're concerned, my dad was Arthur Deane, and I want to keep it that way. If they knew who I really was, none of 'em would trust me.

"Anyway, you hungry, Tom?" she went on, raising her voice again. "Got some rabbits cooking, I have. Just how you like 'em!"

"No, thanks, Alice," I told her. As much as I wanted to be with her, I needed time to collect my thoughts. There was a lot to come to terms with.

She looked disappointed and a little hurt. "Your mam's told us all to keep well away from the house in case we upset Jack and Ellie. Don't want witches too close, do they? Only way we'll see each other is if you come out here to me."

"Don't worry, Alice. I'll do that. I'll come out tomorrow evening."

"Do you promise?" she asked doubtfully.

"Yes, I promise."

"Look forward to that, then. Will you eat your supper with me tomorrow?"

"Of course. See you then."

"Just one more thing before you go back to the farm, Tom. Grimalkin's here. She's coming to Greece with us, too. She wants to talk to you. Over there, she is," Alice said, pointing to the large oak tree just beyond the meadow. "Best you go and see her now."

We hugged as we parted—it was really good to hold her again. Then it was time to face Grimalkin. I looked toward the tree, and my heart began to beat more rapidly. Grimalkin was the witch assassin of the Malkins. At one time she'd hunted me down, ready to kill me, but the last time I'd seen her we'd fought side by side.

Better get it over with, I thought, and with a smile and a nod to Alice, I set off toward the corner of the field. There was a gap in the hawthorn hedge, so I pushed my way through, to find the witch assassin waiting there with her back to the old oak.

Her arms were at her sides, but as usual her lithe body

was crisscrossed with leather straps and sheaths holding deadly weapons: blades, hooks, and the scary scissors she used to snip the flesh and bone of her enemies.

Her black-painted lips grinned to reveal the sharp teeth within; they had been filed to deadly points. But despite all that, she had a kind of wild beauty about her; the grace and aura of a natural predator.

"Well, child, we meet again," she said. "When we last talked, I promised you a gift to mark your age."

In Pendle, she'd told me, on the Walpurgis Night sabbath following his fourteenth birthday, the boy child of a witch clan became a man. I'd turned fourteen on August the third last year, and Walpurgis Night had already passed. She'd promised me something special to mark the occasion, and she'd asked me to go to Pendle to get it. There'd been little chance of that. I hardly thought the Spook would have approved of me accepting a gift from a witch!

"Are you ready to receive it now, child?" Grimalkin asked me.

"It depends what it is," I said, trying to keep my voice as friendly and polite as possible despite what I felt inside.

She nodded, leaned away from the tree, and took a step toward me. Her eyes stared hard into mine, and I suddenly felt very nervous and vulnerable.

She smiled. "It may help if I tell you that your mother agrees that I should do this. If you don't believe me, then ask her."

Grimalkin didn't lie — she lived by a strict code of honor. But was my mam in contact with all the witches in Pendle? I wondered. Bit by bit, it seemed, everything I believed in, everything my master had taught me, was unraveling. What Mam wanted for me seemed to be constantly clashing with the wishes of the Spook. I had another decision to make, and whatever I decided, one of the two would be unhappy. But once again I decided that Mam's needs had to take precedence over those of my master, so I gave Grimalkin a brief nod and agreed to accept the gift.

"Here, child. It's a blade." She held out a leather pouch. "Take it."

While she watched, I unwrapped it to reveal the short dagger within. I saw then that the pouch was actually a sheath and strap.

"You wear it diagonally across your shoulder and back," she explained. "The sheath should be positioned at the nape of your neck so that you can reach for it over your right shoulder. The blade is very potent and can damage even very powerful servants of the dark!"

"Could it destroy the Fiend?" I asked.

Grimalkin shook her head. "No, child. I only wish that it could—I would have used it long ago. But I also have a second gift for you. Come closer—I won't bite!"

I took a nervous step forward. Grimalkin spat into her right hand and quickly dipped her left forefinger into the spittle. Next she leaned forward, traced a wet circle on my forehead, and muttered something under her breath. For a moment I felt an intense cold inside my head, and then a tingling that ran the length of my spine.

"There, it's done, child. It is yours to use now."

"What is it?" I asked.

"My second gift is a *dark wish*. Has your master never told you about such things?"

I shook my head, feeling sure he'd be furious if he knew I'd received such a thing from a witch. "What is it?"

"It is called dark because nobody, even those skilled in scrying, can foretell when and how it will be used or the outcome of using it. It cost me much to create, years of stored power that you can now unleash with a few words. So only use it when you need something badly and all else fails. Begin with the words "I wish" and state what you want clearly. Afterward repeat your wish a second time. Then it will be done."

I felt uncomfortable even thinking about using such dark power.

Grimalkin turned to go. "Remember to use the dark wish with great care. Don't waste it. Don't use it lightly."

With that, she pushed her way through the hedge and set off for the nearest campfire without even a backward glance.

○ ○ ○

I went back toward the farmhouse and found Arkwright chaining up his three dogs in the barn.

"Don't like to do this, Master Ward, but it's for the best. Claw's very territorial. Your farm dogs wouldn't last long if I let her roam free."

"Have you decided? Are you coming with us to Greece?" I asked.

"That I am. My one worry is leaving the north of the County unattended. No doubt there'll be more than one water witch to deal with on my return, but your mam's talked me round. She's a very persuasive woman. So the County will just have to manage. For now, the really important work lies across the sea."

"Has Mam said when we'll be leaving?" I asked. It struck me that she wasn't telling me much at all.

"In two days at the most, Master Ward. We'll be traveling to Sunderland Point and sailing from there. And don't worry about your old master, Mr. Gregory. He's set in his ways, but sometimes there are other means to achieving the ends we seek. If he doesn't come round, then you can always finish your apprenticeship with me. I'd gladly take you on again."

I thanked him for his kind offer, but deep down I was still disappointed. Much as I liked Arkwright, he wasn't John Gregory, and it hurt to think I wouldn't complete my apprenticeship with him as my master.

I turned toward the farmhouse to see Jack bringing in the cows for milking.

"Who was that?" he asked. "Another spook, by the looks of him."

"Yes," I said. "It was Bill Arkwright from the north of the County. Mam sent for him."

"Oh," he said, far from happy. "Seems I'm the last to know who's visiting my own farm these days."

Just then, carried on the breeze from the south, I heard a strange keening noise, halfway between singing and chanting. It was the witches, probably carrying out some sort of ritual.

"Mam says those witches are on our side," Jack went on grimly, with a nod toward the south meadow. "But what about the other lot from Pendle, the ones who aren't? Won't they visit the farm again when you've gone? When I'm alone here with just James and my family? That's what Ellie fears. She's been under such a lot of strain during the past two years. She's close to the breaking point."

I understood that. Ellie had always been afraid that my becoming a spook's apprentice would put them at risk from the dark. Her fears had proved well founded, and last year she'd lost her unborn baby while a prisoner of the Malkins. There was nothing I could say to comfort Jack, so I kept my mouth shut.

CHAPTER VI
A Dreadful Prophecy

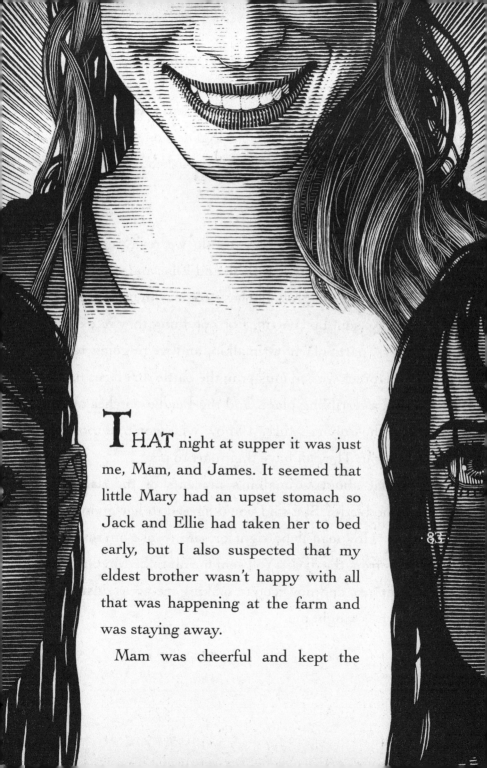

THAT night at supper it was just me, Mam, and James. It seemed that little Mary had an upset stomach so Jack and Ellie had taken her to bed early, but I also suspected that my eldest brother wasn't happy with all that was happening at the farm and was staying away.

Mam was cheerful and kept the

conversation going, but only James really responded much. Finally he went off to bed, leaving me alone with Mam.

"What's troubling you, son?" she asked.

"I'm confused, Mam."

"Confused?"

"Aye. Take the witches . . . do we really need them? They're clearly troubling Jack and Ellie, and without them the Spook would probably have come with us to Greece."

"Sorry, son, but we do. For one thing they're excellent fighters, particularly Grimalkin, and we're going to need all the forces we can muster in the battle that faces us. The Ord is a terrifying place, and the Pendle witches are just about the only creatures I know who won't be too afraid to enter it. They all have their part to play."

"What about Grimalkin's presents of the dark wish and the blade? She said you'd agreed to her giving them to me. How can it be right or safe to use anything that comes from the dark? You sent me off to be Mr. Gregory's apprentice, and now you're making me go against everything he's taught me."

I saw a sadness in Mam's eyes. "Only you can decide whether or not to use those two gifts, son. I'm also doing things I'd prefer not to. I'm doing them to win a great victory. You may have to do the same at some point. That's all I can say. Are you wearing the blade?"

"No, Mam, it's in my bag."

"Then wear it, son. For me. Will you do that?"

"Yes, Mam. If that's what you want, then I must do it."

Mam took my face in her hands and looked at me intently, willing me to understand the truth of what she was saying. "If we fail, the County will suffer terribly. Then the rest of the world will follow. The Ordeen will be let loose, with the Fiend's power behind her. We need everything available to us to stop such evil. This is no time to wonder about where such help comes from. We must grab it with both hands for the greater good. I only wish I could persuade your master to see it the same way. No, son, we have to go to Greece and take the Pendle witches with us. We have no choice."

From that day on I did as Mam asked, wearing the blade

under my shirt in its sheath positioned at the nape of my neck. How could I refuse her? But I felt that I was moving into a much darker phase of my life than I had ever experienced as an apprentice to John Gregory.

The following day, a couple of hours before sunset, I headed for the south meadow to keep my promise to Alice.

She was bending over a campfire near the hawthorn hedge that enclosed the field, some distance from the others. It seemed that she was keeping to herself, away from the other witches. That made me feel better. I didn't want her under their influence.

The rabbits were on a spit, their juices dribbling into the flames.

"You hungry, Tom?"

"Starving, Alice. They smell delicious!"

We ate the rabbits in silence but exchanged smiles. When we'd finished, I thanked Alice and complimented her on the meal. She didn't say anything for a while, and I began to feel more and more awkward. In the past we'd always had plenty to say to each other, but we'd exchanged all our news the day before, and now our conversation seemed to have exhausted itself. There was an uncomfortable distance between us.

"Cat got your tongue?" Alice asked finally.

"If so, it's got yours, too!" I retorted.

She smiled at me sadly. "Things just ain't the same anymore, are they, Tom?"

I shrugged. What she'd said was perfectly true. How could they ever be the same again?

"A lot's happened, Alice. Everything seems to be changing."

"Changing?"

"My apprenticeship to Mr. Gregory is over, Mam's formed an alliance with some of the Pendle witches, and you, my best friend in the whole world, turn out to be the daughter of my enemy."

"Don't," she said. "Don't say it."

"Sorry."

"Look, if we go to Greece and win, then it'll all have

been for the best, won't it? I'll have proved to you and Mr. Gregory that I'm nothing like my father. And maybe when Old Gregory finally realizes that your mam made the alliance for the good of the County, he'll take you back on and you can continue your studies."

"I suppose so," I said. "But I'm uneasy. Uncomfortable. There's a lot to take in."

"It's been bad for both of us, Tom. But we'll come through it, won't we? We always have in the past."

"Of course we will," I told her warmly.

We parted on good terms, but it seemed strange to be leaving Alice in the field with the witches. It was as if we belonged to different worlds. I felt like stretching my legs, so I followed the perimeter of the farm round to the north. The sun was just sinking below the horizon, and as I reached the boundary of Hangman's Hill, I saw three figures waiting in the shadows just beyond the fence. I recognized them as I got closer. It was Mab and her sisters, three witches from the Mouldheel clan.

Mab was leaning back against a tree, staring at me. I

remembered her as quite a pretty girl, but the Mab who faced me now was positively glowing, with a dazzling smile, sparkling green eyes, and golden hair.

Just in time I remembered the two dark magic spells— *glamour* and *fascination*. The first made a witch appear much more attractive than she really was; the second enthralled a man just as a stoat controls a rabbit, so that he is easily manipulated into believing anything the wily witch suggests. No doubt Mab was using those two powers against me, so I resisted, taking a deep breath and concentrating on less favorable aspects of her appearance—her shabby brown dress and dirty bare feet.

When I glanced up again, her hair already looked pale rather than golden and her smile was fading. Her sisters, Beth and Jennet, were sitting cross-legged at her feet. They were twins and, with or without glamour and fascination, were nowhere near as attractive as their older sister. They had hooked noses, pinched faces, and hard, staring eyes.

"You're not supposed to be here, Mab," I told her with a

frown. "Mam wants you all to keep to the south meadow until we leave."

"You don't seem very friendly, Tom." Mab pouted. "We've just come to say hello. After all, we're on the same side now, aren't we? And aren't you going to thank me for saving your life?"

I looked at her in puzzlement. What did she mean?

"That maenad would have killed you but for me," she said. "I scryed it and told Alice to warn you. Knew you wouldn't look at me in a mirror. Just hope we can be friends again now, that's all."

We'd never really been friends, and I remembered that Mab could be cruel and dangerous. Back in Pendle she'd not only threatened little Mary; she'd also intended to murder Alice. This was what repelled me about having to work with malevolent witches. Most used blood or bone magic. They could make do with animals, but they preferred to use people.

"Tell Tom what else you scryed, Mab!" Beth said, getting to her feet and standing beside her older sister.

"Oh, yes, tell him. I want to see his face when he knows!" her twin, Jennet, said, jumping up on the other side of Mab.

"Not sure I should," said Mab. "It'll only make poor Tom unhappy. But maybe not as unhappy as it would have done in the past—after all, he's not as close to Alice anymore. They're not that friendly at all now, are they? But *I* could be your friend, Tom. Closer to you than anyone has ever been. I'd be—"

"What did you scry?" I interrupted. Mab had already proved that she really could use a mirror to look into the future. I was concerned. What had she seen regarding Alice?

"I saw Alice Deane die!" Mab said, her eyes smiling with pleasure. "A feral lamia witch had her in its mouth. Dragged her down into its dark lair, then sucked out all her blood until her heart stopped."

"You're lying!" I snapped, a fist beginning to squeeze my heart and tighten my throat. Mab's prophecies had come true before. I couldn't bear the thought of that happening to Alice.

"No need to lie, Tom. It's the truth, as you'll find out soon enough. I scryed it two weeks ago. I used fresh blood—it was young blood, too. Not often wrong when I do that. It'll happen in Greece on the journey to the Ord. Tell her if you like. Not that it'll make any difference."

"You're not coming with us to Greece!" I said angrily. "I'm going to speak to Mam about you. I don't want you anywhere near me or Alice!"

"You can tell her what you like, but she won't send me away. Your mam needs me. Her foresight is fading, but mine's still strong. I'm needed to find out what the maenads are up to. No, you won't get rid of me so easily!"

Without another word I turned my back on Mab and her sisters and walked back toward the farm. I was seething with anger.

She called out to me, her voice shrill and peevish. "It'll be a bad summer for you, Tom Ward. Lots of nasty things going to happen. You're going to feel more unhappy than you've ever felt before!"

CHAPTER VII
THE JOURNEY BEGINS

AT last it was time to head for
Sunderland Point and begin our long
sea voyage to Greece. Five wagons
were hired to carry us and our tools
and supplies to the coast — one of them
covered with a dark canvas to protect
Mam from the sun.

·95·

The Pendle witches had set off on
foot the day before. Mab and her two

sisters were part of a contingent of seven Mouldheels. There were also nine Deanes and eleven Malkin representatives, including Grimalkin. Alice went with them. We didn't even get a chance to say good-bye.

Brief and sad were the farewells we took of Jack, Ellie, and James. Jack hugged Mam tightly, and when they drew apart there were tears in his eyes. As she climbed up into her wagon, I saw that Mam's cheeks were wet, too. I tried hard to put the sight from my mind, but it seemed like a final parting; they might never see each other again.

I also thought of my last meeting with the Spook. I was now off to a strange land to face great dangers. I might never see *him* again. I wished I could have said good-bye to him properly, to thank him for all his advice and training.

The journey passed without incident, and we arrived at Sunderland Point to find it teeming with activity. The depth of the channel didn't permit large vessels to approach the shore, but out in the river estuary a large three-masted ship lay at anchor. It was the *Celeste*, which had been chartered to carry us across the seas to Greece.

It was supposed to be fast, too, one of the speediest merchant ships operating from County ports.

"Now do you see why I needed the money?" Mam said. "Chartering such vessels doesn't come cheaply. Nor does finding a crew willing to take witches as passengers."

Between the shore and the ship, smaller craft were sailing back and forth with supplies. The evening sun was shining, but there was a strong breeze and I looked nervously at the choppy water.

I heard a welcoming bark, and Claw bounded toward me with her two pups. Bill Arkwright walked close behind them.

"Ready for the voyage, Master Ward? Not a bad day for it," he remarked. "But there's a bit of a swell, and it'll be a lot worse farther out. Be all right once you get your sea legs though."

I said nothing and glanced across at Alice, who was standing near the group of witches. She was clearly as nervous as I was, but she caught my eye and gave me a little wave. I waved back and looked at the witches, who were all staring down at the turbulent water.

The sea wasn't the same barrier to a witch as running water like a river, but the salt was still a serious threat. Immersed in the sea, they would die. Even the spray was toxic to them, so they had put on gloves and leggings, and the normally barefoot Mouldheels were clad in woolen socks. They also wore leather hoods; these were close fitting and had small holes for eyes, nose, and mouth. Yet in spite of these additional garments, I felt sure that the witches would still spend the journey cowering in the *Celeste*'s hold. Mam told me that the crew had been warned about their passengers, but on the shore the witches were attracting a few wary glances and most people kept their distance.

Two large rowing boats were used to ferry us out in groups of six or so. Mam went first, escorted by the captain of the *Celeste*. Next the witches were rowed across, their shrieks and howls at the salt spray slowly fading into the distance. But Alice didn't go with them. She came to stand beside me.

"Mind if I do the crossing with you, Tom?" she asked almost shyly.

"Of course not," I replied.

So we shared the last boat with Arkwright and the three dogs. The animals were excited and difficult to calm, and it took a few stern words from her master to persuade Claw to lie still. The rowing boat pitched and rolled alarmingly, but luckily the crossing didn't take long. Climbing the rope ladder up to the deck proved easy enough, and a basket was lowered for the dogs.

Mam and the captain—a big red-faced man with prominent side whiskers—were standing by the mainmast: she beckoned me across.

"This is Captain Baines," she said with a smile, "the best seafarer the County has."

"Well, I was certainly born and bred in the County, and I got my sea legs when I was younger than you, boy," he replied, "but as for being the best, no doubt some would dispute that. Our part of the world has more than its fair share of good sailors!"

"You're just being modest," Mam said. "And it's not polite to contradict a lady!"

"Then I owe you an apology," said the captain with a bow. "Indeed, I owe your mother a lot," he said, turning toward me. "I have twin boys, just turned five years of age last week. They'd be dead now but for your mother. Maybe my wife, too. Your mam's the best midwife in the County."

It was true. Before she'd returned to Greece, Mam had helped lots of County women with difficult births and saved many a life.

"Well, I certainly would be lacking in courtesy if I didn't show you both around my ship," he went on. "It'll be your home for the next few weeks, so you might as well find out what you've let yourselves in for!"

He showed us the different sections of the hold, including the galley and the quartermaster's stores, and I soon knew exactly what the captain meant. Although the *Celeste* had looked big from the shore, it was actually very small for such a large number of passengers. The crew's quarters, toward the front of the ship, seemed tiny, but the captain pointed out that not all of them would be sleeping at the same time: There were three watches, so at any one time a third of the crew would be on duty. The witches were to be located aft, to the rear of the *Celeste*, and there were separate quarters that I would share with Bill Arkwright. Additionally, there were two cabins. The first belonged to the captain; the second had been reserved for Mam.

Her cabin was small but very well appointed. In addition to the bed, there was an armchair and a table with two straight-backed wooden chairs. All the furniture was bolted to the floor to prevent it from sliding about during storms. The porthole didn't admit much light, so the captain lit a lantern.

"I hope you'll be comfortable here, Mrs. Ward," he said. "And now I must get back to my duties. We'll be sailing within the hour."

"I'm sure I'll be more than comfortable, Captain," Mam said, thanking him with a smile.

I followed Captain Baines back up onto the deck and saw that the tide was rising fast, the wind freshening and the air redolent of salt and tar. Soon the large sails were unfurled, the anchor raised, and with a groan, a shudder, and a flap of canvas, the *Celeste* began to move away from Sunderland Point. At first she didn't roll too much. It was a clear evening and the sun was still just above the horizon, so there was lots to see. To the north, Arkwright pointed out Cartmel and the Old Man of Coniston, the mountain we'd visited the previous year.

"Had some scary times there!" Alice exclaimed.

We both nodded. Arkwright had almost lost his life, and Claw's mate, Tooth, had been slain by the water witch Morwena.

Sailing wasn't as bad as I'd expected, but we were still only crossing Morecambe Bay, which was sheltered from the worst of the wind. The open sea lay ahead, and as we passed the estuary of the river Wyre, I could see a line of choppy white water ahead. The moment we reached it, the ship began to pitch and roll alarmingly. Soon my stomach began to heave, and within ten minutes I'd emptied its contents over the side.

"How long does it take to get your sea legs?" I asked the grinning Arkwright.

"Maybe hours, maybe days," he answered while I gasped for air. "Some poor folk never find them properly. Let's hope you're one of the lucky ones, Master Ward!"

"Going below deck now, Tom," Alice told me. "Sailors don't like women on board at the best of times. Think it's bad luck. I'd better get out of sight."

"No, stay up here, Alice. Mam chartered this ship— they'll just have to put up with it!"

But Alice insisted. I tried going below with her, but the witches were not coping well with the rolling motion. Down in the gloom the stench of vomit was so strong that I quickly fled back up to the fresh air. That night, taking Arkwright's advice, I slept in a hammock under the stars while we headed south down the coast. By dawn I hadn't exactly gotten my sea legs, but I was feeling considerably better and was able to observe the crew as they fearlessly climbed the rigging and adjusted the sails. They had no time for us—it was as if we didn't exist—but I didn't mind:

They were always busy, and when the ship was rolling or pitching badly, it was a dangerous job for those perched high on the masts.

Arkwright knew a lot about seafaring, having made quite a few trips along the coast in his army days. He told me the names of the various parts of the ship: that the left side was called port, the right side starboard; and that fore was the front of the boat and aft the rear. My dad had been a sailor, so I knew most of what he was telling me already, but he'd also taught me manners, so I listened politely to everything Arkwright had to say.

"County ships are always given the names of women," he explained. "Take *Celeste*, the name of this one. As your study of Latin should tell you, Master Ward, it means *heavenly*, and no doubt some women are. But in a big storm a ship can be very unforgiving if she's not handled correctly and treated with respect. Some waves can be the size of a cathedral; they can roll a ship like this over and swallow her up. Ships go missing at sea, lost with all their crew. It happens all the time. It's a hard life being a sailor—in its own way just as tough as being a spook."

We had now sailed into the mouth of a big river called the Mersey, and there, at anchor, we waited for the tide. We hadn't left the County behind yet, it seemed. We were to put in briefly at Liverpool to take on additional supplies.

Unlike Sunderland Point, Liverpool had a large wooden quay where the *Celeste* could berth. Most of us took the opportunity to stretch our legs, but the witches stayed down in the hold. When I set foot on the quayside, I experienced a strange sensation—although I was standing on solid ground, it still seemed to be moving under my feet.

We waited about while the stevedores busied themselves loading up our provisions so that we could leave on the same tide. It was either that or be delayed until nearly nightfall.

Back on board, I stood beside Mam as the crew untied the ship from her moorings. She had sought the shade of the mainmast and kept shielding her eyes against the sun and staring into the distance as if expecting to see something. I followed the direction of her gaze, and out of the corner of my eye saw her face suddenly light up into a smile.

Someone was running toward us. And to my astonishment I saw that it was my master! He was carrying his bag and staff, and his cloak was billowing out behind him. But the *Celeste* was already moving away from the quay, the gap widening with every second. The Spook threw his bag and staff to us. They landed on the deck, and I quickly retrieved them while he eyed the gap uncertainly. It was then that Mam stepped forward and beckoned him onto the ship.

He turned instantly, ran back a little way, then sprinted straight for the edge of the quay. My heart was in my mouth. It seemed impossible that he could leap such a distance. But leap he did. His boots landed on the very edge of the deck, where he tottered and started to fall backward.

Mam stepped forward and grasped his wrist, then steadied him before pulling him to safety. He seemed to fall into her arms as if they'd embraced, but it was just the movement of the ship. He stepped back a little and gave her a little bow before coming to me. I thought he had something to say to me, but he picked up his bag and staff and headed for the steps down to the hold—without even glancing at me.

"I'm glad you're coming with us!" I called after him.

He didn't so much as turn around.

"Is he angry with me, Mam?" I asked.

"More like angry with himself," she replied. "Give him time. But for now I doubt he'll wish to be your master."

"*For now?* Do you mean that I'll be his apprentice again one day?"

"It could happen, but it's far from certain."

A silence fell between us, and we could hear the shouts of the crew as they brought the *Celeste* through the mouth of the harbor and out into the estuary, heading for the open sea. She was beginning to roll again, and squawking seagulls followed in our wake.

"Why do you think he changed his mind, Mam?"

"John Gregory is a brave man who always puts duty above personal needs and wishes. And that is exactly what he's done on this occasion. He's seen what his higher duty is and placed it above his own beliefs. But he's been forced to sacrifice some of his principles, and for a man like him, that's very hard."

Despite what Mam said, I wasn't totally convinced that it was only that. The Spook had always maintained that you couldn't make alliances with servants of the dark. Something else must have changed his mind—I felt sure of it.

CHAPTER VIII
THE YOUNG LADIES

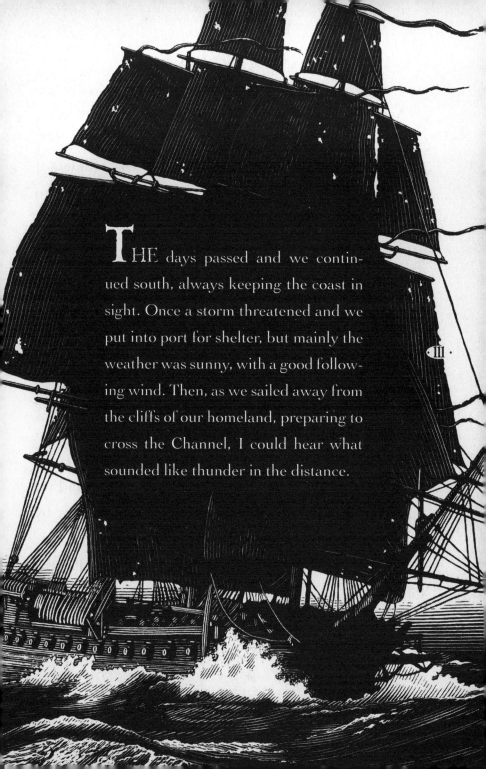

THE days passed and we continued south, always keeping the coast in sight. Once a storm threatened and we put into port for shelter, but mainly the weather was sunny, with a good following wind. Then, as we sailed away from the cliffs of our homeland, preparing to cross the Channel, I could hear what sounded like thunder in the distance.

· III ·

"Another storm?" I asked.

Bill Arkwright shook his head and frowned. "No, Master Ward, those are big guns. Eighteen-pounders if I'm not mistaken. There's a big battle taking place close to the sea. Let's hope it's going our way."

The invader came from an alliance of countries to the east and southeast of our island. It was strange to be so close to the battlefront yet be sailing beyond it into open sea.

After completing our crossing of the Channel, we sailed straight into a big storm in the Bay of Biscay. Thunder cracked and boomed overhead like the cannon shot we'd heard previously, forked lightning rent the sky, and the ship tossed hither and thither upon the furious foam-flecked sea. I wasn't the only one who feared that we would drown, but the crew took it in their stride and we sailed on into calmer waters, the air growing warmer by the day.

Eventually, moving through a strait that Mam called the Pillars of Hercules, we entered the Mediterranean, a vast inland sea.

"Who was Hercules?" I asked Mam. "Was he a Greek?"

"That he was, son—a hero and man of great strength," she answered. "The strongest man in the whole world. See that huge rock to the north? It's called Gibraltar, and it's one of the two pillars. Hercules picked it up and threw it there!"

I laughed. It was preposterous! How big would he have to be to do that?

"You can laugh, son," Mam chided, "but Greece is a land of many strange stories. More are true than you might believe."

"But not throwing the rock!"

Mam didn't reply; she simply smiled mysteriously and turned away. But before she'd taken half a dozen paces, she beckoned me, so I followed her down to her cabin. She hadn't invited me in before, so I wondered what she wanted. It had to be something she needed to say to me in private.

Mam led the way into the gloom of her cabin, lit a lantern, and placed it in the middle of the table, motioning for me to sit down opposite her.

"Now, I think this is the time to tell you a little more of what we face in Greece," Mam said.

"Thank you," I replied. "It's been troubling me that I don't know much about it."

"I know, son, but I'm afraid there's lots that I don't know either. I'm worried that the Ordeen might pass through the portal before we arrive. As I said, she visits every seven years, but not on exactly the same day."

"So we have no way of knowing for certain when she'll come?"

"No, but close to the time there'll be unmistakable signs. First birds and animals will flee the area. Then the sky will turn yellow and whirlwinds will sweep away from the point where the portal opens. It has always been so. Three days and three hours later, we will all be dead, or the Ordeen will have been destroyed."

"Do we really have a chance of success, Mam?" I demanded. It was terrifying. So much depended on what we were preparing to do.

"Yes, son, we do. But it'll be a tremendous challenge.

When the Ordeen appears on the plain south of Kalambaka, her intention will be to ravage that town, slay its inhabitants, and take their blood. Those who escape her servants will be slain and devoured by the maenads. None will escape."

"What about the folk from the town, Mam? Why do they live there if this happens every seven years?"

"Their homes are there, son, and they're poor. All over the world there are people who live close to active volcanoes or in areas afflicted by earthquakes or floods. They have no choice. In Kalambaka, at least they know approximately when the danger will come so they can flee the area. The roads will be thronged with refugees. Of course, some leave it too late to escape; others, the old and the sick, simply cannot travel. And this time, because the power of the Ordeen has increased so much, thanks to the Fiend, even the monasteries will not be safe. The attack comes from both land and air. Flying lamia witches, the vaengir, will find the heights of Meteora no obstacle at all. The Fiend has been sending increasing numbers of them to the Ordeen's side, but at least my sisters won't be among them. He is their enemy, too."

"And what happens when the portal opens?" I asked, filled with curiosity. "Have you seen it happen?"

"Once, son. Just once, many years ago, before I met your dad. But I'll never forget it. First a pillar of fire will extend from the ground to the dark storm cloud above. This usually fades to reveal the Ord within. Then torrential rain will fall, cooling the stones of the citadel. It is then that we must go in. All entities passing through a portal from the dark need a little time to adjust and gather their strength," Mam explained. "That was true of the Fiend last summer, remember. It gave you time to flee from Pendle to the protection of my special room in the farmhouse. So we must take advantage of the same time lag here. Before the Ordeen and her followers have their full powers, we must break into the Ord and destroy both her and them. It's our only hope."

As our journey progressed, the crew's indifference to their unusual passengers turned to open hostility. The captain explained that they had begun to fear and mistrust the Pendle witches. One of the sailors had gone missing on night watch. It had been in the midst of a storm and he'd probably been swept overboard, but they suspected that the witches had taken the poor man's life to satisfy their need for blood. So the voyage grew increasingly uncomfortable, and we were all longing for it to be over.

True to his word, the Spook had discontinued my lessons and hardly spoke to me. Alice he could not bear to look at. Once, when we were talking on deck, he raised his eyebrows, tutted, and went back down to the hold.

So Arkwright took it upon himself to continue my training, concentrating on physical skills as he had back at the mill. But it was a whole new experience to fight with staffs on a deck that pitched and rolled with the swell.

As we got closer to Greece and the temperature increased, the Spook began to sleep up on deck, away from the oppressive heat of the hold. And finally he began to speak to me again. It started with a nod and a half smile, but before long he was giving me lessons once more, so I now had the benefit of two spooks training me.

"Get out your notebook, lad," he said to me as, under a cloudless evening sky and with a light following wind, we sailed across the Strait of Otranto, approaching the Greek mainland at last.

"Well, I mentioned fire elementals to you back in the County and said I'd tell you about them one day," he went on. "We don't have them back home, probably because the weather is so wet. Even in summer we rarely go more than a week without a heavy downpour! But Greece is hot and dry then, and in those conditions fire elementals can thrive. As I say, they are very dangerous and sometimes take the form of glowing orbs, some translucent, others opaque. Take careful note of what I'm saying, because we're certain to meet them in Greece. They'll come through the portal with the Ordeen."

I dipped my nib into the pot of ink and began to write as fast as I could. This knowledge was soon going to be very important.

"As a general rule, the opaque ones are hotter and more

dangerous," continued the Spook. "Indoors, they often float close to the ceiling, but they can also move very fast and are almost impossible to dodge. Contact with them can result in severe burns—and often in a painful death. In more extreme cases, such elementals can reduce their victims to ashes almost instantly.

"And that's not all, lad. Others, called *asteri*, are similar in shape to a starfish, with five fiery radiating arms. These elementals cling to walls or ceilings and drop onto the heads of unsuspecting victims. And once they make contact, you're as good as dead.

"But it's not all bad news. Fire elementals are notoriously difficult to defend against, but a metal alloy blade with the correct percentage of silver can cause them to implode. A spook's staff is particularly useful. Failing that, water can seriously weaken a fire elemental and send it into hibernation until conditions are drier. Water's a good refuge when under attack."

The Spook paused to give me time to write everything up in my notebook. When I'd finished, my curiosity finally got the better of me. Why had my master sacrificed his principles to join us on the journey to Greece? I knew he wouldn't want to talk about it, but I had to ask anyway.

"Mr. Gregory, why did you finally come with us? What made you change your mind?" I asked.

He looked at me, his face filled with anger. Then his expression became sad and resigned. "Your mam wrote to me and told me things I'd rather not have heard. Things I didn't want to believe. After her letter arrived at Chipenden, I struggled with my conscience for a long time and almost left it too late."

I wanted to know more, but before I could speak there was a sudden shout from the lookout far above our heads. We stood up and gazed over the starboard bow. As we were very near the coast of Greece, I thought it meant that land had been sighted.

But I was wrong. The crew began to scurry up the rigging, unfurling every last inch of available sail. A large ship had been spotted to the west, sailing out of the setting sun. It had black sails and was closing on us rapidly. Fast as the *Celeste* was, it seemed that this ship was even swifter. Our crew was agitated and worked feverishly, but still the vessel drew steadily nearer.

The captain watched it for a while with his spyglass. "It's a pirate ship—we've no chance of outrunning it before dark," he said, scratching at his side whiskers. "And I don't fancy our chances if it comes to a fight. We're heavily outgunned."

The pirate ship was bristling with cannon, whereas we had only four guns, two on each side. No sooner had he spoken than we heard a gun being fired. A cannonball hit the water close to our bows, sending up a big plume of spray. The pirates clearly had the armaments to sink our ship with ease.

Bill Arkwright shook his head and smiled grimly. "It's not as bad as it seems, Captain. Just don't return fire. We certainly can't win any fight that involves an exchange of cannon fire, but it won't come to that. The last thing they want is to sink us. They'll want this ship as a prize. No doubt they intend to cut our throats and throw us to the fishes, but when they board us they'll get a nasty surprise."

He turned to me with a grim smile. "Go down into the hold, Master Ward, and let the young ladies down there know the situation."

Wasting no time, I went down to tell the Pendle witches what was afoot. Grimalkin was sitting on the steps sharpening one of her throwing knives.

"We're already preparing, child," she told me. "Mab scryed the threat hours ago. To be honest, we're eagerly anticipating the fight. We've spent too long cooped up down here, and my sisters thirst for blood."

I saw some of the other witches below her, their eyes glinting cruelly as they licked their lips with relish at the thought of the fresh blood that was soon to be theirs. Their fingernails looked as sharp as the blades they were honing, all weapons ready to rend and pierce human flesh.

Back on deck the Spook was standing beside Bill Arkwright, both of them readying themselves for the fight ahead. Arkwright always looked forward to cracking heads. He was actually smiling in anticipation of the impending action. I released the blade from my staff and moved forward to join them. The Spook gave me a nod, and Arkwright gave me a pat on the back in encouragement.

The captain and most of the crew were lined up between the masts, gripping cudgels, but they seemed to have little heart for a fight. We would certainly be glad of the Pendle witches' help. My mouth was dry with fear and excitement, yet I was determined to do my best. But at that moment I felt a firm hand on my shoulder. It was Mam.

"No, son," she said, drawing me away from the others. "You keep well clear of this battle. We can't take the risk of you being hurt. You have more important things to do in Greece."

I tried to argue, but Mam would not be persuaded. It was frustrating that others were free to take risks but not me. I resented being mollycoddled, but I had to obey Mam. So I stood at her side, furious that I couldn't take part in the coming battle.

We didn't have long to wait for the attack. The pirate

ship drew close, and then its crew hurled grappling hooks across the gap and drew the two ships together, their port side crunching hard against our starboard. Some of the pirates paced the deck of their ship with an arrogant swagger. Armed with knives, swords, and big cudgels spiked with nails, they looked pitiless and fierce. Others waited in the rigging, looking down upon us like vultures, considering us nothing more than dead meat.

But before the first of the pirates could leap across, the witches came up from the hold, led by Grimalkin. Wearing their hoods and bristling with weapons, they looked like a force to be reckoned with. Some were drooling, the saliva running from their mouths to drip from the bottom of their leather hoods as they anticipated the feast of blood ahead. Others were baying like hunting dogs, their bodies quivering with excitement. They looked fierce and deadly, none more so than Grimalkin, who led them close to the rail to form the first line of defense. And Alice stood there, too, looking as resolute and determined as the rest.

The pirate captain, a huge man brandishing a cutlass,

was first to jump down onto the deck of the *Celeste*. He was also the first to die. Grimalkin slipped a blade out of a shoulder sheath and hurled it straight and true at his throat. He hardly had time to register surprise before the cutlass slipped from his hands and his lifeless body fell to the deck with a heavy thud.

The rest of the pirates boarded us immediately, and the battle commenced. The Spook and Arkwright were required to play little part in the proceedings; they waited at the rear, their weapons at the ready. The captain and his crew were also redundant, no doubt relieved that their services were not required.

Little of the fight took place on our own deck. After a preliminary fierce skirmish with the witches, those pirates still standing quickly retreated to their own ship. Seeing what they faced, and having witnessed the death of their captain, no doubt they would have preferred to withdraw to a distance and blow us to pieces with cannon shot, but the grappling irons now worked against them. Before they could unhook them and separate the two ships, the witches went onto the offensive. Shrieking and howling with blood lust, they boarded the pirate ship, and the slaughter began. And Alice went with them.

They chased the pirates up the rigging, around the deck, or down into the hold. Those who stood and fought lasted mere seconds before their lifeblood was staining the deck. I strained my eyes to see what part Alice was playing in all this, my stomach churning in anxiety at the thought of the danger she faced. The sun had set by now and the light was fading fast, so she was lost to my sight.

We were spared the worst of the horrors, but we certainly heard the screams of those dying pirates and their unheeded calls for mercy.

I walked forward with Mam to rejoin the others.

"I find it hard to stand by and let such things happen, lad," the Spook complained, giving me a hard glare. I suspected that his words were also directed at Mam, who'd chosen our witch allies, but if so, she made no reply.

"It's a bad business, I'll give you that," I heard Arkwright say, "but how many poor sailors have lost their lives at the hands of those pirates? How many ships have gone to the bottom?"

That was certainly true, and the Spook didn't bother to comment further. At last the cries faded and finally ceased altogether. And I knew that, hidden by darkness, the witches would be taking the blood and bones they needed for their rituals. I knew Alice well enough to be confident that she would play no part in that.

We lay at anchor until daylight, when the blood-spattered witches rejoined the *Celeste* and retreated to their refuge in the hold once more. I noted the contrast between Mab and Alice. The former was gloating, clearly reveling in what had just taken place; Alice stood with her arms folded and looked sick at heart.

CHAPTER IX
WHAT I AM

WE sailed north, tacking against the wind, with the coast of Greece now always visible on our starboard bow. I could see that this was a very different land from the one I was used to. There was some greenery, yes, with clumps of pine and oak and the odd cypress tree spearing the sky, but it wasn't the lush grassland of the County, with its

high rainfall and damp westerly winds. This was a hot, arid country, a desiccated wilderness, the sun burning our heads and necks, the hills parched brown.

We were within less than an hour of the port of Igoumenitsa, but the sea and its denizens hadn't finished with us yet. The first I knew of the danger was a distant sound, high and shrill, audible even above the pounding of the waves against the rocky shore. The Spook and Arkwright stared at each other, eyes widening. At that moment the *Celeste* lurched, hurling us to the deck as the prow began to veer to starboard. We scrambled to our feet as she came about, until, to my astonishment, we were pointing directly toward the coast and a wall of jagged rocks.

"Sirens!" Arkwright cried.

I'd read about sirens in the Spook's bestiary. They were creatures of the sea, females who used their strange, melodious cries to lure sailors onto the rocks and destroy their vessels. They then dragged the drowning sailors into the depths and fed upon their flesh at leisure. A seventh son of a seventh son had a degree of immunity to their calls, but an ordinary sailor could easily be enthralled by their hypnotic voices.

I followed the two spooks forward to the wheel. The cries of the sirens were much louder now, filled with a shrill intensity that set my teeth on edge. I felt the urge to answer their call, but I fought hard against it, and gradually it diminished. Most of the crew were in the prow, staring toward the source of that powerful siren song. The captain was at the helm, his eyes bulging, the muscles of his bare arms knotted as he aimed the ship directly toward the black rocks that awaited us like the huge fangs of a ravenous beast. He gripped the wheel like a madman, his eyes fixed upon the awaiting shore.

I could see the sirens now, sprawled there on the rocks. Beautiful women with bright eyes, golden hair and skin, their allure very powerful, but as I concentrated, trying to slow my breathing, their appearance began to change and I saw them for what they really were. They still had the bodies of women, but their hair was long and green like tangled seaweed, and their faces were monstrous, with huge fangs sprouting from grotesquely swollen lips. But I realized that the captain and crew had been separated from their wives for long weeks, and without the immunity possessed by spooks, they could only see the illusion.

Arkwright seized the captain by the shoulders and tried to drag him away from the wheel. During my training I'd wrestled with Arkwright and fought him staff against staff, so I knew to my cost that he was extremely strong— but even so he couldn't manage to pry the man away. As the Spook went to his aid, some of the sailors left the prow and started to come toward us brandishing cudgels, their intention clear. They were desperate to answer the sirens' call, and aware that we were trying to prevent them.

"Stand back!" cried the Spook, stepping forward to swing his staff in an arc. But the crew kept coming, their eyes glittering insanely. They were in thrall to the sirens' song and would do anything to obey their summons. The Spook struck the wrist of the nearest sailor, sending the cudgel flying from his hand. The man gave a howl of pain and stepped back a pace.

I moved forward to stand at John Gregory's side, holding my staff diagonally across me in a defensive position. Neither the Spook nor I had released our retractable blades. We were facing the crew of the *Celeste*, after all, and didn't want to do anyone any permanent damage. It was for that reason, too, that Arkwright was still wrestling with the helmsman rather than cracking his skull to bring him to his knees.

Suddenly Mam was at Arkwright's side; I glanced back to see her roll something in the palm of her hand and insert it into the left ear of Captain Baines. Arkwright twisted the captain's head, and she did the same to his other ear.

"Now release him!" she cried, shouting above the roar of the waves pounding the rocks, which were dangerously close.

Whatever Mam had done, the change in the captain was sudden and dramatic. He gave a cry of fear, his eyes filled with loathing as the sirens on the rocks now appeared to him in their true shapes, and he began to spin the wheel. In response the boat came slowly about and began to veer away from the sirens. At that moment the crew rushed us, but the Spook and I used our staffs to good effect, bringing two of them down hard on the deck. The next moment Arkwright was at our side, pointing his staff toward them, clearly prepared to use it if necessary. But by then the sirens' cries were already beginning to fade as we sailed down the coast in the opposite direction, the wind now to our rear, driving the *Celeste* fast across the water.

I watched the crews' faces as the allure of the sirens began to weaken and they could be seen in their true shapes. The hideous creatures were hissing with anger, showing their fangs as they began to slip off the jagged rocks into the sea.

"I put wax in the captain's ears," Mam explained. "If you can't hear the siren song, then it has no power. It's a simple but effective method and has been used many times by my people. Sirens are always a risk on our shores, but I thought this stretch of coastline was safe. The power of the dark is certainly increasing."

Within a few minutes the siren cries could be heard no

more. Once the captain had pulled the wax plugs from his ears, Mam explained to the bewildered crew of the *Celeste* what had happened. The ship was brought about, and we continued our journey northward, this time keeping considerably more distance between ourselves and that dangerous shore. We'd not even landed in Greece yet, but already the pirates and sirens had threatened our survival.

We landed at the port of Igoumenitsa late in the morning.

While our provisions were unloaded, we all stayed on board, as if reluctant to leave the safety of the ship. An alien land awaited us, the hot, spice-laden air heavy with the promise of unknown danger.

Then, late in the afternoon, I saw a cloud of dust on the road that led to the port itself, soon followed by a dozen fierce-looking men on horseback who galloped toward the quay. All wore brown robes and had swords at their hips; they were bearded, their faces crisscrossed with scars. Behind them came a wagon covered with black canvas.

The riders halted in a line facing the ship and waited silently. Mam came up from her cabin, hooded and veiled, and stood on the deck looking down at them. After a while she turned to me.

"These are my friends, son. It's a dangerous land, this, and enemies may try to intercept us at any time. We'll need these people if the maenads attack. Come and meet them. . . ."

So saying, she led me down the gangplank to the waiting horsemen. As we approached, they leaped from their horses and ran forward, eager smiles on their faces, to form a circle around her.

Mam turned her back to the sun and lifted aside her veil, then spoke rapidly, her voice warm. I tried to work out what she was saying. It sounded similar to Greek, but I could only catch the odd word. Then she put her left hand on my right shoulder and said *"O yios,"* which means son. And then, a moment later, *"Exi,"* which she repeated. I think she'd just told them I was a seventh son of a seventh son and that I belonged to her.

Whatever she'd said, all their eyes were now fixed on me, and once again their faces were lit with smiles.

"This is Seilenos," Mam said, pointing to a tall black-haired man in the center of the group. "A good friend and a very brave man. His courage is matched only by his love of food and good wine! He's the nearest thing we have in my country to a County spook. He's an expert on lamia witches and fire elementals, which should prove very useful if we manage to get into the Ord."

She spoke to him rapidly—again I couldn't follow the words—and Seilenos nodded at me.

"I've told him that your life is just as important as my own and asked him to do all he can to ensure your safety at all times," Mam explained.

"What language is it, Mam?" I asked. "It's like Greek, but I can hardly understand any of it. They talk so quickly."

"You'll understand most people we encounter without too much trouble, but these people are from the border. It's a dialect from what southerners refer to as 'the barbarous north.'"

"It is all right," said Seilenos, stepping forward and beaming widely. "I speak some of your words, yes? Your good mother tells me you are an apprentice enemy of dark. I teach you as well. I know this land and its dangers."

"Thanks," I told him with a smile. "I'd be grateful for anything that may help."

"Anyway, son," Mam said, "we won't begin our journey east until tomorrow now. We'll spend one more night on the *Celeste*. It'll be safer that way. Best not to set off until we're good and ready. But in the meantime I want to show you something, and I've things to explain. We're going on a little journey, but we should be back here well before nightfall. We'll ride in this. . . ."

She led the way over to the wagon with the black canvas top. The grinning driver climbed down and opened the door for her. I was surprised how cool it was inside. I'd have liked to look out of the window, but it was a small sacrifice to have Mam safe from that burning sun.

Accompanied by Mam's warrior friends, we headed south for about an hour. After a while our pace slowed and we seemed to be climbing. We traveled in silence, not saying a word to one another for the whole journey. I wanted to ask questions, but there was something in Mam's manner that made me hold back. I sensed that she wanted me to wait until we had arrived at our destination.

When we stopped, I followed Mam out, blinking in the bright sunshine.

We were on a rocky hillside; the sparkling blue sea was now far away in the distance. Before us stood a large white-painted house with a walled garden. The paint was flaking from the walls and the shuttered windows also needed a lick of paint. The horsemen didn't dismount but waited patiently as Mam led me toward the front door.

She inserted a key into the lock, turned it, and opened the door. It yielded with a groan and a creak. It was as if nobody had entered this place for years. I followed Mam into the gloom. Once inside, she lifted her veil and led me through the house. As I followed, I caught a movement to my left. At first I thought it was a rat, but it was a small green lizard, which ran up the wall and onto the ceiling.

Mam used a key to open the back door, and after she'd lowered her veil again, we walked out into the walled garden.

It was an astonishing oasis of greenery. Although overgrown and neglected, it was a delight to the eye. A spring bubbled from an ornate stone fountain at its center, and that water gave sustenance to a mass of grasses, shrubs, and small trees.

"See that, Tom?" Mam said, pointing at a small gnarled tree close to the fountain. "That's an olive. Such trees live to a great age, and the olives they bear provide a nutritious oil. That one is well over two hundred years old."

I smiled and nodded, but a wave of homesickness washed over me. The tree Mam had indicated was small—nothing compared to the great oaks, ashes, and sycamores of the County.

"Let's sit in the shade," she suggested, and I followed her to a bench set against the wall, out of the sun. Once seated, she raised her veil again. "Your dad told you about this house and garden, didn't he?" she asked.

For a moment I was puzzled. Then I remembered, and smiled again. "Is this your house, Mam? The one where you stayed with Dad after he'd rescued you from the rock?"

Not long before he died, Dad had told me the story of how he met Mam. He was originally a sailor, and while ashore in Greece, he'd found her bound naked to a rock with a silver chain. He'd protected her from the sun — otherwise she'd have died. Then he'd released her from the rock, and they'd stayed together in this house before returning to the County to be married. The silver chain that had constrained her was the one I now used to bind malevolent witches.

She nodded. "Yes, it's my house. I wanted you to see it, but I really brought you here so that we could be alone together without any chance of being disturbed. You see, there's something else you need to know, son," she continued. "We might not get a chance to talk alone again. This is very hard for me. . . . but I need to tell you what I am."

"What you are, Mam?" I said, my heart hammering in

my chest. I'd waited a long time to find this out, but now, with the truth finally about to be revealed, I was scared.

Mam took a deep breath, and it was a long time before she spoke. "I'm not human, Tom. I never was—"

"It doesn't matter, Mam. I *know* what you are. I worked it out ages ago. You're a lamia witch, like your sisters. One of the vaengir; those who fly. But you've been 'domestic' for a long time. And you're benign. . . ."

"Well, I suppose I expected you to put two and two together and come up with that, but unfortunately you're mistaken. I only wish you were right—"

"Then you must be a hybrid," I interrupted.

"No, Tom, I'm not a hybrid. What I am is far worse than anything you can possibly have imagined."

Mam halted and turned to face me, her eyes glistening with tears. My heart pounded even faster. I couldn't imagine what she was going to say. Whatever it was, it had to be bad.

"You see, son," she continued, "I am *Lamia*. The very first."

I caught my breath, my head spinning. I'd heard her words, but they didn't make any sense. "What do you mean, Mam? I know you're a lamia. You're domestic and benign—"

"Listen carefully to what I'm saying, son. I am *the* Lamia. The mother of them all."

My chest began to hurt as what Mam had just told me began to sink in. "No, Mam! No! That can't be true!" I exclaimed, remembering what had been written in the Spook's bestiary. That Lamia's first children had been killed by the goddess Hera, and that her revenge had been terrible. She'd killed children. Then young men. Taken lives beyond counting.

"I can tell by your face that you know what I've done. You know my crimes, don't you? All I can say in mitigation is that I was driven mad by the loss of my own children. I murdered innocents, and for that I can never forgive myself. But I turned to the light at last and have spent my long life trying to compensate in some way for what I did."

"But you can't be Lamia, Mam! It says in the Spook's bestiary that she was killed by three of her own children, the first lamia witches. They tore her to pieces and fed her to a herd of wild boar. So you can't be her. She's dead."

"Don't believe everything you read in books, son," Mam said. "Much history is passed down by word of mouth and only written up many years later, when the truth has been distorted and embellished. It's certainly true that I later gave birth to triplets, the first lamia witches. It is also true that we quarreled. But we never fought physically. Although their words cut me to the quick, they never raised a finger against me. It pained me, but our family couldn't stay together. They are dead now, but their feral children live on to infest the land of Greece and make its mountain passes more dangerous than anywhere else on earth. That is the truth."

A thought struck me. "But you have feral lamia sisters, Mam. And Lamia didn't have sisters. She was the first. The very first lamia. As you said, the mother of them all—"

"I call them *sisters*, Tom, and that's what they are to me, because we were companions and joint enemies of the Ordeen and the Fiend for many years, long before I journeyed to the County with your dad. But they are really my descendants, children of my children's children many times removed. In spirit, though, they are my sisters. That's how I see them."

I couldn't think straight, didn't know what to say. Suddenly the tears were streaming down my cheeks. Embarrassed, I tried to brush them away. Mam leaned across and put her arm around my shoulders.

"It happened a long time ago, son. Anyone who lives that long is no longer the same being. You evolve and change. Become someone else. That's a truth well worth knowing, for it is exactly what has happened to me. I've little in common with the Lamia who slew so many; I have now served the light for many years. I married your father so that I could bear him seven sons. I bore you as my gift to the County. More than that—my gift to the world. For it is in you to destroy the Fiend and begin a new age of light. When you do that, my penance will be completed. I will have made full restitution for my terrible crimes.

"I know this is hard for you to take in, but try to be brave and remember that you're more than just a weapon to use against the dark. You're my son and I love you, Tom. Believe that, whatever happens."

I couldn't think of anything to say, and we walked back into the house in silence. Mam locked the door, and we strode out toward the wagon. She paused briefly and looked back.

"I won't come here again," she said sadly. "The memories of your dad are so sharp that it's like being bereaved for a second time."

During the ride back to the ship, I tried to digest what Mam had said. I had been told a terrible truth. One that was almost impossible to bear.

CHAPTER X
A DELEGATION OF THIRTEEN

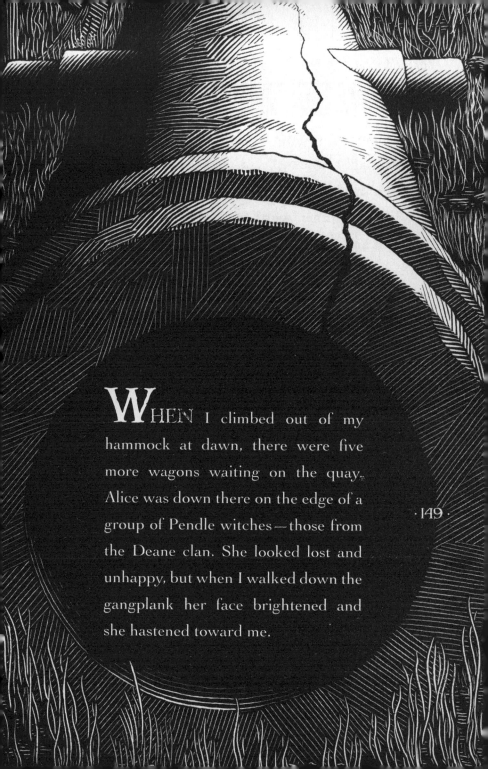

WHEN I climbed out of my hammock at dawn, there were five more wagons waiting on the quay. Alice was down there on the edge of a group of Pendle witches—those from the Deane clan. She looked lost and unhappy, but when I walked down the gangplank her face brightened and she hastened toward me.

· 149 ·

"What's up, Tom?" she asked. "Where did you go with your mam yesterday? Had bad news? You don't look happy at all. . . ."

"Then that's two of us that look unhappy," I told her.

Without another word we began to walk away from the boat and out of earshot of the others. Alice stood and waited expectantly, but I couldn't bring myself to tell her who Mam was. It was bad enough knowing it myself. I felt hurt and ashamed of what she'd once been.

"Mam took me to the house she once shared with Dad," I told Alice. "That's all."

"But what did she tell you, Tom? Must have said something to make you look so low!"

"It was sad—that's all. Going back there made her feel like she'd lost Dad all over again. But she wanted me to see it."

Alice wasn't entirely satisfied with my answer, and as we walked back toward the *Celeste,* I saw Mab Mouldheel staring at us. She could tell that neither of us was happy, and she had a big smirk on her face.

❂ ❂ ❂

It took an hour to load our provisions, and by then the sun was climbing high into the sky. The witches finally disembarked; a few of them managed to find space enough to ride in a wagon, but the majority walked. We set off eastward: Mam's wagon, surrounded on all sides by her escort, led the way. Next came the supply wagons, and then the witches, led by Grimalkin, Alice at her side.

I walked behind with Bill Arkwright and the Spook. Whereas I'd put my bag in Mam's wagon, John Gregory was still carrying his, despite the heat. I wondered again what Mam had written to make him join us so late, leaping onto the boat at the very last moment. What exactly had changed his mind? Did he know the truth about who she was? No, I felt sure that if he'd known my true parentage, he would have had nothing more to do with me. I'd be banished forever, just like Alice.

We traveled all day under the fierce heat of the sun, following the Kalamos river valley toward the town of Yiannena. My spirits were really low. I couldn't stop thinking about Mam's real identity. No one was talkative, though. The sun was intense, and it took all our strength to keep up with the wagons.

We passed through villages with white-painted stone houses and groves of olive trees, and attracted a few curious stares. I wondered if there were spies out there, reporting our progress to the maenads. We were here to do battle with the Ordeen and were therefore their enemies—at some point they were certain to attack. And as our party and the maenads were both heading toward the Ord, it seemed inevitable that our paths would cross at some point.

I was used to the lazy summer drone of insects back home, but here they were everywhere. There were swarms of flying things that got inside my hood and bit me.

"Does it ever rain here?" I asked, looking up at the blue sky and scorching sun.

"It rains at lot in winter, I believe," Arkwright replied, "and it can get cold, too. Your mam says it's a totally different place in spring, with carpets of wildflowers."

"I'd like to see it then," I remarked. "Who knows? Once

we've sorted things out, we may be able to come again one day. I'd love to see more of Mam's country. But what's that whirring noise?" It was in the background all the time and was starting to annoy me.

"Cicadas, a sort of grasshopper," Arkwright explained. "Noisy blighters, aren't they? It's the bigger creatures we need to watch out for, though, Master Ward—like wild boar. Tasty to eat but painful if you get in the way of their tusks! And then there are wolves and even bears."

"Aye, it's a different land to our own," said the Spook. "Greece is far wilder and more dangerous. And that's before we consider the power of the dark. In addition to the maenads, there are lamia witches up in the mountains—lots of 'em—not to mention the Ordeen herself, and the host of fire elementals that will come through the portal with her."

His words made us fall silent, each locked in our own thoughts. Great danger lay ahead, and it had to be dealt with before we could return to the County. I wondered if we'd ever see its green shores again.

We halted a couple of hours before sunset after passing through the village of Kreatopolio, which means *butcher*. It did have numerous butchers' shops, with the carcasses of lambs hanging outside, and we took the opportunity to buy fresh meat. Mam's friends erected three tents—the largest for her; a guard kept watch outside all night. Some of the witches used the other tents, but most of us slept under the stars. I was tired and fell asleep the moment I closed my eyes.

Although we needed to reach our destination as soon as possible, Mam had decided that we should rest here for a day before heading on. She feared the maenads. Scouts would go out the following morning to see if there was any immediate danger.

We rose early and ate just before the sun came up. Breakfast was simple, just some white sheep's cheese called feta and a couple of slices of bread without butter.

"I could murder a plate of bacon and eggs!" I complained to Arkwright.

"So could I, Master Ward," he replied, "but I believe some of the lads not needed for scouting are off hunting wild boar this morning. So perhaps we'll eat better later. If not, there's always the lamb we bought yesterday."

After breakfast the Spook, Arkwright, and I walked a little way from the camp and found a clump of olive trees under which to shelter from the fierce morning sun. But the Spook seemed agitated and couldn't keep still. He soon got to his feet.

"We're not being told enough!" he complained. "I'm going to talk to your mam, lad!"

He was away about an hour. When he returned, his expression was grim.

"Well?" Bill Arkwright asked. "Did you get any answers?"

The Spook laid down his staff and hunkered down between us in the shade of an olive tree. He took a long time to reply.

"It seems that once the Ordeen arrives through the

portal, a delegation from the local area enters the citadel of the Ord," said the Spook. "It's a ritual that never changes. The delegates hope to appease her and mitigate the effects of her visitation. But the truth is, nothing they do ever makes any real difference."

"Then why do they bother?" I asked. "What's the point of it if they achieve nothing?"

"It's because they're human, lad. Human beings have hope. No matter how desperate things are, they convince themselves that they can change things for the better, that this time their visit will alter the outcome.

"The Ordeen needs human blood to wake her from her deep sleep on the far side of the portal. Few of the delegates return, and those who do rant and rave in a delirium. The horror of the experience deranges their minds. Kalambaka is planning to send a delegation of thirteen people, the usual number, but your mam has other ideas. Thirteen of *us* will be going in their place."

Arkwright whistled through his teeth. "Did she say which of us?"

The Spook stared hard at me. "She just named one so far, lad. You. You'll be part of that delegation."

The thought scared me, but I tried not to show it. I hoped the Spook, Arkwright, or Mam would be with me. Then at least I wouldn't be alone.

"No doubt it's some sort of trick. A way to get inside and take the enemy by surprise?" Arkwright asked.

"Aye, that's the idea. She's not thought it through yet, but she's hoping to create some sort of diversion. The main attack would be launched while the delegation pretends to go about its business. She's going to hire mercenaries—a lot of 'em. Savage warriors from the north."

Arkwright soon went off with the dogs, and I was left alone with the Spook. He looked ill at ease and kept muttering to himself and shaking his head.

"What's wrong?" I asked.

"Wrong? Too much is wrong. This is just about the most dangerous situation I've ever walked into with both eyes open, lad. If we survive a likely attack by maenads, we have to cross the Pindhos Mountains, and they're likely to be crawling with feral lamia witches. And all before we even set eyes on the Ordeen. . . ."

His reference to lamias made me think of Meg, the love of my master's life, and her sister, the feral Marcia. They'd both sailed back to Greece the previous year. Maybe our route would take us close to where they were staying? I wondered if he was still missing Meg.

"Will you go and see Meg while we're here?" I asked.

The Spook bowed his head, and for a moment I thought he wasn't going to answer—or would tell me in no uncertain terms to mind my own business. But then he looked up and I saw sadness in his eyes; even before he began to speak, I knew that he had been considering it.

"I've thought about it, lad, but decided against it. You see, she told me where she was heading. By now she'll be living in a remote farmhouse far to the south. Because she's kept her distance from people, she'll have changed back to her feral form. I'd hardly recognize her now. A year or so and she'll be no different from her sister, Marcia. She's lost to me now. She might as well be dead. The woman I knew and loved is certainly gone, so I'd like to keep my last memories of her just as they were. . . ."

He shook his head sadly, and I could think of nothing to say that might make him feel better. But to my surprise he was smiling as he got to his feet.

"Do you know, lad, my old bones have never felt better! It must be the heat and the dry air. No doubt they'll soon start aching again once we get back to the County. But for all that, I'll be glad to be home!"

Late that afternoon Seilenos and three of his men returned after a successful boar hunt. The other warriors had been out scouting or guarding the perimeter of the camp.

That night we dined under the stars, on wild boar and lamb. "All's well for now," Mam said. "There's plentiful game in the area, and the men report that there's no sign of enemy activity. Tomorrow we press on toward Meteora."

Seilenos looked across at the Spook, who was merely picking at his food. "Eat up, Mr. Gregory!" he said with a smile. "We have dark to fight soon. Need to build up strength!"

The Spook looked back at him dubiously. I could tell he didn't really approve of Seilenos. "Back home in the County, we spooks don't eat much when the dark threatens," he replied, his manner cool. "When things become critical, we fast, denying ourselves food so that our minds and spirits are better prepared to face our enemies."

The Greek spook shook his head. "That I cannot understand!" he cried, throwing up his hands in bewilderment. "You weaken yourself by such foolish practices. Food and wine give strength. Is that not so? You will need your strength to face the salamander!"

"What's a salamander?" I asked.

"Highest and most powerful form of fire elemental is this salamander. More powerful even than asteri. A big lizard, it is, basking at the heart of fierce flames. It spits fire, too. Also blows scalding steam from its nostrils. Need lots of food inside you to fight such a formidable thing. Eat up, young spook! You will need all your strength soon. Do your wives not feed you well at home?" Seilenos asked, looking at Arkwright and the Spook in turn.

"I have no wife," Arkwright growled.

"We County spooks don't marry," John Gregory explained. "A wife and children would distract us from our vocation, which is to fight the dark."

"A pretty wife could be a distraction, yes," Seilenos agreed. "Fortunate it is that my wife is ugly and has a sharp tongue!" he went on, giving me a wink. "I've five little ones to bring up, too. That's why I travel with you. To escape wife and earn money from your good mother!"

I was hungry and ate until I was full. Even so, compared with Seilenos, I picked at my food. He ate until his belly seemed sure to burst, applauded by his men, who seemed to delight in his insatiable appetite. When I settled down to sleep, he was still eating—and drinking a good deal of wine.

I thought over what the Spook had reported earlier. Mam hadn't mentioned her plan at supper, so she must still be thinking it through. Why had she picked me to be part of the delegation? The thought was frightening, but I had to trust Mam's judgment.

Soon after dawn, we continued our journey eastward.

We traveled for three days, each stage of our journey more wearisome than the previous. It was hot and dusty, the sun beating down mercilessly. After the third day we skirted the town of Yiannena.

At last we saw a ridge of mountains on the horizon, the ones we needed to cross in order to reach Meteora. Two nights later, as we made camp on their lower slopes, those high Pindhos Mountains loomed very close. Tomorrow, well before noon, we would start to climb. Beyond the mountains awaited the plain of Kalambaka, where the Ordeen would emerge from her fiery portal. Every mile brought us closer to that ultimate danger.

CHAPTER XI
Night Attack

I lay wrapped in my cloak some distance from the cooking fire. It had been a hot day, but the stars were bright and the air was starting to cool a little. Just as I started to sink into sleep, I was awakened very suddenly by a loud noise.

It sounded like wild laughter but ended in a frenzied scream. I looked

out into the darkness beyond the fire. Immediately the sound was repeated from a different direction and I lurched to my feet, snatching up my staff.

It was maenads—I felt sure of it. They were preparing to attack. Other people were stirring about me. In the light of the embers I saw Bill Arkwright's shaven head as he kicked dirt across to extinguish the orange glow of the fire, plunging us into relative darkness. In the distance the other fires were also being doused, so that the enemy had only starlight to see us by. I saw Arkwright crouch down to make himself less of a target, and I did the same.

There were more shrieks and yells, this time from behind us and much closer. We were surrounded: the maenads were moving in, about to attack. A shadowy figure ran straight at Arkwright, and he struck out at her with his staff. The maenad fell at his feet with a grunt, but others were sprinting toward us from all directions. I could hear their feet thumping on the dry earth. I whirled to meet an attacker at my left shoulder, swinging my staff in an arc. I caught her on the head, and she overbalanced and fell away. I pressed the catch in my staff and the blade emerged with a click. It was a fight to the death now. Maenads were all around, some stabbing at me with long cruel blades, others charging with bare hands. Some had killed already. The mouth of one was dripping with blood, and she had pieces of skin and flesh trapped between her teeth. I whirled round, trying to keep them at bay. There were too many to fight off, and I'd no hope of help. Everyone else was in the same predicament. We were heavily outnumbered.

My only hope was to break out of the circle, so I attacked, lunging forward, spearing my staff toward the figure directly before me. She fell back, and I leaped over her body into an open space. The maenads were still shrieking behind me. I needed to link up with some of the others — Bill Arkwright and the Spook or even the Pendle witches — and fight alongside them.

A shadow loomed up from my right, and before I could spin to defend myself a hand gripped my wrist fiercely and tugged me away into the darkness.

"Just follow me, Tom!" cried a voice I knew so well.

It was Alice!

"Where are we going?" I demanded.

"Ain't time to talk now. Got to get away first."

I followed at her heels. We ran away from the camp, heading roughly east. The sounds of pursuit faded, but when Alice showed no sign of slowing down, I caught her up and grabbed her arm from behind.

"I'm not going any farther, Alice."

She turned to face me, her features in shadow but her eyes glittering in the starlight.

"We've got to go back, Alice. They'll need all the help they can get. We can't just leave like this. We can't abandon them and think only of ourselves."

"Your mam said that at the first sign of trouble I had to get you away. Especially if the maenads attacked. 'Get Tom to safety,' she said. 'If anything happens to him, it's all for nothing anyway.' Made me promise that, she did."

"Why would it be all for nothing? I don't understand."

"Whatever your mam's plan is for defeating the Ordeen,

you're an important part of it, Tom. So we've got to keep you safe. We need to keep heading east. We'll be up in the mountains before dawn. They won't find us there."

Alice sometimes hid things from me but had never told me a direct lie. I knew that she was following Mam's instructions, so reluctantly I continued east. I was still worried about the attack on the camp. There had been so many maenads down there, but I knew the defenders would put up a good fight. There was Mam's warrior guard, but also the witches from Pendle, the Spook, and Bill Arkwright— he would certainly do his best to break a few skulls.

"Why didn't you or the Pendle witches sniff out the attack?" I demanded accusingly. "And surely Mam or Mab would have known what was coming and raised the alarm, too. What went wrong, Alice?"

Alice shrugged. "Don't know the answer to that, Tom."

I felt uneasy but said nothing more, keeping my worries to myself. Mam had already told me that her foresight was waning. I felt sure that the Fiend was weakening all our powers, making our mission more and more impossible.

"Come on, Tom. Let's move!" Alice cried, an urgency in her voice. "More than likely they'll still be following. . . ."

So we ran on a little farther before slowing to a steady jog.

As we reached the foothills, the moon came up above the solid bulk of the dark Pindhos Mountains rising before us. No doubt somewhere ahead there was a route through them, but we weren't back in the County and didn't have either a knowledge of the terrain or a map to refer to. All I knew was that Meteora was somewhere to the east beyond this range. So we climbed as best we could, hoping to find our own way through.

We'd been climbing through a pine wood for about ten minutes—my body was starting to sweat with the exertion—when Alice suddenly came to a halt, her eyes wide. She sniffed the air three times. "There *are* maenads following us. Ain't no doubt about it. They must have a tracker."

"How many, Alice?"

"Three or four. Aren't too far behind either."

I looked back, but even with the moonlight bathing the

slope, I could see nothing of our pursuers through the trees. However, Alice was rarely wrong when it came to sniffing out danger.

"The higher we get, the more chance we've got to hide and throw 'em off our trail," she said.

So we turned and hurried on. Soon the trees were left behind us, and the ground became steeper and more rocky. The next time I looked back, I could see four shadowy figures moving swiftly up the trail. They were closing on us fast.

We were following a narrow track between two huge crags rising up on either side when, suddenly, we saw a cave ahead, its dark maw leading downward. The path led straight into it. There was nowhere else to go.

"We could lose 'em down there in the dark. Hard to track us, too," Alice suggested. Swiftly she sniffed the entrance to the cave. "Seems safe enough, this one. No danger at all."

"But what if it's a dead end, Alice? If there's no way through, we'll be trapped down there in the darkness."

"Ain't got much choice, Tom. We either go in, or turn back and face 'em on the path!"

She was right. We had no alternative. I nodded at her, and after using my tinderbox to light the candle I always carried with me, we entered the cave. The descent was gradual at first, and the air was much cooler than outside. Every so often we paused for a second but could hear no sounds of pursuit. It wouldn't be long before the maenads came after us, though. And what if we reached a dead end? That didn't bear thinking about.

But the path up to the cave entrance was well-worn, suggesting there was a way through. The tunnel sloped downward more steeply now, each step taking us deeper underground. Suddenly we heard a faint rhythmical tapping within the wall, somewhere to our right. Almost immediately there was a reply from the left wall.

"What's that, Alice?"

"Don't know," she said, her eyes wide. "Ain't the maenads. They're back there. Unless there are more of 'em already in the tunnel."

The tapping became more frantic, building into an insistent beat made by some insane many-armed drummer.

The sounds were sometimes above but mostly to the side, as if somebody or something was keeping pace with us, moving along the tunnel. But we could see nothing. Either the things making the sounds were invisible or they were somehow inside the rock. Could they be some sort of elemental? I wondered.

Eventually the tapping noise faded, which made me feel a lot better. Now the tunnel had narrowed and was really steep, the floor uneven and strewn with loose rocks. After a few minutes we emerged into a wider passageway that sloped from left to right. Until now the cave had been dry, but here water cascaded down the far wall and dripped from the roof above, and there were puddles on the ground. We followed the downward slope.

Soon the water underfoot became a shallow, fast-flowing stream, and we followed its course. We pressed on, our mood darkening as our confidence began to ebb away. The depth of the water steadily increased; eventually it came above our knees, the current so strong that I found it difficult to stay upright. By now we could hear the maenads calling to one another behind us, the sounds getting nearer and nearer.

Stumbling along, thigh deep in water, we reached what at first glance appeared to be a dead end. But the water level didn't seem to be rising any further—if there was no escape route, it would surely have already reached the roof of the cave. Only as we got closer did I notice the extreme turbulence of the water. It crashed against a wall of solid rock before swirling back on itself. It was a large whirlpool.

Somewhere below, we could hear a great echoing roar of falling water. It must be dropping through a hole into a cavern somewhere farther underground. Then we heard shouts and shrieks of anger from behind us. The maenads were closing on us, and we were trapped against the rock face.

Desperately I held the candle aloft and searched the walls that hemmed us in. There was a steep upward slope of scree to our right, a dry area above the water. To my relief, I saw that it led up to a small tunnel. I pointed toward it, and Alice immediately started to scramble up the loose rocks. I followed at her heels, but our pursuers were very close now. I could hear their feet scrunching up the scree, then pounding along the tunnel behind us.

They'd catch us in moments, I thought. Was it better to turn and face them now? The tunnel was very narrow: Only one could confront me at a time. That lessened the odds against us. I decided that it was indeed time to turn and fight.

I handed the candle to Alice. Then, holding my staff before me at forty-five degrees, I released the blade, remembering all that Arkwright had taught me. Breathe slowly and deeply. Spread your weight evenly. Let the enemy come to you and make the first move. Be ready with the counterstrike. . . .

The maenads were getting ready to attack, working themselves into a frenzy, issuing a torrent of words in Greek. I couldn't understand it all, but I got the general meaning. They were telling me what they intended to do to me.

"We'll rip out your heart! Drink your blood! Eat your flesh! Grind your bones!"

The first maenad ran straight at me, brandishing a knife and a murderous wooden spike. Her face was twisted into something beyond anger. She lunged. I stepped back and felled her with a hard blow to the temple. The one behind her moved toward me more cautiously. She had insane eyes but a cunning face and was waiting for me to make the first move. She wielded no weapon; her hands were stretched out in front of her. If she managed to get a grip on me, she would immediately start to tear my body to pieces. The others would rush in to help, and that would be the end of me.

She opened her swollen lips to reveal the sharp fangs within, and a nauseating stench wafted over me—far worse than the breath of a witch who used blood or bone magic. The maenads fed on carrion as well as fresh meat, and she had strips of putrefying flesh between her teeth.

Suddenly I heard a loud tap somewhere above—nothing to do with the maenads. Almost immediately it was answered by another, much louder and closer. The sounds began to build toward a deafening crescendo. Within seconds it was all around us, a cacophony of rhythmical tapping on the rock. It was getting louder and louder, an insistent, threatening thunder.

The maenad lost patience and ran at me. I used my staff like a spear, jabbing it into her shoulder. She shrieked and staggered back. All at once, perhaps loosened by the thunderous noise, rocks began to fall around us, and there was an ominous rumble overhead.

Something struck me a glancing blow on the head and I fell backward, half stunned. I struggled up onto my knees and caught a quick glimpse of Alice's terrified face; then the tunnel came down with a grating, grinding, rumbling roar, and everything went black.

I opened my eyes to see Alice bending over me. The candle had burned very low and was now little more than a stub. There was a bitter taste in my mouth. A piece of leaf lay under my tongue, some healing herb from Alice's leather pouch.

"Getting really worried, I was," she remarked. "You've been unconscious for ages."

She helped me to my feet. I'd a bad headache and a lump the size of an egg on the crown of my head. But of our attackers there was no sign.

"The maenads are buried under that pile of rubble, Tom, so we're safe for now."

"Let's hope so, Alice—they're really strong and any who've survived will start to move those rocks to get at us!"

Alice nodded and glanced at the rockfall. "I wonder what those sounds were. . . ."

"I don't like to think about it, but whatever caused them probably brought down the tunnel."

"Need to find a way out of here quickly, Tom. That candle ain't going to last long."

That's if there was another way out. If not, it was all over for us. We'd never be able to shift that rockfall. Some of the slabs were too big even for the two of us to lift.

We continued down the tunnel as quickly as we could;

the candle was starting to gutter. Soon we'd be in dark-ness, maybe never see daylight again.

It was then that I realized it wasn't flickering just because it was burning low. There was fresh air blowing toward us. But how big would the gap in the rock be? I wondered. Would we be able to get out? Gradually, as we climbed, the breeze became stronger. My hopes soared. And yes—within moments there was light ahead. There *was* a way out!

Minutes later, grateful to be free of what might have been our tomb, we emerged onto a high path. The moun-tainside was lit by the moon, which had become paler with the approach of dawn. I took the candle stub from Alice, blew it out, and thrust it into my breeches pocket against further need. Then, without a word, we continued east along a path that was taking us deeper into the mountains.

We had to press on and find a way through to the plain on the other side. I just hoped that Mam and the others had survived the maenad attack. If they had, they'd con-tinue on toward Meteora, and that's where we'd find them.

CHAPTER XII
LAMIAS

EVENTUALLY we reached a fork in the path. Both tracks led roughly eastward toward the plain, but which one should we take?

"Which path, Alice?" I asked.

She sniffed each in turn. "Ain't much choice," she said with a frown. "Neither one's safe. A dangerous place, this."

"What sort of danger?"

"Lamias. Lots of 'em."

Lamias lurked in mountain passes such as this, preying on travelers. The thought of them made me very nervous indeed—I remembered what Mab said she'd scryed: Alice being killed by a feral lamia on the journey toward the Ord. I was torn between telling her about it and keeping it quiet. But why tell her? I asked myself. She was alert to the danger from lamias anyway, and knowing would only make her more fearful.

But I was still fearful that Mab would be proved right.

"Perhaps we should stay here for a while, Alice," I suggested, looking up at the sky, which was already brightening. "The sun will be up soon. It can't be much more than half an hour or so before dawn."

Lamias couldn't stand sunlight—we'd be safe then—but Alice shook her head. "Reckon they'll have sniffed us out already. They'll know we're here, Tom. Stay in one spot and they'll come at us from all sides—they might arrive before the sun comes up. Best keep moving."

What she said made sense, so, on impulse, I chose the left-hand path. It rose steeply for a while before descending toward a small valley where sheer cliffs reared up toward the sky on both sides. Even when the sun came up, this area would remain in shadow. As we scrambled down, the pale moon was lost to view and I began to grow nervous. To our right was the dark entrance to a small cave. Then I began to notice the feathers scattered around us.

I'd seen that before, back in the County. It was a sign that feral lamia witches were close. When human prey wasn't available, they made do with smaller creatures such as mice and birds, using dark magic to place them in thrall while they ripped them to pieces and drank their blood.

Soon, to our horror, we saw more signs of danger: a second cave, fragments of dead birds—their wings, beaks, heads, and legs littering the blood-stained rocks outside it. But I noticed that the remains were old, not fresh kills.

"We've taken the wrong track, Alice! We need to go back!"

"Either that or move forward a lot faster!" she argued, but it was already too late.

We heard a chilling hiss and turned to find something big scuttling along the rocky path behind us. It was a feral lamia. The creature, at least one and a half times the length of my own body, was crouched on four thin limbs with large splayed hands, each elongated finger ending in a sharp, deadly talon. Long, greasy hair hung down onto the scaled back and across the face, too. What I could see of its features told me that the situation couldn't be worse. This was not the bloated face of a lamia witch that had recently fed, making it sluggish and less aggressive. No, it was gaunt, cadaverous, its heavily lidded eyes wide open and showing a ravenous hunger.

I turned, stepped in front of Alice, and raised my staff—lamias didn't like rowan wood. I drove it hard and fast toward its head. There was a dull thud as the end made contact and the creature backed away, hissing angrily.

I followed, jabbing at it again and again. It was then that I heard another angry hiss from behind; I turned to see a second lamia approaching Alice. Almost immediately a third scuttled up onto a large boulder to our right.

Rowan wood wouldn't be sufficient now, so I pressed the recess near the top of my staff and, with a sharp click, the retractable blade emerged from the end.

"Keep very close behind me, Alice!" I cried. If I could force the lamia back to where the path widened, we could race past it and make our escape.

Wasting no time, I drove my staff hard at the lamia ahead of me. My aim was true, and the blade pierced its right shoulder, sending up a spray of black blood. It screamed and retreated, so I advanced again, stabbing quickly, keeping it at bay, trying to maintain my concentration. Lamias are incredibly fast, and this slow retreat could at any moment turn into a rapid frenzied attack. The lamia could be on me in a second, its talons pinning me down, ravenous teeth biting into my flesh. So I had to focus and await my chance to drive my blade through its heart. Step by step, I continued to advance. *Concentrate!* I told myself. Watch! Focus! Get ready for the first hint of a surge toward me.

There was a sudden scream from behind. Alice! I risked

a quick glance over my shoulder. She was nowhere to be seen! Turning away from the wounded lamia, I began to run back along the track in the direction of that scream. There was no sign of her, and I halted on the path. Had I gone too far? I wondered.

Desperate, with my heart hammering with fear for Alice, I quickly retraced my steps until I came to a cleft in the rock. There were feathers and bird fragments on the ground in front of it. Had she been dragged inside? A shout from within confirmed that she had, but her voice sounded distant and somehow muffled. I eased myself through the gap and moved into the increasing gloom. I came to another cave, far smaller than the others—just a dark hole descending steeply into the ground.

Suddenly I saw Alice looking back at me. Her eyes locked with mine, and I saw her fear, pain, and desperation. The lamia's jaws were gripping her right shoulder and there was blood at her throat. It was dragging her down, headfirst, deeper into its lair. The last thing I saw was Alice's left ankle and pointy shoe disappearing from view. It happened so quickly. Before I could even move she was gone.

I rushed over to the opening, threw down my staff, fell to my knees, and thrust my left hand downward in a desperate attempt to grasp Alice's ankle. But she'd already been dragged too far. I reached into my pockets for the candle stub and my tinderbox. I'd need some light to follow her into the darkness. There was a lump in my throat. The lamia's teeth were in deep, and it might already be starting to drain her blood, I thought. It was exactly what Mab had predicted. And she'd said that Alice would die down there in the darkness. The witch would suck her blood until her heart stopped.

I heard a scrabbling noise from below. I was probably already too late. Frantic with fear for Alice, I suddenly remembered the dark wish that Grimalkin had given me. It was wrong to use it—it meant invoking the dark. But what choice did I have? How could I stand back and let Alice die when I had the power to save her? Tears welled in my eyes, and my throat began to constrict with emotion.

I couldn't imagine life without Alice. I had to do it.

But *would* using it save Alice? Would it really be strong enough?

"I wish Alice to be unhurt, safe and well!" I cried, and then repeated the wish quickly as Grimalkin had instructed. "I wish Alice to be unhurt, safe and well!"

I don't know what I expected to happen. Certainly not for Alice to simply appear safe and well at my side. I was hoping to see her crawl to safety from the lamia's lair. But all I could hear was the distant whine of the wind. Grimalkin had said that the wish contained years of stored power. Surely something should be happening by now?

But there was nothing, nothing at all, and my heart sank into my boots. The wish hadn't worked. Had I done something wrong? I looked down into the dark maw of the lamia's lair, and regret began to gnaw at my stomach. Why had I wasted my time using the wish? Why had I been so stupid? I should have lit my candle and crawled after her right away.

I opened my tinderbox, and it was then that I sensed

something right behind me and remembered the third lamia. In my haste to save Alice I'd forgotten all about it! I turned round. . . .

But it wasn't a lamia. No, it was something far worse. Standing there and smiling down at me was the Fiend himself.

He was in the shape of Matthew Gilbert, the murdered bargeman. Matthew had been an easygoing, burly man with large hands and a warm smile. The top two buttons of his shirt were open, revealing the brown hair on his broad chest. He looked every inch the genial fellow who had once plied his trade along the Caster-to-Kendal canal. But the Fiend had visited me in that form before, so I knew exactly who I was facing.

"Well, Tom, isn't this a special day? One I've waited a long time to arrive. You've finally used the dark!"

I stepped back in alarm at his words and shook my head—though I knew I was lying even to myself. How could I deny it? The Spook had warned that the Fiend would try to win me to his side, corrupting me bit by bit until my soul was no longer my own and I belonged to him. And he'd suggested that Alice was the most likely means to his achieving this end. And now it had happened. I'd used the dark to save Alice.

"Don't try and pretend that you haven't! After all, you've just used a dark wish. Do you think I don't know that? Your use of dark magic alerted me to what was happening, so I came right away. The wish has already saved Alice. She'll be with you soon—just as soon as I leave and allow time to return to normal. You are already free to move, but nothing else is. Look about you. Maybe then you'll believe me."

The Fiend could distort the flow of time, sometimes stop it altogether. I looked up through the cleft in the rock and saw a bird, some kind of hawk, high in the air near the crag above, but it wasn't moving. It was still and frozen against the pale sky.

"You were lucky to escape and reach these mountains," the Fiend continued. "The attack took you all by surprise. The Pendle witches who oppose me didn't detect the threat. Not even that clever little Mouldheel scryer. Your mother's power came to nothing because I darkened her foresight — I've been doing it for many months now. How can she hope to prevail against an enemy who has my support? Tell me that!"

I said nothing. It was bad enough facing something as terrible and powerful as the Ordeen. But behind her, ready with his even greater strength, stood the Fiend. Mam couldn't hope to beat him. The whole enterprise seemed doomed to failure.

"You've fallen silent, Tom. You know I'm right. So now I'll tell you more. I'll explain just how bad things really are. It's your birthday soon. You'll be fifteen, won't you?"

I didn't reply, but he was correct. I'd be fifteen on the third of August, which was now little more than a week away.

"Your mother is relying on you to carry through her doomed scheme," he continued. "Do you want to know what part you're to play in this foolishness?"

"I trust Mam," I told him. "I'm her son and I'll do whatever she wants."

"*Whatever?* That's generous, Tom. Very generous indeed. But you'll need to be generous—extremely generous—because she needs a lot from you. Your life, no less. On your fifteenth birthday, you are to be sacrificed in order to fulfill her desperate need for victory."

"You're lying!" I shouted, shaking with anger. "Mam loves me. She loves all her children. She wouldn't do that."

"Wouldn't she, Tom? Not even for the greater good? Individuals are expendable. She believes in the light and is prepared to do anything to defeat the dark. Even to sacrifice the thing she loves most. That's you, Tom. That's what she's going to do!"

"She wouldn't do that. She just wouldn't . . ."

"No? Are you so sure? A special blood sacrifice might just give her a chance. And your blood is very special, Tom. The blood of a seventh son of a seventh son."

I didn't answer. I'd said enough already.

The Fiend was enjoying my discomfort. "Not only that," he continued. "You are your mother's son as well. And she is not human. Do you know what she is?" He smiled.

"She's told you already, I can see that. You're so easy to read, Tom, like an open book. So you know what she's done in the past. How cruel and bloodthirsty she once was—a true servant of the dark. And despite her conversion to the light, she's reverting back to her original form. Think how easy it will be for a murderous creature like that to sacrifice you for a cause she believes in!"

Everything grew dark, and I felt as if I was falling through space—and about to experience some terrible impact. It was as if I'd been thrown off a cliff and was hurtling toward the rocks below. I was terrified, expecting to be smashed to pieces at any second.

CHAPTER XIII
MY BLOOD

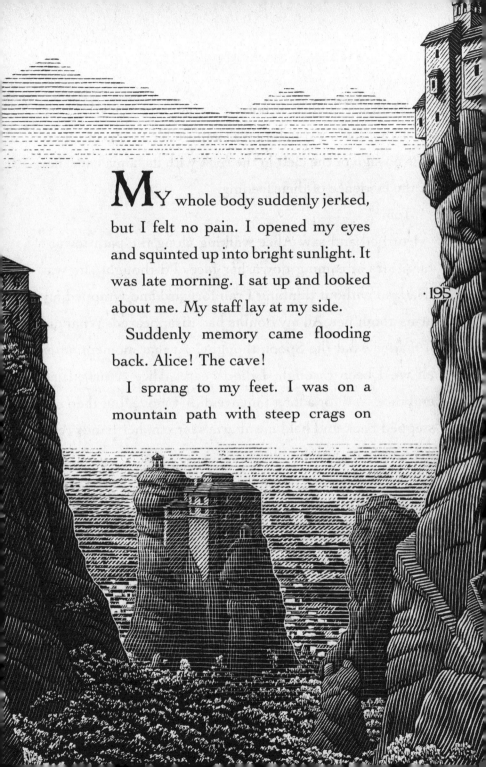

MY whole body suddenly jerked, but I felt no pain. I opened my eyes and squinted up into bright sunlight. It was late morning. I sat up and looked about me. My staff lay at my side.

Suddenly memory came flooding back. Alice! The cave!

I sprang to my feet. I was on a mountain path with steep crags on both sides. Whether or not it was the same track I'd been following the night before was impossible to say, but there was no sign of the cleft in the rock with its lamia cave, nor of the evidence of their feeding.

"Tom!"

I turned and saw Alice walking along the path toward me, tears streaming down her face. I'd thought she was dead, so without thinking I ran forward and wrapped my arms about her. All my doubts had disappeared. What did it matter what the Spook thought? At that moment, after all we'd been through, I didn't care. Alice returned my embrace, and for a long time we didn't move, but then she stepped back and held me at arm's length, her hands resting lightly on my shoulders.

"Oh, Tom—did last night really happen? It was dark, and the lamia's teeth were tearing at me. I was growing faint with loss of blood and I thought it was all over. I was dying. Then, the next moment, the sun was shining. And there isn't a single mark on my body. Was it just a nightmare?"

"It did happen," I told her. "But you see, Grimalkin gave

me two gifts, a blade and a dark wish. So when the lamia dragged you into her lair, I used the wish to save you. Then your father appeared."

So I told her what the Fiend had said, as much as I could remember; how he'd told me I was to be sacrificed. But I still didn't tell Alice that Mam was the original Lamia. I couldn't say it out loud. It hurt too much.

"He's just playing games with us," Alice said bitterly. "Using everything to his advantage as usual. As for you being a sacrifice—don't even give it a moment's thought. Your mam has risked everything to protect you. Even last night she sent you away from danger. Lying, he is, Tom. Lying as always."

"Maybe. But he wasn't lying last spring when he told me you were his daughter, was he? And what he said last night is possible. Even though Mam loves me, she might well sacrifice me and accept the pain—if it brought victory. Maybe she's been protecting me so that she can sacrifice me when she needs to."

"Your mam wouldn't do that, Tom."

"Not even if it was the only way to defeat the dark? Remember, she had me for that reason. She once told the Spook that I was her 'gift to the County.' I was born for a purpose."

"But she'd ask you first. Just like she asked you to give her the money from the trunks and come to Greece with her."

I paused, remembering Mam's love for her family. "I think you're right, Alice. If it's meant to happen, then she will ask me."

"And what would your answer be, Tom?"

I didn't reply. I didn't even like to think about it.

"We both know you'd say yes."

"But it would all be for nothing anyway," I said bitterly. "The Fiend will support the Ordeen with his own power while he lessens Mam's. He's already damaged her. Now she can't see into the future any longer. That's why she needs Mab. Even if the Ordeen was to be defeated, there's still the Fiend to reckon with. It all seems so hopeless."

Without another word, we set off eastward once more, following the meandering path through the mountains. It was a long time before we spoke again.

We finally descended through a pine forest, then crossed the arid plain toward Meteora. I knew that the monasteries were built on high rocks, so even if we'd wandered too far south, we should still be able to see them from a good distance.

On the second day of our journey, we thought we saw dust rising into the sky on the horizon. It could have been Mam's party—or maybe it was the maenads who'd attacked them. So, to avoid the risk of capture, we kept our distance.

Then at last, to the northeast, we saw the rocks of Meteora. The closer we got, the more spectacular they appeared. Rising from green thickets of trees and scrub, huge pillars of rock, sculpted by the elements, towered above us. And perched on their summits were the famed monasteries. It seemed impossible that such buildings could have been constructed on those perilous heights, let alone made secure enough to withstand the ravages of weather and time.

The small walled town of Kalambaka lay at the foot of the rocks, bordered to the south by groves of olive trees. Shielding my eyes against the sun, I searched the horizon. Mam had feared that we might be too late, but there was as yet no sign of the Ordeen's citadel.

We skirted the town and made our camp deep within the thickets below the rocks, hiding away from any watchers. Only the monks could look down on us from their strongholds.

The town was lit by lanterns strung on ropes between the houses; they moved to and fro when the wind was up. That first night we spent hours watching them: the stars above slowly wheeling about the sky from east to west while the lanterns danced below. We ate well, too. Alice caught some rabbits and they proved to be as succulent as any we'd tasted in the County.

On the second night, while we were eating, Alice sniffed danger and stood up quickly, her finger to her lips. But her warning came too late.

A massive shape came out of the trees into the clearing where we were eating. I heard a snort and a clash of metal, and at that moment the crescent moon appeared from behind a cloud, conjuring up a gleaming silver apparition before our startled gaze.

It was a horseman dressed in chain mail, two great swords attached to his saddle. And what a horse he rode! This was no heavy lumbering beast such as those used to draw barges or pull wagons back in the County; it was a thoroughbred, fine and high stepping, with an arched neck and a form built for speed. Its rider was a warrior from head to toe; he had an aquiline nose and high cheekbones, long hair, and a full mustache that obscured his mouth.

The rider drew his sword, and for a moment I thought he intended to attack, but he simply indicated that we should leave the clearing. We didn't argue; we simply turned and headed into the trees.

At dawn we realized that this warrior was a scout, clearing the way for his followers. A large group of them — a thousand strong at least — were soon approaching across

the plain. Their armor gleamed in the sunlight like bur-
nished silver, and the dust erupted behind them like a
storm cloud. They looked formidable.

They set up camp at the edge of the trees just north of
the town. Who were they? I wondered.

"Do you think they're something to do with the Ordeen,
Alice? Maybe more of her supporters?"

"Not sure, Tom, but your mam never mentioned anything about enemy warriors such as these, did she?
Only that she was going to hire mercenaries to keep
us safe from the maenads. That could well be them. In
which case they're on our side. Didn't expect so many
though."

"It would be nice to think it's the mercenaries, but we
can't risk approaching them."

So we kept our distance, retreating farther into the trees,
wondering who they were — friends or foes. As we waited,
Alice turned to me, reached into the pocket of her dress,
and held up a small earthen jar. It was the blood jar she'd
once showed me back in the County.

"I've been thinking about the Fiend a lot recently," she said. "We could make him keep his distance — from you at least — by using this."

There were two methods that witches employed to keep the Fiend at bay. One was to bear him a child. Grimalkin had done just that, and as a consequence he was forced to keep away from her. The other was to use a blood jar. Alice claimed that this one contained a few drops of blood from the dead water witch Morwena, who'd been the Fiend's daughter. If this was mixed with my blood, and carried by me, it would mean that he could have no contact with me.

I shook my head firmly. I'd used the dark already with the wish, and that was bad enough. Bit by bit it was happening; the Spook's fears were coming true. I was being compromised. Then a thought struck me. I remembered what my master had said months ago, after I told him that Alice might be the Fiend's daughter. He'd suggested that she couldn't have taken any of Morwena's blood; she'd probably simply used her own. The blood from any of the Fiend's offspring would do.

"It's your blood in that jar, isn't it, Alice?"

For a moment she seemed about to protest. Then her expression changed to one of defiance.

"Yes, Tom, it *is* my blood. You feel better now you know the truth? Feel good to show me up for a liar? Well, Morwena's blood or mine, it makes not the slightest difference. Mix a few drops of your blood with this, and once the jar's in your possession you won't have to face anything like that night in the mountains again, will you?"

I lowered my gaze.

"There's something else, too," she continued. "We'd have to stay together forever then. The blood jar would protect you—and me too if I stayed close to you. But if I wandered too far away from it, the Fiend would be there in a moment to take his revenge, because he'd know what I'd done. It wouldn't bother me much, Tom, being close to you. In fact I'd quite like it. And we need to take advantage of anything we can. Anything just to give us a chance."

"You mean well, Alice, so I'm not going to quarrel with you. But nothing's changed. I still feel the same way—I can't risk using the dark again. And do you think it would be good to be bound together like that? I'd always be afraid that something might separate us. I wouldn't dare let you out of my sight! How could we live like that?"

I didn't bother to add that we'd probably be separated as soon as we got back to the County anyway—if indeed we managed to survive this battle. If I continued as the Spook's apprentice, there was no way my master would ever allow Alice to live with us at Chipenden again.

Alice nodded sadly and pushed the jar back into her pocket again.

About an hour after dawn, Alice suddenly sat up and pointed at something in the distance. "Look over there," she said, turning to me. "I think I can see your mam's wagon!"

Straining my eyes, I searched the far boundary of the warriors' camp. At last I saw what could have been a dark wagon.

"Are you sure, Alice?" I asked.

"Difficult to see from here, but I think so," she replied.

I had been tormenting myself, wondering how I could possibly rescue Mam from such a host of captors, but now my fears were suddenly dispelled. Alice had been right after all. I continued watching, and after a while a small party left the camp on foot and went toward the rocks. There was someone walking at their head. A woman, heavily veiled and hooded against the sunlight.

"It's your mam, Tom! I'm sure of it!" Alice cried.

Just behind the hooded figure walked a man with a staff. I could tell by his gait that it was the Spook. There were others following at a distance. I recognized Seilenos and two more of the escort that had met us at Igoumenitsa. If it was indeed Mam, she didn't seem to be a prisoner at all.

We made our way down through the trees and out into the open. The veiled figure saw us immediately, waved, then beckoned us forward. When we got closer, she pushed her veil aside, turning her back to the sun. Alice was right. It was Mam.

She smiled—though she seemed a little withdrawn and

formal. There was a wildness about her eyes, and in the bright sunlight her face seemed even more youthful than before. The faint laughter lines around her mouth had disappeared altogether.

"Well done, Alice," she said. "You did well to get yourselves to safety. For a while it went hard with us, but we fought off the maenads until these warriors came to our aid. They're mercenaries, bought with more of the money you returned to me, son. They were riding west to meet us and arrived just in time to drive away our enemies. As I said, Tom, the maenads are numerous, and we'll need these men if we are to keep them at bay and complete our journey."

"Is everyone all right?" I asked. "Where's Bill Arkwright?"

"Aye, lad," answered the Spook. "Apart from a few cuts and minor wounds, everyone's fine. Bill's discussing tactics with the leader of those mercenaries. They're working out how best to deploy our forces as we approach the Ord."

"Now come with us," Mam commanded. "There's no time to waste. We're going to visit one of the monasteries. There are things we need to know."

"Is it that one, Mam?" I said, pointing up at the nearest one, perched on a high pinnacle to our right.

"No," she said, shaking her head and pulling the protective veil across her face again. "That one's called Ayiou Stefanou. Although it's spectacular and the closest to the town, it's not the highest or most important. No, we have a long journey ahead of us."

We walked for hours, the impressive rounded cliffs and pinnacles of Meteora always in our sight. At last we approached an imposing monastery built on a high, broad rock.

"That's Megalo Meteorou directly ahead," Mam said. "The grandest of them all. It's about six hundred and fifteen feet high, almost twice the height of Priestown Cathedral's steeple."

"How was it possible to build on a rock that high?" I asked, gazing up at it in amazement.

"There are lots of stories, son," Mam told me, "but that monastery was founded by a man called Athanasios hundreds of years ago. Monks had lived in caves hereabouts

for a long time, but this was the very first of the monasteries to be built. One story is that Athanasios flew on
the back of an eagle to reach the top." She pointed up to
where two eagles rode the thermals high above.

"It sounds a bit like the story about Hercules throwing
that big rock!" I said, smiling.

"No doubt it does, Tom. It's much more likely that he
was helped by the locals, who were skilled rock climbers."

"So how are we going to get up there?"

"There are steps, Tom. Lots of them. It'll be a hard
climb, but imagine how difficult they must have been to
cut into the rock! Just Mr. Gregory, you, and I will make
the climb. Alice must wait behind. The monks know me
well—I've talked to them many times—but women aren't
generally welcome up there."

The escort waited below with the disappointed Alice
while I followed Mam and the Spook up the stone steps.
There was no rail, and a sheer drop threatened to the side.
At last we came to an iron door set in the rock. A monk
opened it wide and admitted us to further flights of steep

steps. Finally we reached the summit and saw a large dome ahead of us.

"That's the *katholicon*," Mam said happily.

I knew the word, which meant a church or main chapel. "Is that where we're going?"

"No, we're going to visit the Father Superior in his private quarters."

We were led toward a small building and then into a spartan cell, where a monk with a gaunt gray face and a head shaven even closer than Bill Arkwright's squatted on the stone floor. His eyes were closed, and he hardly seemed to be breathing. I looked at the bare stone walls and the straw in the corner that served as a bed—not the accommodations I'd expected for the important priest who ruled the monastery.

The door closed behind us, but the Father Superior made no attempt to acknowledge us or move. Mam put a finger to her lips to indicate that we should be silent. Then I noticed the monk's lips moving slightly and realized that he was saying his prayers.

When he finally opened his eyes and regarded us each in turn, I saw that they were the color of the bluebells that brighten the County woodlands in spring. He gestured that we should join him on the floor, so we sat down facing him.

"This is my friend, Mr. Gregory, an enemy of the dark," Mam said, nodding toward the Spook.

The monk gave him a faint smile. Then his eyes locked upon mine. "Is this your son?" he asked. He spoke in Greek, in a dialect I found easy to understand.

"Yes, Father," Mam replied in the same language, "this is my youngest and seventh son, Thomas."

"Have you a plan to enter the Ord?" asked the monk, turning to Mam again.

"If you could use your influence to persuade them to stand aside, some of my party could take the place of Kalambaka's delegation."

The monk frowned. "To what purpose?" he demanded. "What would you hope to achieve by taking such a risk?"

"A few of the Ordeen's servants are already awake when

the Ord first appears—just the ones who receive the delegation. We will distract them, and while they are diverted, a larger attack will be mounted. We are hoping to reach the Ordeen and destroy her before she is fully awake—"

"Will you take part in the sacrificial blood ritual? Would you go that far?"

"There is more than one way to breach a citadel's defenses. I will employ the same device used by the ancients—a *wooden horse*," Mam added mysteriously.

I hadn't a clue what she meant, but the monk's eyes suddenly lit up in understanding; then he fixed his gaze upon me once more.

"Does the boy know what is required of him?" he asked.

Mam shook her head. "I will tell him when the time is right. But he's a loyal and obedient son and will do what is necessary."

At those words my heart sank. I remembered what the Fiend had told me. Had he been telling the truth? The Father Superior had used the term "sacrificial blood ritual."

Was I to be sacrificed in order to gain victory?

The Spook now spoke for the first time. "It seems to me that there's a great deal we haven't yet been told. No doubt we'll be finding out the worst soon enough," he said, giving Mam a withering glance. "But what can *you* tell me, Father? Have there been signs yet to indicate precisely when the Ord will pass through the portal?"

The Father Superior shook his head. "No, but it will be soon—days rather than weeks, we believe."

"We've little time to prepare," Mam said, rising to her feet. "We must take our leave of you. So I must ask you once again, Father—will you ask the delegation to stand aside so that we may replace them?"

The Father Superior nodded. "I will do as you ask. No doubt they'll be happy to be relieved of a duty that for most is a death sentence. But before you go, I would like you to hear us pray," he said. "The boy particularly. I sense that he has little idea of our power."

So we followed the Father Superior from his bare cell toward the magnificent dome of the *katholicon*. I was a little irritated by his comment. How did he know what I thought? I'd never really believed that prayers could achieve anything, but I'd always added my "Amen" when Dad had said grace before our family supper. I respected those who had faith and prayed, just as my dad had taught me. There were many ways to reach the light.

The church was splendid, with its ornate marble and beautiful mosaics. About a hundred monks were standing facing the altar with steepled hands as if already at prayer, though they hadn't yet begun. Suddenly they began to sing. Their prayer was a hymn. And what a hymn!

I'd heard the choirboys sing in Priestown Cathedral, but in comparison to this it had been little more than a tavern singsong. The voices of the monks rose up into the dome in perfect accord, to swoop and soar there like angels. You could sense the incredible strength of all those voices singing in harmony. A powerful sound with a single purpose.

Had those prayers *really* had the power to keep the Ordeen at bay? Apparently so. But the power of the dark had grown, and this time the bloodthirsty goddess would not be confined to the plain. Unless we could destroy her first, she would attack the County. But the odds against our success were very high.

We took our leave of the Father Superior and left the *katholicon*, the hymns of the monks receding behind us. It was then that I caught a glimpse of the Spook's face. It was twisted with anger as it had been when he'd left me at the farmhouse and rushed back to Chipenden. I sensed that he was getting ready to speak his mind, and that Mam would receive the full force of its withering blast.

CHAPTER XIV
PORTENTS

"THE blood ritual ... what does it involve?" demanded the Spook, staring hard at Mam.

We were in her tent, seated on the ground in a circle. Alice was on my left, the Spook to my right. Also present were Bill Arkwright and Grimalkin. The Spook had given Mam a piece of his mind as soon as we returned to camp. Politely but firmly, he'd demanded to know exactly what we were all facing, especially the delegation; he'd even accused Mam of holding back important information that we badly needed.

This meeting was the result of those hot words. Mam was grim and unsmiling. I sensed there were things she didn't want to say—certainly not to this gathering. I think she would have preferred to speak to me alone.

"I don't know everything, far from it," she admitted. "What I know I've learned from talking to the survivors of previous delegations. Some of the accounts were contradictory, probably because their minds had been damaged by the experience. It seems that the servants of the Ordeen demand blood. And they'll want *your* blood, Tom."

"*My* blood? Why will they want my blood?"

"Because you'll be the youngest, son. You see, each time a delegation visits, they take the blood of its youngest member. And we really do want to give them your blood—that's important."

"You expect your son to give his life?" the Spook demanded angrily.

Mam shook her head and smiled. "This time they won't be killing the donor—although that's what has happened in the past. This time they'll just get a cupful of blood." Her gaze moved from the Spook to me. "Do you know the story of the fall of Troy?" she asked.

I shook my head. Although she'd taught me Greek, Mam had spoken little of her homeland; my life back at the farm had been filled with tales of the County, its boggarts, witches, and wars.

"In ancient times, we Greeks fought a long and terrible war against Troy," she continued. "We besieged the city for many years, our forces camped outside its impregnable walls. At last our people crafted a great wooden horse and left it on the plain before Troy and sailed away, pretending to have given up the fight. That huge wooden horse was assumed to be an offering for the gods, and the Trojans dragged it into their city and began to celebrate their victory.

"It was a trick. The horse was hollow, and that night,

when the Trojans had retired to their beds, exhausted and drunk with wine, the Greeks who'd hidden inside it crept out and threw open the gates of the city, allowing their returning army to enter. Then the slaughter began. Troy burned, and the war was finally won. Son, *you* will be my Trojan horse. We will trick the Ordeen's servants and breach the defenses of the Ord."

"How?" I asked.

"The Ordeen needs a sacrifice of human blood to awaken her from her sleep in the dark beyond the portal. Your blood will animate her, give her life. But your blood is mine also; the blood of her sworn enemy will be flowing through her veins. It will weaken her. Limit her terrible power. Not only that. Sharing the same blood will make you like kin. You will have access to places that would not normally be open to you. And so will I. The Ordeen's defenses—traps, snares, and other dark entities—will be weakened. Those who guard her have senses that are attuned to blood. They may not all see you, or me, as a threat. That is what I hope to achieve."

"You say just a cupful of Tom's blood?" said the Spook. "Previously a life's been taken. Why should it be different this time? Tell me that!"

"There's an invitation for one of the delegation to come forward in combat," said Mam. "The rules aren't completely clear, but victory for the delegation champion means that the life of the donor is no longer forfeit."

"Has the delegation's champion ever won?" the Spook persisted.

"Usually there's nobody brave and strong enough to volunteer. This time our champion will be Grimalkin."

"And what if she loses?" Arkwright asked, speaking up for the first time.

"I will win," said Grimalkin calmly, "so the question needn't be answered."

"That's not good enough!" he persisted. "You don't know what you might face inside that citadel. Maybe some demon, some dark entity that can't be defeated by a mortal."

Grimalkin smiled grimly, parting her lips to show her

sharp, pointed teeth. "If flesh clothes its bones, I will cut it. If it breathes, I will stop its breath. Otherwise"—she shrugged—"we will all die."

Mam sighed and then finally answered Arkwright's question. "If Grimalkin loses, the lives of all the delegation are immediately forfeit, and our main attack will fail. Every one of our party will be slain, along with the inhabitants of Kalambaka and the monks. Then, seven years from now, the Ordeen will be free to use her portal to materialize anywhere she pleases."

For a while after that, nobody spoke. The enormity of what we faced and the disaster that would follow our defeat were awful to contemplate. It was the ex-soldier, Bill Arkwright, who shook us from our stupor.

"Let's assume that Grimalkin succeeds," he began. "As far as the journey itself is concerned, I've discussed the deployment of the mercenaries with their leaders. There should be no problem in keeping the maenads at a distance. But what about the actual attack? How are the rest of us to get into the Ord?"

"There's only one entry point that would give our attack any real chance of success," Mam explained. "Fifty paces to the left of the main gate, high on the wall, is a huge gargoyle. It's a skull, with horns like a stag's antlers branching from its forehead. Beneath it is a tunnel leading to the inner courtyard of the Ord. That tunnel is the route into the Ord taken by the delegation—it's the easiest way into the citadel. The Pendle witches will attack first. Soon afterward, our mercenaries should be able to ride through and lay siege to the inner defenses."

"What if it's too heavily defended?" Arkwright asked.

"That's a chance we'll have to take. If we attack soon enough, all should be well. As we know, servants of the Ordeen who receive the delegation awake as soon as the Ord has cooled. But they will be distracted by the delegation and hopefully slain by the Pendle witches soon after Tom's blood has been drunk. That's what I hope for, anyway. As for the rest of her servants, it is hours before they are fully alert. We must reach the Ordeen and slay her before she regains her strength."

"How will those on the outside know that the delegation has completed its work?" Arkwright asked.

"Grimalkin will use a mirror," Mam told him.

I saw the Spook's face tighten, but he said nothing.

"Once we're inside the Ord, do we know where to find the Ordeen?" I asked.

Even before she shook her head, I could tell by Mam's face that she didn't know. "We assume she will be somewhere away from the main entrances that is easy to defend. It seems likely she will be sleeping at the top of one of the three towers, but there is also a domed structure beyond them. Once inside the inner citadel, we should be able to search out the Ordeen, though we will still have to contend with denizens of the dark."

For a long time after hearing those grim words, nobody spoke. It seemed to me that we had very little hope of success, and I'm sure we all shared that view, perhaps even Mam. Then I started to think about the delegation. Would Mam be part of it?

"The delegation . . . who's going with me, Mam?"

"Grimalkin, Seilenos, and ten more of my escort. There'll be great danger, and not all of you will come back. I only wish that I could go with you and share those perils, but the Ordeen and her servants know me as their enemy. I fear I'd be recognized immediately, and our plan would fail. However, I've told Grimalkin all I know about the likely dangers. For example, you'll come upon a table heaped with food and wine—but you should neither eat nor drink. That's important."

"Is the food poisoned?" I asked.

"Not poisoned. Enchanted. It's charged with dark magic. So beware," Mam warned, her voice hardly more than a whisper. "Touch neither food nor drink. Those who eat the food of the Ordeen can never go home—"

"If Tom's going into danger, then I want to go, too!" Alice cried out, speaking for the first time.

Mam shook her head. "Your place will be by my side, Alice."

"No, that ain't good enough!" she said, springing to her feet. "I have to be with Tom."

"You stay away from him, girl," said the Spook.

"Stay away? He'd be dead if it weren't for me—and you all know it."

Mam shook her head. "Sit down!" she commanded.

"Ain't going to sit down until you give me what I want!" Alice retorted, almost spitting out the words. "You *owe* me this! And there are things even *you* don't know yet!"

Mam came to her feet to face Alice, anger in her face. At that moment the tent canvas began to flap. It had been a calm evening, but now a wind was getting up. Moments later, it was gusting furiously, threatening to tear the fabric from its supporting poles.

Mam led the way outside and looked up at the sky. "It begins," she said, pointing toward the horizon. "That's the first of the portents. The Ordeen is preparing to move through the portal."

A gale was blowing strongly from the south, and on that horizon there was an unmistakable yellow tint to the sky. It looked like a big storm was brewing. This was the first of the signs. Mam was sure of it. So we made our preparations. We would start our journey at dawn.

○ ○ ○

It was a restless night, disturbed by animals fleeing from the south. At one point our camp was invaded by a pack of scampering, squealing rats. Birds shrieked with panic as they flapped their way north into the darkness.

About an hour before dawn, unable to sleep, I stepped outside to stretch my legs. Seilenos stood there, looking up at the sky. He saw me and came across, shaking his head.

"Well, young spook, we win or die this day. A dangerous land, this. Land of many mysteries, too. Much danger ahead. You stay close to me and be all right. Seilenos, he know what to do. Ask me anything. I explain. Lamias and elementals I know all about. I will teach you. . . ."

I remembered the mysterious sounds in the tunnel before the roof came down. I was curious to know what had been responsible. "After the attack on the camp, Alice and I hid in a cave and had to fight off some maenads, but there was something else—strange tapping noises all around us. Then there was a rockfall that nearly killed us."

"Tapping? What kind, this tapping? Fast or slow?"

"It started slow, but then got much faster. It had a sort of rhythm to it and built to a crescendo so that the rocks fell, nearly killing us."

"Lucky to escape with your lives, young spook. Dangerous elementals, those. Live in caves and called tappers. Try to drive humans away. First use fear. Frightful tapping sounds. Next bring down big rocks and try to crush you. When hear tappers—run fast!"

That was probably good advice, but we'd been faced with dangerous maenads and were forced to stand and fight. Seilenos patted me on the shoulder and headed for one of the fires where breakfast was being prepared. I stayed where I was, waiting for the sun to rise.

Not that I saw it, for at dawn the sky was filled with a yellow haze. The Spook told me we needed to fast in order to prepare to face the dark, so we didn't eat breakfast. Even Bill Arkwright, never one to go for long without food, confined himself to one thin slice of bread, but Seilenos ate his fill, grinning and shaking his head when he saw that we'd left our plates of lamb and boar untouched.

"Eat up! You need strength. Who knows when we eat again?"

"As I told you, we do things differently in the County — and for good reason," growled the Spook. "I'm about to face what might well be the greatest danger from the dark that I've encountered in all the years I've been practicing my trade. I want to be fully prepared, not so full of food that I can hardly think!"

Seilenos just laughed again and continued to stuff large slices of meat into his mouth, washed down with red wine.

As we prepared to head south, Alice joined me, a little smile lighting her face.

"Your mam's changed her mind, Tom," she said. "I'm to be part of the delegation after all."

"You sure you want to do this, Alice? Wouldn't you be safer with Mam? I don't want anything to happen to you."

"And I don't want anything to happen to *you*. That's why I'll be by your side. You're safer where I am, Tom. Trust me. And we do want to be together on your birthday, don't we?"

I smiled and nodded. I'd forgotten all about my birthday.

Today was the third of August. I'd just turned fifteen. But Alice hadn't finished yet. I could sense that she was about to say something else. Something I wouldn't like. She kept glancing at me sideways and biting her bottom lip.

"You're going into the Ord with Grimalkin, who's a witch assassin, a servant of the dark. And you used the dark wish she gave you to save me. So what's the difference between doing that and using the blood jar to keep the Fiend at bay?" Alice demanded. "Take the jar. A birthday present from me to you."

"Leave it, Alice!" I shouted in annoyance. "It's hard enough without you saying things like that. Don't make things worse, please."

Alice fell silent. I felt as if I was sinking ever downward. Even Mam was forcing me to compromise with the dark. I knew she had little choice and I had to be part of it—nonetheless, all the Spook's fears seemed to be well founded.

CHAPTER XV
THE APPROACH TO THE ORD

WE made our way south, fighting against the human tide of those fleeing the Ord. Refugees were everywhere. Some were on foot, clutching possessions or carrying children; others had loaded what they could onto small carts, which they pulled or pushed by hand. Many kept glancing back and called out warnings, telling us to flee

· 233 ·

with them; they were desperate and fearful for themselves and their families.

We walked all morning across that arid landscape under the sickly yellow sky. Dark whirlwinds had been visible on the horizon, moving north and destroying everything in their path, but luckily they hadn't passed close to us. And now the wind had dropped, the air growing warmer and more oppressive by the minute. I was carrying my staff as well as my bag, which I had retrieved from Mam's wagon. Mam's escort rode just behind her, and behind them were the Pendle witches, led by Grimalkin. Bill Arkwright and the Spook walked to the right of Alice and me, the three dogs following in their wake. And far to our rear, at least a couple of hundred yards distant, were the mounted mercenaries.

Alice and I were both weary and afraid of what was to come, so we hardly exchanged a word. At one point Bill Arkwright came up alongside me.

"Well, Master Ward, how does this compare to the County? Have you changed your mind yet? Would you like to live here?" he asked.

"I wish I was back home," I told him. "I miss the green hills and woods—even the rain!"

"Aye, I know what you mean. This is a parched land, all right, but from what your mam said I think we'll be getting some rain soon enough."

He was referring to the deluge that would come soon after the appearance of the Ord. "There's something I'd like to ask you, Master Ward. If anything happens to me, would you take care of the dogs? No doubt Mr. Gregory wouldn't want them at Chipenden—a boggart and dogs don't mix too well! But you'd be able to find them a good home somewhere, I'm sure."

"Of course I will."

"Well, let's hope it won't come to that. Let's hope we're all safely back home in the County before too long. There's danger ahead, worse than we've ever faced before, I fear. So just in case we don't meet again, here's my hand in friendship. . . ."

Arkwright held out his hand, and I shook it. With a nod and a smile toward Alice, he left my side. I felt sad, it was as if we were saying good-bye forever.

But there was another good-bye to face, this one from the Spook. Awhile later, he too moved across to walk beside me. As he approached, I noticed Alice fall back to join Grimalkin, who was now behind us.

"Are you nervous, lad?" my master asked me.

"Nervous and scared," I told him. "I keep taking slow, deep breaths, but it doesn't seem to help much."

"Well, it will, lad, it will. So just keep at it, and remember all I've tried to teach you. And once we get inside that citadel, stay close to me. Who knows what dangers we'll find there?"

He patted me on the shoulder, then moved away again. I wondered if that was because he didn't like walking too close to Alice. Soon afterward we paused for a short rest, and I wrote down what Seilenos had told me about tappers in my notebook. It helped to calm me down. No matter what danger threatened, I had to keep up with my training.

When we set off again, I had one more visit—one that

both Alice and I could well have done without. Mab and her two hook-nosed sisters approached us.

"What you been up to, Tom?" Mab asked, looking sideways at me. "That's no dead girl walking beside you. She should be dead by rights, that Alice Deane. Saw it happen. Saw that witch lamia sucking her blood and tearing her with its teeth. Only something from the dark could have saved her. That's the only thing I couldn't have seen coming. What you been up to, Tom? Must have meddled with the dark, I think. That's the only thing that could've done it! What does Mr. Gregory think about that, eh?"

Alice ran and pushed Mab backward so that she almost overbalanced and fell. "Things are bad enough without having to listen to you talk rubbish. Get you gone! Leave Tom alone!"

Mab turned to Alice and stretched out her hands in front of her, clearly intending to scratch her face, but I quickly stepped between them. Mab shrugged and backed off.

"We'll be on our way," she said, her mouth twisting into a smile. "Leave you to think over what's been done and what's been said. You're close to the dark now, Tom. Closer than you've ever been before."

With that Mab and her sisters moved away, leaving me with my thoughts. I continued to walk with Alice, but neither of us spoke. What was there to say? We both knew that I'd been compromised by the dark. I was just glad that the Spook hadn't overheard what Mab had said.

Late that morning the weather began to change. The wind got up again, blustering into a gale that screamed about our ears. We journeyed on through the heat, but we were now very uncomfortable.

Soon Alice pointed directly ahead. "Look at that, Tom. Ain't ever seen anything like that before!"

At first I could see nothing; then a menacing shape loomed up on the horizon.

"What is it? A cliff? Or a black ridge of hills?" I asked.

Alice shook her head. "It's a cloud, Tom. And a strange dark one for sure. Ain't natural, that! Don't like the look of it one little bit."

In normal circumstances such a fearsome cloud would have heralded a violent storm, with a heavy downpour to come. But as we drew nearer, I could see that it was curved at its rim like a great black plate or shield. The wind ceased again, and the temperature began to drop alarmingly; whereas before we'd been scorched by the heat, now we began to shiver with cold and fear. We were suddenly plunged into a twilit world, our faces deep in shadow.

I looked about me: Alice, Arkwright, and the rest of our company, including the Pendle witches, were walking very slowly, with bowed heads, as if oppressed by the weight of the darkness above us. Only the Spook held his head high.

Although there was now not a breath of wind, I could see that the ominous and unusual cloud was in turmoil, churning and swirling far above as if some giant was stirring it with a massive stick. Soon I could hear a high, shrill shriek; suddenly, on the distant horizon, I saw a column of orange light.

"That's what Mam told us about, Alice," I exclaimed, pointing ahead. "It's the pillar of fire. The Ord must be somewhere within it!"

We were at least three miles away from the fiery column, but I could soon feel its warmth on my forehead despite the drop in temperature around us. We were heading for an immense crimson vortex, a gigantic throbbing artery connecting sky to earth. It looked dramatic and disturbing, and seemed to be thickening and flexing rhythmically; I was afraid that it might suddenly explode outward to engulf us all. Lightning forked up from its base, bifurcations of white and blue like the jagged branches of trees reaching out into the black cloud above.

Although fixed in the same spot, the column was rotating widdershins, against the clock. Swirling dust formed a mushroom at its base, and at its apex combined with the substance of the swirling cloud. The shrill whine grew to a raucous screech and there was now a sharp smell, at first difficult to name. It bit high into my nostrils and I could taste it on the back of my tongue.

"It smells like burning flesh!" exclaimed Alice, sniffing the air. "And sounds like souls screaming in Hell. They're burning! All burning!"

Yet, if so, it was the reverse of what my senses told me: this was creation rather than cremation, flesh reborn of fire. If what Mam had told me was correct, the Ordeen and her servants were entering our world in the midst of those flames. It was a fiery portal. The heat upon my face abated somewhat; the fury lessened as the colors shifted across the spectrum, crimson slowly transmuting into bronze.

"There's a huge building!" cried Alice, pointing fearfully ahead. "Look! Inside! You can see it inside the flames! That's the Ord!"

Alice was right. I could see the vortex slowing and shrinking, but the process was one of definition rather than collapse; now almost transparent, it allowed us to make out the shape of the Ord that lay within, that dark dwelling place of the Ordeen.

It had three twisted spires of equal height, so tall they

almost reached up into the cloud. Behind them, as though protected, was the dome Mam had talked about. And both towers and dome rose from a massive edifice that resembled a great cathedral, though far larger and more magnificent than Priestown's, the biggest church in the County. And while a cathedral sometimes took decades to build, this seemed to have been formed in a matter of moments.

The pillar of fire had now disappeared altogether. We moved on, getting closer and closer to the dark mass of the Ord, which rose up before us like some gigantic, terrifying beast. Although the outer darkness increased again, there was a strange new light radiating from inside the Ord. It was now lit from within by a bronze glow that was increasing in power even as I watched. Now, for the first time, I was able to appreciate the detail of the structure. Each twisted spire had long, narrow windows, arched at the top like those of a church. They were open to the air, and through them the inner fires shone more brilliantly.

"There are horrible things moving inside the windows,"

Alice whispered, her face filled with awe and terror. "Things from Hell."

"It's just your imagination, Alice," I told her. "It's too far away to see anything properly."

But notwithstanding my rebuke, I *could* see movement at some of those windows, indeterminate shapes that flickered like wraiths against the light. I didn't like to think what they might be. Then my eyes were drawn to the main entrance—the largest of the cavernous doorways that gave access to the structure. It was high and arched, and although it glowed brightly, deep within it was a darkness so complete that I was suddenly seized by dread of what it concealed. The Ord had come through a portal from the dark, and anything might lurk within it.

We were nearing it now. The citadel was immense, rearing up before us to block out the darkness of the sky.

A shouted order rang out from behind us, and we turned to see the warriors come to a halt before changing their formation into two crescents, horns facing the Ord. They looked formidable, with their glittering mail and weapons.

They had performed the first of their two tasks well. The maenads had been kept at bay; occasionally, small patrols had peeled off from the main force to drive them away and hunt them down. Now these mercenaries faced an even more dangerous assignment: They were soon to ride straight into the heart of the citadel and fight the dark beings within.

We walked on. It had been agreed that the mercenaries wouldn't approach until it was time to attack. I gazed at the citadel, searching along its outer wall, and finally my eyes found the secondary entrance that Mam had described. Above it was a gargoyle skull with huge antler horns. This was where the delegation would enter. If we failed, the Ordeen's servants would surge out through the main entrance to ravage the area.

Suddenly I felt the first drops of moisture on my face, drops that quickly became a torrent of warm rain falling through the utterly still air. As it descended, drumming furiously on the hard, dry ground, steam began to rise from the Ord, and the fanciful idea came to me that some invisible blacksmith, having completed his work, was now quenching the heat to temper it for his intended purpose.

Within moments a dense white mist was rolling toward us and the visibility was reduced to a few feet. Everything became eerily silent. It wasn't long before Grimalkin loomed out of the mist, along with Seilenos and the other members of Mam's escort who would make up the thirteen of the delegation.

Mam turned to me, patting me on the shoulder in reassurance. "It's time. You'll need to be brave, son. It won't be easy. But you have the strength to come through it."

"Won't the maenads have warned the Ordeen that we're approaching? Won't they tell her that we have an army of mercenaries with us?"

Mam shook her head. "No, they can't contact the Ordeen directly. They simply wait for her arrival and then take advantage of the horror that she brings, feasting on the dead and dying."

"But won't we have been seen anyway? Won't those already awake within the Ord guess what we intend to do?"

"Although ours is larger than normal, an armed escort always accompanies the delegation to the Ord, so it's nothing new. To the watchers inside, these assembled warriors are just flesh and blood waiting to be devoured. They won't expect the attack we've planned."

Mam suddenly hugged me tightly. When she let me go, there were tears in her eyes. She tried to speak; her mouth opened, but no words came out.

Someone moved out of the shadows behind her. My master. He laid a hand on my shoulder and drew me to one side.

"Well, lad, this is it. I don't like your mother's methods and I don't like the company she keeps, but I do know that she belongs to the light and she's doing what she's doing for the good of us all. Whatever you face in there, remember all I've taught you, be true to yourself, and don't forget that you're the best apprentice I've ever had."

I thanked him for his kind words, and he shook my hand.

"Just one other thing," he said as I turned to go. "I don't

know why your mother is sending that little witch in with you." He gestured at Alice. "She seems to think the girl will protect you. I truly hope so. But don't for one moment forget who her parents are. She's the daughter of a witch and the Devil. She's not one of us and never can be, no matter how hard she tries. You'll do well to remember that, lad."

His words struck at my heart. But there was nothing I could say in reply, so I merely nodded, picked up my bag and staff, and went over to where Grimalkin was waiting with Alice and the others. She led us into the mist, heading to the Ord.

CHAPTER XVI
FILL THE CUP!

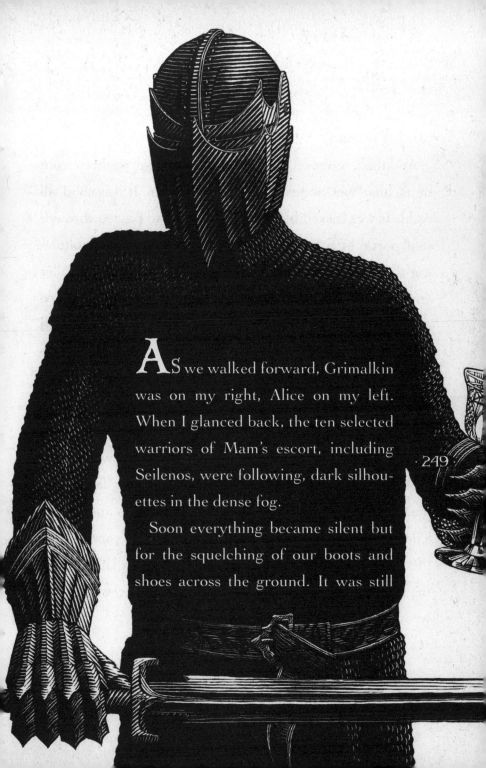

As we walked forward, Grimalkin was on my right, Alice on my left. When I glanced back, the ten selected warriors of Mam's escort, including Seilenos, were following, dark silhouettes in the dense fog.

Soon everything became silent but for the squelching of our boots and shoes across the ground. It was still raining—not as heavily now, but the ground was rapidly turning to mud.

And then, too soon, the walls were suddenly right in front of us, huge wet stones glistening in the rain. It was solid, all right: It was incredible to think that it had passed through that portal of fire into our world. We turned left, following the wall for a little way until we reached the smaller entrance. Grimalkin did not falter as she led us forward under the gargoyle and into the Ord. A tunnel stretched away ahead of us, but she turned into a doorway on the left and we followed her into a hall of such vastness that the center of the high vault above was lost in darkness. The light here was dim. I could see no torches, but there was an even diffusion of low light. Directly before us was a long table covered with a cloth of red silk; upon it lay dishes made of silver and bronze, heaped with fruits and meats. There were thirteen ornate high-backed chairs carved from the whitest ivory and upholstered in rich black silk, and on the table before each chair was a golden goblet, exquisitely wrought and filled to the brim with red wine.

As the light increased, so the colonnades to our right and left came into view, and I could now see that the floor between the rows of pillars was a fine mosaic depicting great serpents entwined about one another. I was following those meandering forms across the floor when I stopped in shock.

In the middle of the floor was a dark pit. For some reason that opening filled me with dread. I began to shake with fear. What did it contain? I wondered.

We all sat down but, remembering Mam's instructions, ignored the food and drink on the table. The chairs had been positioned on one side of the table so that we all faced the pit.

We heard echoing footsteps, distant at first, then getting nearer and nearer. A head slowly rose into view out of the pit, as if lifted by a giant hand. Someone was climbing up the steps within it. A dark figure stepped out onto the mosaic floor, a warrior encased from head to foot in black armor. In his left hand he carried a long blade; in his right, a large crystal chalice.

He walked toward us with measured steps, and I had a few seconds to study him. There was no vent in that black helmet for either mouth or nose, but two thin horizontal slits were positioned where his eyes should have been. But I could see no eyes—nothing but darkness. His armor was black chain mail, and his boots were both unusual and deadly. Their toes ended in sharp barbed spikes.

He halted by our table, and when he spoke, fear gripped my heart. The voice that boomed out was cold and arrogant, with a harsh metallic quality.

"Why do you not eat the food provided to sustain you? Why do you not drink from the wine so freely given?" he demanded reproachfully, his words echoing from ceiling to floor and wall to wall.

His questions brought us all to our feet, but it was Grimalkin who spoke for the rest of us.

"For your hospitality we thank you," she replied, her voice calm and dignified. "But, as yet, we neither hunger nor thirst."

"That is your decision to make, but despite that, an exchange is

required for what we have freely provided. Fill the chalice so that my mistress may live!"

So saying, the dark warrior held the vessel out to the witch assassin.

"With what shall we fill it?" Grimalkin asked.

At first the warrior did not reply. His head turned, and he seemed to look along the row, checking each of us in turn. Then my heart filled with dismay. I was still unable to see his eyes, but I knew beyond all doubt that his gaze had settled upon me.

"My mistress needs sustenance. She must drink warm blood from the body of the youngest here!" he declared, pointing his blade directly at me. *"Surrender his life. Fill the cup from his heart's blood!"*

I began to tremble again. Despite everything I had been told, even though I knew that Grimalkin would fight for my life, I was afraid. All sorts of doubts began to whirl through my head, and a cold fear clutched at my heart. Was I going to die here? Had the Fiend spoken the truth after all? Had this been Mam's intent all along—to make a sacrifice of me? Perhaps her slow reversion to the feral state had leached away any human love she might have had for her son.

Grimalkin shook her head. "You ask too much!" she cried in a loud, commanding voice. "We demand the right of combat!"

The warrior inclined his head. *"That is your right. But do not undertake such a challenge lightly. If I win, all your lives are immediately forfeit. Do you still wish to proceed?"*

Grimalkin bowed her acceptance of the terms. And suddenly everything grew dark. I heard sighs and whispers all around, and then, as light filled the hall once more, I saw that the warrior now stood armed and ready in the middle of the mosaic floor. He no longer carried the chalice. In his right hand he hefted a long blade; in his left, a spiked metal orb on a long chain.

Grimalkin drew two long blades and, with consummate grace, leaped across the table, landing like a cat. She began to pad toward the armored figure, a slow, deadly stalking of her opponent. And it seemed to me that a smile played about the lips of the witch assassin. This was what she lived for. She would enjoy combat with this knight. She liked to test her skill against a worthy opponent, and I knew that she had found one who would push her to the limit. Grimalkin was not afraid to die. But if she failed and was killed, then we also would forfeit our lives.

Her adversary stepped forward and began to whirl the spiked orb around his head. The chain spiraled higher and higher, the heavy metal sphere at its end scything through the air with enough force and velocity to remove Grimalkin's head from her body.

But not for nothing was Grimalkin the assassin of the Malkin witches. Timing her attack to perfection, she stepped inside the orbit of the whirling orb and struck straight at the left eye slit of the helmet, her blade rasping against metal to miss by less than the width of a finger.

The warrior's sword was as swift as Grimalkin's blades, and they exchanged savage blows, but she was in too close for him to wield the orb. It hung uselessly on its chain while she used two blades against his one. For a while she seemed to have the upper hand and pressed him hard.

Then it was the warrior's turn to gain the ascendancy. The witch assassin had no armor, and now, in retreat, that drawback became apparent. Twice he directed kicks at her body, the spike threatening to disembowel her, but she spun like a wheel, with great economy of movement, staying too close for him to use the chain and orb. Again and again her blades struck her opponent's body with metallic clangs but were deflected by the armor that encased it. It seemed impossible that she could survive, let alone win. What chance had she against such a heavily protected foe? Her legs and arms were naked, her flesh vulnerable.

It suddenly struck me that she had given up something that would have been greatly to her advantage. Had she retained the blade and dark wish, she could have employed them now. She had made a great sacrifice indeed.

Now Grimalkin whirled away from her enemy, moving counterclockwise in a circling retreat to our table. I became concerned. The tactic seemed ill-advised. At this distance the warrior could once more wield his deadly orb effectively against her. He began to whirl it above his head, faster and faster, readying himself for the killer blow. Grimalkin stepped closer to him, as if placing herself in the perfect position and waiting for the spiked orb to crush her. My heart was in my mouth. I thought it was all over.

But when the weapon descended, the witch assassin was no longer there. The orb struck the table a terrible blow, sending dishes and goblets crashing to the floor. And then Grimalkin committed herself, aiming directly for the slit in the helmet that marked the position of her enemy's unseen left eye. Her blade struck home, and a great scream of pain filled the hall.

In an instant all became dark, the air freezing cold. Powerful dark magic was being used. I felt dizzy and reached out to the table to steady myself. The great hall was silent as the echo of that shriek faded. But then, in the darkness, I saw two glittering eyes moving toward us from the direction of the pit.

Again the light steadily increased, and we were all

seated at the table—although I couldn't remember having sat down. The goblets and dishes that littered the floor had been returned to their proper places. Grimalkin was back in her original position at the table.

The dark warrior was once more standing directly before us, carrying the crystal chalice and his long blade. Was it the same man? Had he been returned to life by dark magic? Is was as if the fight with Grimalkin had never happened.

"My mistress needs sustenance. She must drink warm blood from the body of the boy!" he declared, pointing his blade directly at me again. *"Fill the cup!"*

As the fearsome warrior held out the crystal chalice, my heart fluttered in my chest with fear.

"We've won, child!" Grimalkin whispered into my ear, her voice filled with triumph. "He no longer demands your life—just that we fill the cup. It's exactly what we want."

Silently the warrior placed the crystal goblet on the red silk of the tablecloth. Grimalkin picked it up and withdrew a short knife from its leather scabbard. She turned toward me. "Roll up your sleeve, child. The right arm . . ."

With shaking fingers I did as she asked. "Now take the chalice and hold it under your arm to catch the blood."

I lifted my bare arm and positioned the exquisitely wrought vessel beneath it. Grimalkin made a small cut into my flesh. I hardly felt it, but blood began to drip downward; however, it stopped flowing before the chalice was half full.

"Just one more cut and it's done," she said.

I felt the blade again and sucked in my breath as the sharp pain bit. This time my blood cascaded freely, and to my surprise the vessel suddenly became much heavier. It filled rapidly, but no sooner had the blood reached the rim than the flow suddenly ceased. I saw that it had already congealed into a thin red line against the pale flesh of my arm.

The witch assassin placed the cup on the table; the warrior picked it up and carried it toward the pit. We watched him descending the steps until he was lost to view, then waited in silence until he was some distance from the hall. We couldn't risk his hearing a disturbance and turning back. It was vital that my blood be given to the Ordeen. The minutes passed slowly, but at last Grimalkin smiled and pulled a small mirror from her sleeve, preparing to signal our success.

However, before she could do so, everything went dark, and I felt a sudden chill again. Once more bright, glittering eyes moved toward us from the direction of the pit. Had the servants of the Ordeen guessed our intent?

Suddenly I was aware that, notwithstanding the intense silence, the hall was now full of people. And what strange and terrifying people they were!

The men were very tall, with long, pointy noses and chins and elongated faces. They must be demons, I thought, with their cavernous eyes, and their dark, loose clothes that hung from their bodies like gossamer sails stretched over willowy trees. At their belts were imposing, curved swords.

The demons brought to my mind an old County proverb.

Pointy nose and pointy chin,
Darkness surely dwells within!

By contrast, the women were sleek, with voluptuous curves, revealing skin that glistened as if freshly anointed. And they were dancing, whirling rhythmically to the beat of a distant unseen drum. These women danced alone while the men brooded on the edge of the dancing space or lurked in the gloom of the pillars, watching with hungry eyes.

I looked back along the table and saw that everyone in our party seemed transfixed by the dancers. Their strange movements held some sort of enchantment. Grimalkin still had the mirror in her hand but seemed powerless to use it. We were helpless. Had we gotten so close to success only to be thwarted at the last moment?

And then I realized that some of Mam's escort, Seilenos among them, were eating greedily from their plates and gulping wine from the golden goblets—despite the warning they'd been given. I knew then that the Greek spook lacked the willpower and determination of John Gregory. It would now surely be his undoing.

I turned back to the women dancing before the pit and saw that whereas each had previously danced alone, now they spun in twos, woman with woman, following the mosaic patterns of the long serpents. The drumbeat was getting louder, faster, and more frantic, and now there was more than one drum. It made me want to tap my feet, and I felt a strong urge to rise from my seat. I looked across to Alice and saw that she too was gripping her seat, stopping herself from joining the dancers. I slowed my breathing and fought the impulse to move until it began to subside.

Then I saw that one of the dancers was actually a man — one I recognized. It was Seilenos. Just moments earlier I'd seen him eating the forbidden food; now he was suddenly part of that wild dance. I lost sight of him for a moment, but then he whirled back into view, this time much closer to our table. And I could see that a woman had her mouth against his neck, her teeth biting deep into his flesh; blood was dribbling onto his chest. Terror showed in his bulging eyes; they rolled wildly in their sockets. His belly seemed to be convulsing, and his clothes were torn, revealing deep wounds across his back. The woman was draining Seilenos of blood. He was spun back into the press of bodies, closer to the pit, and I didn't see him again.

I was grateful that I had been well taught by the Spook and had fasted before entering the citadel. Seilenos's love of food and wine had cost him his life—maybe even his soul!

Then, to my right, I saw Grimalkin again, her face straining with the immense effort of fighting the powerful dark magic that bound us all. She slowly brought the mirror to her mouth. She breathed on it and, rapt with concentration, began to write with her forefinger. It was the signal to begin the attack.

CHAPTER XVII
FIRE ELEMENTALS

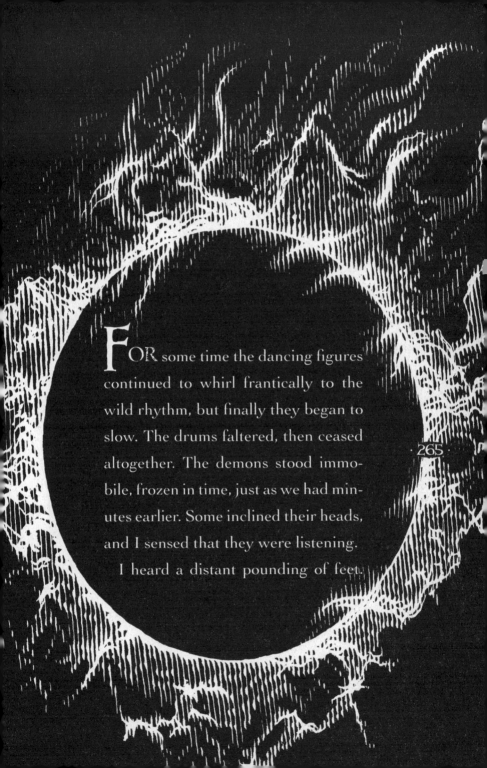

FOR some time the dancing figures continued to whirl frantically to the wild rhythm, but finally they began to slow. The drums faltered, then ceased altogether. The demons stood immobile, frozen in time, just as we had minutes earlier. Some inclined their heads, and I sensed that they were listening.

I heard a distant pounding of feet.

Closer and closer it came. The doors were flung back with a crash, and the Pendle witches burst into the hall, long knives at the ready, their faces savage and eager for battle. There were Mouldheels among them, but no sign of Mab and her two sisters. Why hadn't they joined the attack? I wondered.

Once again, Grimalkin vaulted across the table and joined the fight. Any enchantments possessed by the demons were either not used or ineffective against the combined wild onslaught of the witches. To right and left they cut, wielding their blades to powerful effect. Their enemies resisted, drawing their swords and fighting back, but within moments several of them lay dead, their red blood pooling on the floor.

It all happened so quickly that we had no time to join the fray. One moment there was ferocious fighting, the next the demons were retreating down the steps into the pit. But it was an orderly retreat. Some fought a rearguard action while the women escaped. Soon only the witches remained, gazing down the steps into the darkness.

Alice gripped my arm tightly as we moved to join them, but already they were turning their backs upon the pit.

"It's too dangerous to follow them," Grimalkin said. "I expect that's exactly what they want. They gave up and retreated far too easily. No doubt they want to lure us down into the darkness and ambush us. We'll take the route advised by your mother, child. I suggest you wait here until the mercenaries have launched their attack. They're on their way now, so we'll go ahead and press on deeper into the citadel."

With that, she led the blood-spattered witches out into the tunnel, to the inner courtyard.

"Best do as she says, Tom," Alice said, still holding my arm tightly. "We'll follow on in a few moments."

Some of the survivors of Mam's escort nodded in agreement. Without their leader, they seemed nervous. The bodies of Seilenos and two more of Mam's escort lay in pools of blood, unseeing eyes staring up at the high ceiling.

"Let's move closer to the door," Alice said, looking

nervously to the steps. "Now that the witches have gone, those demons might come back up."

It seemed a good idea, so we all headed for the open doorway.

Within moments we heard horses galloping toward us. We watched as the mercenaries thundered in through the entrance and along the tunnel to begin their attack. It took a long time for them to pass. As the last hooves echoed into the distance, we left the hall and followed them to the inner courtyard.

I looked back briefly. There was no sign of Mam, the Spook, or the others. Surely they should be here by now? I thought.

We hadn't taken more than a couple of dozen paces along the tunnel when the sound of galloping could be heard again. It was getting louder and louder! The warriors were coming back. They were in retreat already! What had gone wrong?

A riderless mount swept past, almost trampling Alice beneath its hooves. Its eyes rolled in fear, and it was foaming at the mouth. More horses galloped by, some with riders, their weapons gone, eyes wide with terror. Yes, they were in retreat all right. There was no doubt about it. This was a rout. What had made those warriors turn and flee like that?

As more and more thundered toward us, I realized that we were in real danger of being crushed. I pushed Alice into a niche in the tunnel wall, shielding her with my body. The horses buffeted against us, filling the tunnel with the beat of many hooves. It seemed to go on forever, but at last all was silent again and I stepped away from the wall.

"You all right, Alice?" I said as I picked up my staff and bag.

She nodded. "Where's your mam's escort?" she asked.

I looked around. Three more of them were dead, their bodies trampled, but of the remainder there was no sign. And where were Mam, the Spook, and Arkwright? Were they in the tunnel behind us? Had they been crushed in the stampede? A lump came into my throat.

I called out, "Mam! Mam!" But there was no reply, just an eerie silence.

"We should follow the witches," Alice suggested. "Maybe your mam and Old Gregory have been delayed. They might not even have been in the tunnel when those horses came through."

I nodded and we went on. I was still worried about Mam, but also afraid of what might be waiting ahead. Whatever it was, a thousand mounted warriors had fled in fear rather than face it. Was it the Ordeen herself? Had she received my blood and awakened already?

We were approaching the end of the tunnel now, and mist began to swirl toward us. A strange fear gnawed at my insides. Waves of cold swept through me like a gale trying to force me backward.

"Do you feel it, Tom?" Alice asked.

I nodded. For a spook, any degree of fear was dangerous when facing the dark. It made the enemies of the light much more powerful.

We struggled on. I tried to block out the fear by thinking

of happy times in my childhood: sitting on Mam's knee, or Dad telling me stories about his time at sea. We forced ourselves forward until at last, from out of the mist, the high inner wall of the Ord loomed up before us, its huge stones still steaming.

We'd reached the wide cobbled courtyard. There were dead horses on the ground; warriors, too, their eyes wide open and staring, their faces twisted with terror.

"What killed them, Alice?" I cried. "There are no marks on them. No wounds at all."

"Died of fright, they did, Tom. It froze their minds and stopped their hearts. . . . But look! There's an open gate."

Ahead of us, set into the wall, stood a wide wooden gate. It was open, but darkness waited within. As I stared at it, despair washed over me, and I couldn't find the will to take a single step nearer. It had all been for nothing. The warriors had fled or died, and now there was no chance of entering and destroying the Ordeen before she drew on her mantle of power again.

We stood staring at the open gate. What could Alice and

I do alone? And how long before the Ordeen awoke?

"I haven't got the strength to go in," I told Alice, knowing that I was in thrall to the powerful dark magic that had been used against the mercenaries. "I'm not brave enough for this. . . . I haven't the will. . . ."

Alice's only reply was to nod her head wearily in agreement.

Although neither of us voiced our thoughts, it seemed certain that the Pendle witches had already gone through ahead of us. But we still didn't move. I was wondering what could have happened to Mam and the others. The heart and courage had gone out of me.

I don't know how long we'd have remained standing there, but suddenly I heard footsteps behind and turned to see a tall hooded figure carrying a staff and bag emerge from the tunnel. To my astonishment, I saw that it was the Spook. At his heels was Bill Arkwright, who looked resolute, as if in the mood for breaking a few heads. But there was no sign of his three dogs.

Arkwright nodded, but the Spook strode straight past

us without even a glance in our direction. Then, as he reached the gate, he turned and looked back at me, his eyes glittering fiercely.

"Come on, lad, don't dawdle!" he growled. "There's work to be done. And if *we* don't do it, who will?"

I forced myself to take a step nearer; then another. With each one it grew a little easier and the shackles of fear began to loosen and fall away from my mind. I realized that while the warriors had fled or died, our line of work—plus the fact that spooks were seventh sons of seventh sons—gave us the strength to resist. But above all it was the Spook and his determination that had helped me to conquer my fear.

As for Alice, her training as a witch would help, and although my master hadn't invited her to join him, we both stepped through the gate and entered the darkness beyond.

"Have you seem Mam?" I asked the spooks.

They both shook their heads. "We got separated when those horses stampeded out of the tunnel toward us. Don't you worry, lad," said the Spook. "Your mam can look after herself. No doubt she'll follow along later."

They were kind words but did little to make me feel any better.

"Where are Claw and her pups?" I asked Bill. "Are they safe?"

"Safe enough for now," he replied. "There's no point in bringing them into this place. They've been trained to deal with water witches and suchlike. What chance would they have against a fire elemental?"

Now I heard a distant roar of cascading water and, much nearer, the echoes of large drops pattering down on stone. There was also the hiss of steam. A deluge had fallen onto the Ord, and much of it had found its way inside. I reached out a hand and touched the wall. The stones were still very warm.

The Spook opened his bag, pulling out a small lantern, which he lit and held aloft. We looked around, and I immediately saw that there was more than one path open to us. Wreathed in tendrils of mist, a narrow passage lay ahead,

sloping upward; to our right was another, this one perfectly level. The Spook paused. He seemed to be listening.
I thought I heard a faint cry in the distance, but it wasn't
repeated, and after a few moments he turned to face me.

"I think upward is the way we should go. I expect we'll
find the Ordeen in one of the towers. What do you say?"
he asked, looking at Arkwright.

The other spook gave the briefest of nods and my master set off, striding out determinedly. We followed, Alice
close by my side.

We had been walking for only a few minutes when the
passage came to an end. There was solid stone ahead,
but to our left I saw an opening. Without hesitating, the
Spook went through and held up the lantern. We followed
him and found ourselves in a large room full of stone slabs
occupied by what I took to be sleepers, lying on their
backs. Unlike the passageways, this chamber wasn't in
total darkness; it was filled with a faint yellow light that
had no apparent source.

The supine figures looked human, but their bodies were

long, their faces elongated, with pointy chins and noses and deep-set eyes. These were the demons we'd seen watching the dancers in the hall. But now, as the lantern bathed the nearer ones in light, I saw that rather than sleeping, they were dead.

Their throats had been cut and they were lying in pools of their own blood, which had also splattered down onto the stone floor. As we walked slowly forward, picking our way between the slabs, we saw bloody footprints. Some were made by pointy shoes, but there were marks of bare feet, too—the feet of the Mouldheel witches.

"The Pendle witches aren't the allies I'd wish for, but at least we've nothing to fear now in this chamber," the Spook remarked.

"The Ord's huge," I said. "There must be lots of chambers. Just think how many other creatures there must be like these. . . ."

"It doesn't bear thinking about, lad. We must press on. At least if danger threatens, those ahead will encounter it first and give us some warning."

The Spook and Arkwright led the way out of the chamber, but just as I was about to follow, I heard a cry behind me and turned to see Alice transfixed, her face a mask of terror. One of the demons had suddenly sat up on his stone slab; he was gripping her arm tightly and glaring at her malevolently.

He was bleeding from the throat, but evidently the cut hadn't been deep enough and he had awakened to find intruders in his domain. His eyes glittered fiercely, and he reached for the curved blade at his belt. He was going to use it on Alice! I ran forward and jabbed him hard in the chest with the end of my staff. He gasped at the contact with rowan wood and opened his mouth; saliva and blood gushed out. He drew his blade, so I jabbed him again. The weapon went spinning from his hand. He released Alice's arm and rolled away from me across his stone bed to land on his feet in a low crouch. He slowly turned to face me, his eyes just above the level of the slab.

Before I could react, he leaped up. No human could have jumped so high and with such speed. He flew over the slab and dropped onto me, sending the staff spinning from my hand. I fell backward, twisted away and rolled clear. I saw that the demon was about to attack again and realized I had one chance. It would take too long to get out the silver chain that lay hidden in my breeches pocket, but I might just be able to reach over my shoulder and draw the knife that Grimalkin had given me. But no sooner had the thought entered my head than I realized I was too late. The demon was upon me.

Two things happened simultaneously. There was a click, and something shot forward above my head and speared the creature in the throat. He slumped to his knees, choking, and then fell to one side. After a long, shuddering breath he was still.

Alice came to my side; she was holding my staff. The click I'd heard was her releasing the blade, which was now covered in blood. The Spook and Arkwright came running back into the chamber. They looked at the dead creature and then at Alice.

"Looks like Alice just saved your life, Master Ward,"

Arkwright said as I climbed shakily to my feet.

The Spook said nothing. As usual he begrudged Alice any praise. Just then there was a groan from the far corner of the chamber. Another of the Ordeen's servants began to stir.

"Those witches haven't been as thorough as we thought," the Spook observed. "Let's move on. There's no sense in staying here a moment longer than we need. Time is short—and who knows what lies ahead?"

Beyond the door was another passageway, which led upward once more. We began to climb, the Spook in the lead. Suddenly he raised his hand and came to a halt, then pointed to the wall on our left. A small glowing sphere, a bubble of translucent fire, was floating there at head height. It was no bigger than my fist, and at first I thought it was attached to the wall. As I watched, it floated across the passage and disappeared into the stones.

"What was that?" I asked. "A fire elemental?"

"Aye, lad, I suppose so. Having lived in the wet County all my life, I've not set eyes on one before. From what I've read, they can be very dangerous indeed, but because of all the water that's fallen on the Ord—and found its way inside—it should be some time before they become fully active. All the more reason to press on just as fast as we can! Where's Seilenos? He knows all about such things."

"He's dead," I explained, shaking my head sadly. "Despite Mam's warning, he ate the food and drank the wine at the table, and he was killed by one of the demons."

"Greed killed the poor man," said the Spook gravely. "The County way is the best when facing the dark. It's a pity. We badly needed his expertise here."

The passage continued to rise even more steeply, and once again we encountered a stone wall barring our way with an opening to the left. Inside the next chamber, the lantern revealed more stone slabs with demons lying upon them. All had been slain in the same way as the others and there was a lot of blood, but as we advanced between the slabs, Alice gave a gasp of horror.

This time the witches hadn't found things so easy. One of their own number was dead. There wasn't much left of her either. All that remained was her legs below the knees and her pointy shoes. Above them, her body had been reduced to black ashes, which were still smoking. The air was tainted with the stench of burned flesh.

"What did that?" I asked. "That glowing orb we saw before?"

"That or something like it, lad. Some sort of fire elemental for sure. Let's hope it's moved on elsewhere. The Ord is coming to life faster than we hoped," said the Spook, and then his eyes widened in alarm.

A ball of fire had appeared in the air five paces ahead of us. It was much more threatening than the translucent orb we'd seen earlier. This was slightly larger than a human head and was opaque, throwing out flames, pulsing rhythmically, alternately expanding and contracting. It started to glide to us, growing rapidly as it did so.

The Spook struck at it with his staff, and it retreated a little way before approaching again. Once more he thrust at it, missing it by less than an inch, and it shot forward over our heads at tremendous speed and broke against the far wall in a shower of orange sparks.

Striding quickly, the Spook led the way out of the chamber. I glanced back and saw that the fiery orb had re-formed at the base of the wall and was starting to float toward us again. Beyond the doorway were steep stone steps that we climbed as fast as we could. I glanced back again anxiously, but the elemental didn't seem to be following us. I wondered if it was confined to the chamber in some way. Maybe its duty was to guard it?

The steps curved up in a spiral. Were we already inside one of the three spires? I wondered. There was no way of telling, because there were no windows. I was becoming increasingly nervous. Even if we did succeed in destroying the Ordeen herself, this route was full of elementals . . . and who knew what other creatures? We'd have to come down these steps again, and by then anything that lurked in the shadows would probably be fully awake and dangerous. How could we make our escape?

Moments later we encountered another threat. A dead Mouldheel lay before us on the stairs, identifiable from her bare feet and ragged dress. Where her head and shoulders had been, a glowing orange fire elemental shaped like a starfish writhed and crepitated, moving slowly downward to consume the remainder of her body. It was one of the asteri the Spook had warned me about.

"Looks like it dropped onto her head as she passed beneath it," he observed. "Not an easy way to die . . ."

Pressing our bodies back against the stone walls, we went on, giving the dead witch and her terrifying slayer as wide a berth as possible. But then the Spook pointed ahead. There were four or five similar elementals clinging to the high ceiling, pulsing with fire.

"Not sure whether it's best to move slowly or run for it," he muttered. "Let's try it slowly and keep close together. Ready with your staff, lad!"

The Spook took the lead, with Alice following him and Bill Arkwright bringing up the rear. We held our staffs at the ready. My mouth was dry with fear. We climbed slowly and steadily, passing beneath the first two star-shaped elementals. Perhaps these were still dormant or had been affected by the deluge? We could only hope. . . .

Just when we thought we'd escaped the danger, we heard a hissing sound and a large elemental dropped straight toward the Spook's head. He whirled his staff, and with a shower of sparks the blade cut it into two pieces. They fell onto the steps behind us. I glanced back to see them crawling toward each other, attempting to re-form into one creature again.

We hurried on but kept checking the ceiling for danger. At last we reached a landing. Facing us were three cavernous doorways, and I realized that these must be the entrances to the three towers.

"So which way is it to be?" asked the Spook, staring at each flight of steps in turn.

"It's anybody's guess!" Arkwright replied with a shrug. "This place is so big—we'll run out of time before we can search it all. It doesn't look good."

"Alice could sniff out the danger," I suggested.

The Spook frowned—clearly he considered that a use of the dark.

I spoke quickly before he could refuse. "Mam would want us to use every possible means in order to survive and slay the Ordeen!"

"And I've already explained that I don't like all your mam's methods and don't choose to employ them myself!" my master snapped.

"Let Alice do it," I begged softly. "Please."

"I think we've little choice but to let the girl try," Arkwright said.

The Spook closed his eyes as if he was in pain, then gave a barely perceptible nod.

Alice immediately went to the foot of the central flight of stairs and sniffed loudly twice. "Can't tell what's up there," she admitted, "because that's the way the witches went. They've tainted the air, so I ain't able to tell what's beyond them."

"Then it would make sense to take those steps," suggested the Spook. "At least then we might get some warning if they run into trouble. Won't they have sniffed it out as the safest route anyway?"

But before Alice could answer, there was a sudden scream from the central tunnel, and we could hear someone running down the steps toward us. The Spook raised his staff, and there was a click as he released the retractable blade.

A moment later, a shrieking witch ran out onto the landing, her hair on fire, her pointy shoes clattering on the marble floor. I doubt she even saw us. Still screaming, she continued down the steps and was lost from view. Then a second one appeared, a barefoot Mouldheel, one of Mab's followers. Arkwright intercepted her, grabbing her ragged sleeve and threatening her with his staff. Her eyes were filled with terror, her face grimed with soot, but she seemed unhurt.

"Let me go!" she cried.

"What happened?" he demanded.

"Fire demons! We had no chance. They're dead. All dead!"

With that she tore herself free and ran on down the steps. If she was right, all the witches were dead—even

Grimalkin. The power of the Ordeen was such that they hadn't been able to sniff out the danger, and they'd been no match for the fire elementals.

Alice checked the left-hand stairs and shook her head. "Danger up there!" she said. At the right-hand opening she nodded slowly. "Seems all right . . ."

So we began a cautious ascent, the Spook once again taking the lead. We seemed to be climbing forever; my legs grew weary and felt as heavy as lead. It was terrifying to imagine this whole structure passing through a portal, full of dark entities—some of them unknown and not even recorded in the Spook's Bestiary. And what if the Ord were suddenly to return through the portal, carrying us all with it? It was a scary thought, and I wished we'd done what was necessary and were on our way out rather than penetrating ever deeper, with a host of unknown dangers ahead of us.

At last we reached the top of the stairs, to be faced with a large, circular bronze door. On it was embossed a huge skull. There was neither lock nor handle, but the

Spook placed a hand against the carving and pushed. The door slid open soundlessly. Holding the lantern high, he stepped into a small octagonal room. We looked around in puzzlement. There was no other door. What was this place? What function did it serve?

Almost immediately I received an answer. This was a trap! Without warning, the ground opened beneath my feet, and I heard Alice cry out in fear. Then the lantern went out, my stomach lurched, and I fell into nothingness.

CHAPTER XVIII
A Bargain

I landed on soft earth, the impact driving all the breath from my body and jolting my staff and bag out of my grip. It was totally dark — I couldn't even see my hand in front of my face. I got to my knees. There was mud beneath me, the dampness starting to soak into my breeches. I called out to the Spook and Alice but received no reply.

However, I wasn't alone. I sensed a movement in the darkness, close by. Whatever it was traveled on more than two legs, scuttling delicately toward me. With a start, I felt something touch my ankle just above my boot. It was a gentle touch, almost a caress, and I wondered for a moment if perhaps this was something I didn't need to fear after all. But then that first delicate contact became a grip of steel, and I felt sharp teeth tearing into my leg. I waited for whatever it was to bite through to the bone, even sever my foot, but it began to drag me along behind it. I didn't dare resist. Helpless, I bumped across the earth, then felt the ground beneath me change, giving way to a hard, cold surface. I could hear the legs of the creature clicking and clacking across it. Then it stopped, released my leg, and scuttled away.

Nearby, people were laughing. I had the impression that their laughter was directed at me, in an attempt to provoke me in some way. I lay perfectly still and said nothing. I'd lost my staff and bag in the fall, and but for the silver chain in my breeches pocket, I was defenseless.

Suddenly the ground beneath me began to sway alarmingly, and I heard the creaking of chains. Instinctively I sat up and stretched out my hands at my sides for support. The mocking laughter seemed to be receding below me. Either that, or I was somehow being carried aloft. The sounds became fainter and fainter, then faded away altogether. There was a slight movement of air on my face now. I *was* moving upward into the darkness!

Feeling like a tiny mouse in a cat's basket, I kept perfectly still and silent. The slightest movement might precipitate an attack. Anything could be lurking in the darkness, and I didn't want to draw attention to myself. But then I became aware of shapes about me; it was growing lighter. I had feared the dark, but the light now showed me how hopeless my predicament was.

The surface beneath me was metal, pitted with rust and scratches. As the light intensified, I saw that I was sitting in a deep, circular metal dish, suspended from the apex of the spire far above me. Three rusty chains were fastened to its outer edge; apart from its great size, it was very much like the bait dish spooks used to lure a boggart into a pit. Was I bait for some creature—some large predator? I wondered fearfully.

There were other chains nearby, and they also seemed to be in motion. Above me I heard a deep rumble. How far was I from the ground? As I moved to peer over the edge of the dish, it began to sway alarmingly. Below was a yawning gulf. And all around me I could see other dishes rising up into the spire. I was trapped. There was no way down.

The walls were also getting gradually closer as the spire narrowed. Now I could see the texture of the stones—and something else. There were creatures clinging to the walls, so many that they resembled a colony of insects, the teeming center of a hive. What were they?

The higher I rose, the closer the curved walls pressed in toward me. Only then did I understand exactly what I was seeing. My heart lurched with fear. I was gazing at a great horde of lamia witches, the vaengir.

There were hundreds of them. Each had four limbs, the

heavier back ones armed with savage claws, the forelimbs resembling human arms with delicate hands. A pair of black insectile wings were folded across the back, concealing an inner, lighter pair. After the deluge, they were fluttering them in order to dry them. Outside, on the plain, it would soon be dark, and once their wings were dry they'd be able to leave the Ord and venture out of the cloud shield to attack Kalambaka and the monks of Meteora.

I could see the lamias watching me through their heavy-lidded eyes, gaunt cheeked and restless; they were eager to feed. The rumbling from above grew louder, changing slowly into a grinding and clanking that hurt my eardrums. I looked up. Above me was a huge spindle, which was spinning slowly, hauling up the chains, drawing the metal dishes upward.

I glanced down at the other vessels and saw that there were human forms sprawled in some of them, whether alive or dead, I couldn't tell, because they were too far below me. None of them seemed to be moving. Suddenly I understood.

We were food for the lamias! Food to give them strength for their flight! The horror of what I faced set my whole body trembling. I was going to be torn to pieces. Slowly, taking deep slow breaths, I forced my fear to subside. There were other people to think about. Were the Spook, Arkwright, and Alice in the same situation as me, being drawn aloft to feed the ravenous lamia hordes?

There was a jerk, and the grinding and rumbling ceased. I looked down again and realized that I was right in the center of the tower, the highest of about thirty dishes.

Then I felt my dish begin to ascend once more. I glanced at the other dishes below me, but they weren't moving; I was leaving them behind. Moments later I passed a large, static metal cylinder wrapped with rusty chains, one of the mechanisms by which the other dishes had been lifted. I must be suspended from some different system. Now, above me, I saw something that looked like a boiling black cloud, much like the one above the Ord, but inside it. I flinched away as I drew nearer. It filled me with fear. A moment later I was within it, unable to see anything. The dish came to a halt, and I was suspended there for several moments in absolute darkness.

Then the black cloud began to recede, thinning as it did so, and I was able to see my surroundings. I was still within the rusting metal vessel. Below was the yawning void through which I had ascended. I had been drawn up into a small room of black marble. It was no more than a cube, with no doors or windows and only two items of furniture: a large circular mirror on the wall to my left—and a throne.

I began to tremble because I'd seen that throne before. It was the one the Fiend had been sitting in when I'd talked to him on the black barge back in the spring. It was intricately carved. On the left arm was a fierce dragon, its claws lifted aggressively; on the right was a fork-tongued snake, its long body trailing down the side of the throne to coil about the claw-footed leg.

I stepped out of the dish onto the marble floor, looking straight ahead, afraid to glance down at the gulf below. As I did so, a sudden chill ran the length of my spine, a

warning that I was in the presence of a dangerous servant of the dark. I knew what was happening because
it had happened to me before. I couldn't move. I wasn't
even breathing but felt no compulsion to do so. Time had
stopped. Stopped for me as well as for my immediate envi-
ronment. That could mean only one thing. The Fiend.

And suddenly there he was, sitting on that ornate throne,
once more in the shape of Matthew Gilbert.

"I'm going to show you something now, Tom," he said,
his voice filled with malice. "The future. What will happen
in the next few hours. Only you can stop it. Look into the
mirror!"

I felt my heart surge in my chest. I was breathing again,
but all around me was utter stillness. Although I felt free to
move, time was still frozen. Unable to help myself, I did as
he commanded and looked at the mirror. Everything grew
dark, and for a moment I felt myself falling, but then I was
looking down on the metal dishes from somewhere just
above, able to see them all, my eyes clearer and sharper
than they'd ever been.

Some dishes were filled with blood; others held people. Flesh and blood—it was all food. Food for the lamias. I could see the Spook in one; he wasn't holding his staff and looked old and frail, gazing upward with terrified, despairing eyes. In another was Alice, gripping the edge of the dish with white knuckles. But Mam wasn't there, and somehow that gave me hope.

No sooner had that thought entered my head than I heard the beating of many wings and the flock of vaengir flew down onto the dishes with outstretched claws. They formed a dark, ravenous mass of thrashing wings, obstructing my view, but I heard Alice cry out.

I was helpless, unable to go to her aid. I could do nothing for any of them, not even cover my own ears to block the awful sound of screams and tearing flesh.

Now the view changed, and I was outside the Ord, watching the servants of the Ordeen ride out of the gates. There were thousands of them, scimitars and spears at the ready, their elongated faces fixed with cruel intent. They were all male; of the females there was no sign. Time seemed to speed up, and I saw them approaching Kalambaka, over-taking the warriors who had fled the Ord. These they cut down without mercy or lifted up in order to drink their blood before casting the broken bodies back into the dust. Behind them came the maenad hordes, gorging upon the flesh of the dead and dying.

In the walled town they attacked all those who had been unwilling or unable to flee. Unarmed men and women suffered the same fate. Children, even babies, were torn from their mothers' arms, drained, then dashed against the bloodstained walls. Once again, maenads pounced on the broken bodies and tore at the flesh of the victims. Next I saw the vaengir swoop down upon the monasteries of Meteora; their lofty heights were no protection against such a ferocious aerial attack. I saw bodies fall like broken dolls; the floor of the *katholicon* ran with blood. No more would hymns soar like angels to fill the dome; no more would the monks' prayers strengthen the light. The Ordeen was now free to emerge anywhere she chose. Now the County too was at risk.

"That is the future, Tom!" cried the Fiend. "The events I showed you will begin to unfold in just a few moments, beginning with the deaths of your master, Alice, and Arkwright. That is, unless you take the necessary steps to prevent it. I can help you. I require something from you, that's all. I simply want you to give me your soul. In return I offer you a chance to destroy your mother's enemy."

The vision faded, and I was left staring at my own reflection. I turned back toward the Fiend. "My soul?" I asked in astonishment. "You'd own my soul?"

"Yes, it would belong to me. Mine to use exactly as I wished."

Own my soul? What did that mean? What were the consequences? To be dead and trapped forever in a living hell? In the dark itself?

The face that stared at me from above the throne was no longer smiling. The eyes were hard and cruel.

"Three days from now, if you survive, I will come to collect your soul. That will give you time enough to do your mother's will and reach a place of safety. I will not kill you.

No, the terms of this contract are such that when I come for you as agreed, your breath will leave your body and you will die, your soul falling into my hands. And your soul will endure in my possession and be subject to my will. The hobbles that bind me will no longer be important. I will not kill you myself, so my rule here will not be limited to a mere hundred years. You will have agreed to forfeit your life so you will be removed from the world of your own volition. Thus I will be free to use my own devices to work toward eventual domination of this world. It will take time, a long time, but I am patient."

I shook my head. "No. It's madness. You're asking too much. I can't agree to that."

"Why not, Tom? It's the obvious thing to do. Make that sacrifice and surrender your soul into my keeping. You will achieve so much: I can give you the chance to avert all the deaths I've shown you. And you will prevent any future danger to the County. It's your decision, Tom. But you saw what is about to happen. Only you can stop it!"

Only by agreeing could I prevent the deaths of Alice,

Arkwright, and the Spook. And thousands more would die, the Ordeen would triumph, and seven years from now, when she took revenge on Mam and destroyed everything and everyone she held dear back home, it would be the turn of the County to endure a similar fate. But to prevent that, I'd have to suffer the loss of my own soul. It was a terrible thing. But would the sacrifice be worth it? What did the Fiend mean by a "chance"?

"How much of a chance would I be given in return for my soul?" I demanded. "What would you do to help me now?"

"Two things. The first is to delay the Ordeen's awakening. An hour is the best I can do. Of course, some of her servants awake long before her. Others are already beginning to stir. Those you must avoid or deal with as best you can. But secondly, and most importantly, I would tell you the location of the Ordeen."

More than once in the past I'd been given similar chances by servants of the dark. Golgoth, one of the Old Gods, had offered me my life and soul in exchange for freeing him from the pentacle that bound him. I'd refused. I counted for nothing; my duty was always to the County. In Pendle, the witch Wurmalde had also demanded something from me—the keys to Mam's trunks. She hoped to find tremendous power for the dark in them. Despite the fact that the lives of Jack, Ellie, and their daughter, Mary, depended on my agreement, once again I'd refused.

But this offer was different. It wasn't just my own life at stake, nor the lives of members of my family. Yes, my soul would belong to the Fiend, the dark personified. But I also would be saving the County from a future visitation. And only if he won me to his side could the Fiend rule the earth until the end of time. That wouldn't be the case—he'd simply own the part of me that was immortal. The Ord was a huge, complex structure. Knowing the precise location of Mam's enemy would give us a real chance of success, I thought.

I was very tempted to agree to his offer. What else could I do? And it would buy time, something we all needed very badly. Besides, there was one thing that gave me hope.

There was no evidence that Mam was dead, and if she still lived, then anything was possible. Perhaps she would find a way to save me, some means by which I could be freed from the bargain I was about to make.

"All right," I said, shuddering at the thought of what I would be surrendering into the Fiend's control. "I'll pledge my soul in return for what you offer."

"Three days from now I'll return to collect it. So, is it agreed?"

I nodded. "Yes. It's agreed," I said, my heart sinking into my boots.

"So be it. Then here is the information you need. The Ordeen is not to be found within any of the three towers. They are home to her servants and contain only traps and death for any who enter. However, there is a dome behind them, on the roof of the main structure. That's where you'll find her. Take care in crossing that roof, though—it contains many dangers. And remember, you have just one hour before the Ordeen awakes."

Having delivered the second part of what he'd promised,

the Fiend smiled and gestured that I should take my place in the dish again. No sooner had I done so than the room began to darken, the cloud thickening and boiling about me. The last thing I saw was his gloating face. But what else could I have done? I asked myself. How could I have allowed so many to die? At least this gave us some chance of averting such a bloodbath. What was my soul compared to that?

I'd made a bargain with the Fiend. In three days' time, unless Mam could help me, I'd have to pay a terrible price for this chance at victory.

CHAPTER XIX
YOUR FATE

T HERE was a lurch, and the dish began to descend, the cloud quickly dissipating to reveal the inside of the twisted spire again. The lamias were still there, clinging to the stones, but did not move. As I passed a cylinder it began to turn slowly, rumbling and creaking as it yielded the chains of other dishes to the pull of gravity. I

glanced over the rim to watch them edging down ahead of me. Even as I studied them, looking for the ones that had held the Spook, Alice, and Arkwright, they disappeared from view.

I remembered the pitch blackness of the lower regions, and no sooner had I done so than the light about me faded; my descent now took place in complete gloom. Finally, with a jolt, my dish reached the ground.

For a moment I didn't move. I waited in the darkness, hardly daring to breathe. I heard dull thuds nearby as other dishes made contact with the soft ground. I remembered the creature that, cloaked in darkness, had fastened its teeth around my leg and dragged me to the saucer. What if it was still lurking in the vicinity? I forced myself to be calm. The unseen creature had served its purpose, placing me where I could be taken up to meet the Fiend. Surely it would let me be now? After all, we'd struck a bargain and I'd been given just one hour to find the Ordeen before she was fully awake. But could I trust the Fiend? Would he keep to our agreement?

There was a movement to my right and I cringed away, but a moment later a light flared and I could see a figure holding up a lantern. To my relief, it was the Spook. He approached me slowly, glancing uneasily from side to side. Close behind him was Arkwright. As I clambered up from my metal vessel, my feet sinking into the mud, another figure came out of the darkness toward the lantern: Alice.

"I thought it was all over for us then," the Spook observed. "One moment I'm waiting to be drained of blood, the next I'm back here. Seems too good to be true . . ."

He glanced at us all in turn, but I said nothing, though I could feel Alice's eyes watching me closely.

"Then let's see what else we can find," my master said. "I'd feel better with my staff in hand."

We followed the Spook, staying within the yellow circle of light cast by the lantern. Within moments we'd found his staff and bag, then Arkwright's, and finally my own belongings.

"I feel a lot better with this at the ready!" Arkwright exclaimed.

"It's almost as if someone's helping us," observed the Spook. "I wonder if your mam's playing some part here."

"It would be nice to think so. I just hope she's all right," I said, hoping he wouldn't guess at my part in what had happened.

"Well, it does seem like we've been given a second chance," he continued, "so let's make the most of it. I don't know how long we've got before this place is fully awake, so let's hurry on. But the question is—in which direction?"

I now knew where to find the Ordeen, but how could I tell him without revealing the source of my knowledge?

"We need to get to the foot of those three flights of steps again," my master continued. "Each one must lead up into a different tower. This last one was a trap. The center one contained elementals that killed the witches. That leaves only one."

"My instincts tell me that we won't find her in a tower," I said, choosing my words carefully. "Each one will surely contain a trap like the one that nearly did for us. I think she'll be in the dome on the roof of the main structure—the one that Mam mentioned. Mam said that if the Ordeen wasn't in the towers, she could well be there."

The Spook scratched at his beard and pondered what I'd said. "Well, lad, as I've told you many times before, you should always trust your instincts. So as both you and your mother agree, I'm inclined to go along with it. But how do we get out of here?" he asked, swiveling his head and holding the lantern higher.

Apart from that illuminated area, we were surrounded by darkness; we couldn't even see the walls. But the Spook set off at a rapid pace, and we followed. From a narrow window we glimpsed a grim view down onto a nightmare landscape of buttresses and turrets and dark pools of water. We didn't linger but pressed on through a narrow doorway and down some steps until we were standing on the roof of the Ord's main structure behind the towers.

There were a number of small turrets and odd prominences ahead of us, but beyond we could see the dome rising up. We walked in single file, the Spook in the lead, Alice behind me, and Arkwright bringing up the rear. Far above, the dark cloud continued to boil and a faint drizzle was drifting into our faces. The Spook still held up the lantern—though at the moment it wasn't needed because the stones of the Ord radiated a bronze glow.

There was a lot of water on the roof. In hollows it had formed deep pools. Soon we were walking down a gentle incline alongside a gulley full of still water; shelves of stones rose up on either side, hemming us in.

Suddenly a pale yellow light shone down on us from above. I looked up and saw the waning moon just before it was covered again. We were approaching what looked like the entrance to a tunnel, but when I went in, I could see that we were not totally cut off from the sky.

Again the moon came into view, shining through what appeared to be the bars of a cage. It was almost as if we were within the skeleton of a gigantic animal, looking up through the arch of its ribs. Clinging to the stone were the unquiet dead. Some hung by their hands; others clung with all four limbs. And on the ground all around us we could see more of the dead.

"Oh, I don't like this place one bit!" Alice complained, her eyes wide and fearful.

Being the Spook's apprentice, I'd encountered lots of trapped souls before, but this was far worse. Some were clearly human — abject wretches in tattered rags, either holding out their arms to us and crying out for help or just jabbering incoherently. That was bad enough, but others were only partly human and resembled creatures out of a nightmare. One took the form of a naked man, but he had many legs and arms, like a large, twitching spider, and his skin was covered in boils and warts. Another had the head of a bewhiskered rat but a sinuous body that ended in a tail rather than legs.

"What are they?" I asked the Spook. "And what are they doing here?"

He turned to face me and shook his head. "There's no way to be sure, lad, but I suspect they're mostly trapped souls. Some of these spirits may have been here many years, bound to the Ord as it's passed through the portal again and again. Others have descended so far from their former humanity that they're barely recognizable. We call them abhuman spirits because their souls have degenerated and fallen away from what they once were. I'm afraid that even if we had time, there's nothing to be done for these unfortunates. I don't know what crimes they committed on Earth to be trapped in this place, but they're so far from the light that they can no longer reach it now. Only the destruction of the Ord would free them."

Trapped souls? I felt sick to my stomach at the thought that in three days' time I might suffer a similar fate.

With a shake of his head, the Spook moved on until we'd passed beyond that fearful tunnel; the wailing and jabbering voices faded into the distance. The gulley came to an end, but beyond it the roof descended more steeply now. Directly ahead was the dome that contained the sleeping Ordeen. I could see a narrow entry at its base—a small, dark oval that filled me with dread. It had no door, but when the Spook tried to lead the way inside, he recoiled suddenly as if he'd walked into an obstruction.

He rubbed his forehead for a moment, then stepped

back and jabbed at the opening with the base of his staff. He seemed to be striking at empty air, but there was a dull thud as it made contact with some invisible door.

"I can feel some sort of barrier," he said, exploring the area with the palm of his hand. "It's quite smooth but very solid. We'll just have to hope that there's another way in."

But when I tried to touch what he was indicating, my hand passed beyond the Spook's. I took a deep breath and stepped forward, crossing the barrier with ease. Immediately I felt a great distance between me and the others. I could still see them through the doorway, but they were like shadows, and there was no bronze glow illuminating everything. I was in a totally dark and silent world—what I sensed was a vast enclosed space.

I stepped back through to their side and was instantly engulfed by sound; it reminded me of when Arkwright had taught me to swim. He'd thrown me into the canal, and I'd thought I was drowning. As he pulled me up by the scruff of my neck, I'd come out of the silent underwater world to be buffeted by sound. Now it was the same;

there were anxious voices and Alice's cries of alarm.

"Oh, Tom! I thought we'd lost you. You just seemed to disappear!" she told me, her voice filled with distress.

"I could see you," I said. "But you were just like shadows and I couldn't hear you."

At that Alice approached the invisible barrier and tried to pass through, without success. Arkwright also tested it, first with his staff, second with his hand. "How is it that Tom can get through and we can't?" he demanded.

The Spook didn't answer him directly. He stared at me with glittering eyes. "It's your mam's doing, lad," he said. "Remember what she told us? That by giving your blood you'd have access to places you'd not normally be able to go? She was desperate for you to come back to Greece with her. Maybe there's something here in the Ord that only you can do. Certainly you're the only one able to cross this barrier."

The Spook was right. My blood now ran in the Ordeen's veins and arteries. I could now enter places normally barred to outsiders, and so could Mam. This was part of her plan.

"We're running out of time. Maybe I should go on alone?" I suggested.

I was scared, but it seemed the only way. I thought the Spook would object, but he nodded. "It might be the only way for one of us to reach the Ordeen before she wakes, but if you go on, lad, you'll go alone—and who knows into what danger."

"I don't like it, Tom!" Alice cried.

"I think it's a chance we just have to take," continued the Spook. "If we don't find and destroy the Ordeen, then none of us will escape with our lives. What's it like in there? What did you see?"

"Nothing—it's just dark and very quiet."

"Then you'd better take the lantern," he said, handing it to me. "You go on, lad, and see what you can do. We'll try and find another way in."

I nodded, took the lantern, smiled in reassurance at Alice—and stepped through the invisible barrier again. I was really scared, but it had to be done. I glanced back at the shadows of the Spook, Arkwright, and Alice, then went forward resolutely into that silent world. But it was no longer totally quiet now that I was in it. My footsteps echoed back at me from the darkness, and I was aware of my own breathing and heartbeat. Gripping my staff and bag firmly in my left hand, I held the lantern aloft with my right. Anything could be lurking beyond that yellow circle of light.

I must have walked for about two hundred yards or so without encountering any wall or obstruction, but I was aware of a change. My footsteps no longer echoed. And then, ahead of me, I saw a big doorway with steps leading upward beyond it.

I held my breath and came to a halt. Someone was sitting on the bottom step, looking in my direction. It was a young girl with fair hair falling onto her shoulders, a raggedy dress, and bare feet. She stood up and smiled at me. She was about my own height and looked hardly older than Alice, yet despite the smile there was a certain fierce authority in her expression.

It was Mab Mouldheel. It seemed that the account of her death was mistaken. But how had she gotten here? How had she passed through the barrier?

CHAPTER XX
THE TRUTH OF THINGS

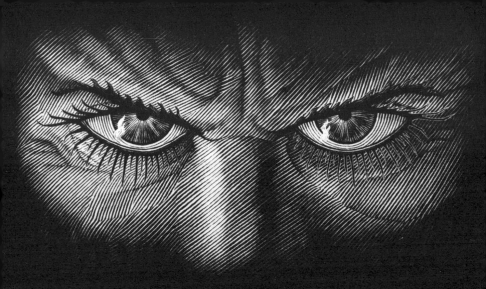

"WHAT took you so long?"
she asked. "I've been waiting here for
ages."

"Why would you be waiting for
me?" I asked warily.

"Because you have things to do and
time is short! Your mam's waiting,"
she replied. "Here, I'll carry this. . . ."

With those words she took the

lantern from me and, seizing the sleeve of my cloak, began to pull me. For a moment I resisted but then allowed myself to be tugged up the narrow spiral steps. Faster and faster we went, until we were almost running.

Suddenly I started to worry. Why had I allowed her to control me like this? Was Mab using some sort of dark magic to bind me to her will?

"Where are your sisters? And why weren't you with the rest of the Mouldheels?" I demanded, bringing our flight to a sudden halt. I didn't trust her at all. Perhaps the Fiend had betrayed me, failed to keep his word. What if Mab was delivering me into the clutches of the Ordeen, who was already awake?

"We separated into different groups as we entered the Ord," Mab explained. "Beth, Jennet, and I followed at a distance. Now they're safe and sound and as far away from this ugly place as possible. But I stayed. Risked my life, I have, to do this. You should be grateful."

"To do what?"

"Find the Ordeen for your mam. Scryed it for her, I did.

Hardest thing I've ever done. Now come on, Tom. No time to delay. Time's short, and your mam's waiting up there!" she cried, trying to pull me up once more.

"Wait!" I shouted, resisting. "You knew where the Ordeen was? Yet we weren't told? We wasted our time and then fell into a trap. Why didn't you warn us? We could all have been killed!"

And there was worse, although I didn't tell Mab. I'd just surrendered my soul to find out where the Ordeen was.

"No, Tom. It wasn't like that at all. Only scryed that once we were inside the Ord. I could only do it by using the blood of one of the Ordeen's servants. I cut the throat of one of the sleepers. Didn't take me long.

"Then we knew that the Ordeen wasn't in any of the towers. Knew she was here. So your mam decided to risk taking the most direct route. She led me out of the tunnel and along the wall. Went in through the main entrance, we did, bold as brass! Lots of danger inside, though—nasty insect things with six legs and huge pincers and lots of eyes. Didn't come near your mam, though. They kept their distance. Then we came up against a barrier here. Your mam could get through, but I couldn't. Used her power to smash it so I could get in. Cost her a lot, too — drained some of her strength. Just shows how badly she needs me. 'Bring Tom to me as quick as you can!' she said. "So come on. No time to waste!"

With that, she began to tug me after her again. I didn't resist, and soon we were running up the steps again at full pelt. We halted on a gloomy landing. Before us stood a doorway, and darkness beyond.

"You go inside," Mab said. "Your mam's waiting there to talk to you. She told me to wait outside. She wants to see you alone."

I didn't want to go in, but I held out my hand for the lantern. Mab shook her head. "Doesn't want you to see her yet. Not like this. She's changing. Just halfway there, she is. Not nice to look at . . ."

I didn't like the way she said that about Mam, and I felt like striking her with my staff. Was Mam changing into her full Lamia shape?

"Go on!" Mab snapped.

I scowled at her and, clutching my staff and bag, went forward into the darkness of that forbidding chamber and waited for my eyes to adjust. But even before I was able to make out the shape in the corner, I could hear labored breathing. Was that Mam? She sounded as if she was hurt.

"Mam! Mam! Is it you?" I cried.

"Yes, son, it's me!" a voice replied. It sounded hoarse and somewhat deeper than I remembered. And weary and full of pain. But without doubt it was Mam.

"Are you all right, Mam? Are you hurt?"

"There is some pain, son, but it's only to be expected. I'm changing. I can choose my shape, and I'm taking on one that might just give me a chance against the Ordeen. But it's been harder than I thought. Much harder. I still need a little time to ready myself. You must delay her."

"Delay her? How?" I demanded.

"First with words. You'll be an enigma to her, a puzzle that she'll be desperate to solve. That's your first defense. Later, your chain and staff might buy us further time. Are you still wearing the blade, Tom? And have you used the wish?"

My heart sank right down into my boots at her words. I suddenly realized that Mam had wanted me to use the Grimalkin's gifts against the Ordeen. But I had to tell her the truth.

"I still have the blade, but I used the dark wish to save Alice. A feral lamia had her in its jaws. She'd have died otherwise."

I heard Mam sigh wearily. "Combining the wish and the blade might have given you a real chance against the Ordeen. But if you survive this, son, you made the right decision. You'll need Alice by your side. As a last resort, use the blade anyway."

"What did you mean by me being a puzzle to the Ordeen?" I asked. "I don't understand. Why will I be that?"

"Don't you remember what I told you? The reason we gave her your blood? She will know you and not know you. You will seem like kin. Someone she should know but does not. You'll be able to hold her attention and allow me to ready myself and strike first. She drank your blood, taking it into her own body in order to gain new life. It's changed her. It makes you close. Already that's weakened her. That's why you were able to pass through the barrier. That's why I was able to enter this place too. We share the same blood, Tom."

Her voice was changing now. Becoming less human. Once again, I had my doubts. I'd been tricked so many times before and was wary.

"Is it you, Mam? Is it really you?" I demanded.

"Of course it is, Tom. Who else? But I don't blame you for doubting me. I've changed and continue to change. I've taken on many forms in my long lifetime, and now I'll take my final one. The process is accelerating even as we speak. I'm no longer the woman I was. I remember being your mother. I remember being a wife to your father. But I'm already something different now. Don't be sad, Tom. All things change eventually. Nothing lasts forever. All we can do is make our final moments together worthwhile.

"For much of my long life I've planned the destruction of the Ordeen. And now it's almost within my grasp. You gave your blood to her—gave it bravely. That was why I brought you to my homeland. But there is one more thing you can do that might make a difference. Delay her. Buy me time. Mab will guide you to the place where she will shortly awaken. Soon I'll use the last of my strength against her. I will hold her in a death grip. But if I succeed in doing that, you must flee the Ord immediately. Will you do that? Do you promise, Tom?"

"Leave you, Mam? How could I do that?"

"You must do it, son. You must escape. Your destiny is to destroy the Fiend. That's what I've worked so long to achieve. If you die here with me, it will all have been for nothing. I'll bind the Ordeen fast until her strength fails. Once that happens, the Ord will collapse back through the portal. It will be destroyed, and if she can't get free, it will be the end of her, too!"

"But you'll be destroyed as well! Is that what you're saying, Mam?"

"Yes, it'll be the end of me, too, but the sacrifice will be worth it. I will have achieved what I set out to do so long ago. So do you promise? Please! Let me hear you say it. . . ."

I felt shocked and full of grief. Mam was going to die here. But how could I refuse her when it would be the last thing she'd ever ask of me?

"I promise, Mam. I'm going to miss you so much. But I'll make you proud."

At that moment, a shaft of moonlight came through the window to illuminate Mam's head. It was still just recognizable, but her cheekbones were higher and sharper than ever, the eyes more cruel. I could just make out the shape of her body and a little of the substance. She was crouching close to the ground. There were scales, sharp claws, folded wings. . . . Even as I watched, she was becoming less and less human, transforming before my eyes into her final Lamia shape.

"Don't look at me, Tom! Don't look at me! Turn away now!" Mam cried out, her voice full of pain and sorrow.

I had seen something similar to this before—and heard Mam utter those words. The Bane that had lived in the labyrinth beneath Priestown Cathedral had once afforded me a terrible vision, showing me Mam in this shape. And I remembered his exact words.

"The moon shows the truth of things, boy. You know that already. All you have seen is true and will come to pass. All it takes is time."

The Bane had been right: I was now in a waking nightmare. It had come to pass, all right.

I hesitated, and Mam cried out again, "Go and do what I ask! Don't let me down now! Remember who you are and that I love you!"

So I turned my back and fled the chamber, filled with an anguish of my own.

Outside, Mab gave me a triumphant little smile. "Told you she wasn't nice to look at," she said. "Now I'll take you to the Ordeen."

Trembling at what I'd seen, I followed Mab up more steps. It hurt me to think of the pain Mam was feeling and the change she was undergoing. But I had little time to dwell on that as we emerged onto a balcony with a low stone balustrade and Mab pointed at another flight of steps leading down beside it.

"There she is!" Mab hissed. "The Ordeen!"

Far below was what looked like the interior of a church; all it lacked was rows of pews. A straight aisle passed between ornate marble pillars toward a white dais, where a woman in a black silk gown reclined upon a black marble throne. Tall black candles in golden holders lined the aisle, and behind the throne were hundreds more, flames burning steadily in the still air. Beyond the pillars were shadowy alcoves in the walls, within which any manner of dangers might lurk.

I looked at the woman again. Her eyes were still closed, but she might awaken at any moment. My instincts told me that this was indeed the Ordeen.

When I turned to face her, Mab put a finger against her lips. "Keep your voice very low," she warned softly. "She'll soon start to stir. Go down the steps and do what your mam asked before it's too late. Do it or none of us will get out of here alive."

I realized that there was no more time for words. So, putting down my bag, I turned my back on Mab Mouldheel and started to descend the steps, trying to make as little noise as possible. Once I reached the bottom, I walked along the aisle, heading toward the black throne. Despite all my efforts, the noise of my boots echoed back loudly from the arched ceiling. I wondered if the sleeping Ordeen was guarded—I glanced right and left at the shadowy alcoves beyond the pillars, but nothing moved. There was no threat there.

The nearer I got, the more I was aware of the intimidating power of her presence; an intense cold rose slowly up my spine. Mam said that I had to do my best to hold the attention of the Ordeen until she was ready to come to my aid and destroy her enemy. But what if she attacked me on sight? So, readying myself for danger, I switched my staff from my left to my right hand, then eased my silver chain out of my breeches pocket and thrust my left hand beneath my cloak to conceal its threat.

Now that I was closer, a stench wafted toward me. The Ordeen had the appearance of a woman, but there was something of the wild animal about her—a fetid, musky odor that almost made me retch.

I halted before her throne. Her eyes were closed, and she still seemed to be sleeping. Was this my chance to strike before she awoke to her full strength? Why not use my advantage? But would any of my weapons prove effective?

Silver was usually a powerful tool against servants of the dark, but I wasn't dealing with a mere witch—this was one of the Old Gods, a much more powerful being. Could a silver chain bind her? It seemed unlikely. My staff, with its blade forged from a silver alloy, could hurt her. But I would have to spear her heart, and she would be fast and strong. I might not get the chance. I still had the blade that Grimalkin had given me, but I'd used the dark wish. Even though Mam had understood that I'd needed it to save Alice, I'd sensed her disappointment at its loss. The blade might hurt the Ordeen, but my best chance of damaging her badly was now gone.

I decided to employ my weapons in that order: chain, staff, and then blade. But first I would attempt to bind my enemy with words. I would use everything at my disposal to delay her until Mam was ready to attack.

Yet even as those thoughts whirled around within my head, the Ordeen opened her eyes and looked straight at me before sitting upright on her throne. Her lips began to suffuse with blood, becoming swollen and bright red; her eyes were the dark blue of the sky an hour after sunset.

She was awake.

CHAPTER XXI
A SHARP TOOTH

THE Ordeen came to her feet and glared down at me angrily, her expression wild and arrogant.

"An insect creeps into my domain," she said softly. *"I sense it shiver and shake with fear. All I need do is stretch out my finger and smear it against the cold marble floor. Shall it be done?"*

It was then that I noticed her jaws.

The lower one was particularly powerful and wide, the muscles bunched below her ears. When she opened her mouth, I saw that her teeth were very sharp, the canines particularly. They weren't long like those of a water witch, but they were curved, and once she bit into flesh there'd be no escape from her terrible jaws. I glanced down at her hands. They were very large for a woman, and the veins were prominent. And instead of fingernails she had sharp talons.

I knew that she was trying to terrify me, so I took a slow, deep breath and attempted to control my fear—always a spook's first task when dealing with the dark. I felt it subside and then, as my trembling eased, I took a step toward her. She didn't expect that, and I saw her eyes widen in surprise.

"Who are you, insect?" she demanded. *"I feel that I know you somehow. I sense that we have met before. How did you get here? How did you pass by my servants and the traps and barriers to come so close to me?"*

"I crept in like a little mouse," I replied. "I'm too small and unimportant for anyone to notice me."

"Yet what is that staff you hold in your hand? A staff of rowan wood that hides a fang within! A metal blade impregnated with silver."

"Do you mean this?" I asked calmly, pressing the recess in my staff so that the blade emerged with a loud click.

"That's a very sharp tooth for a little mouse," she said, descending the first step of the dais. *"But still you are a mystery. You're a stranger to this country. Where is your home?"*

"Far across the sea in a green land where rain is never very far away."

"What is your parentage? Who begat you?"

"My father was a farmer who worked hard to bring up his family and taught us right from wrong. He's dead now, but I'll never forget him. And never forget what he taught me."

"I feel I know you. You could almost be my brother. Do you have sisters?"

"I've no sisters, but I do have brothers—"

"Yes! I see it now. There are six! Six! And you are the seventh! And your father before you was a seventh son. So you have gifts. The ability to see and hear the dead. The facility to block"

the long-sniffing of a witch. You are a natural enemy of the dark. Is that why you are here, little mouse? To slay me with your staff? However sharp, you'll need more than one small tooth to destroy me. . . ."

How did she know these things? Was she reading my mind? It was frightening, because within moments she seemed set to learn who I was. And through me, she'd become aware of Mam. Immediately my fears proved well founded.

"Wait! There's more," she continued. *"Much more! You have other gifts. Gifts from your feral mother. A speed that mocks the tick of time. The ability to smell the approach of death in those afflicted by sickness or injury. A long moon shadow that shows what you'll become. But what mother could give you such things, little mouse? I see her now! Through you I know her. Your mother is Lamia, my mortal enemy!"*

I saw the intent in her eyes. She was going to slay me on the spot. Quickly—quicker than ever before—I slid my silver chain onto my wrist and withdrew my hand from my cloak. She didn't react. I was moving, but the Ordeen wasn't.

She was just staring at me, anger creasing her brow.

The moment expanded. Time flickered and froze. I felt strange. I was the only thing moving in an utterly still world. I wasn't breathing. My heart wasn't beating.

Was this what the Ordeen had meant by "a speed that mocks the tick of time"? Had I really inherited it from Mam? Was it something similar to what the Fiend used? That same trick had allowed me to pluck a blade from the air the previous summer when Grimalkin had hurled it at my head.

Taking careful aim, all my focus on the target, I cracked the chain and hurled it straight at her. I had no fear at all that I would miss. Moving targets are difficult to hit, but she was as immobile as the practice post in the Spook's Chipenden garden.

The chain fell in a perfect spiral over her head and tightened against her body. Her eyes widened and seemed to bulge in her sockets, and she slumped to her knees, in obvious pain. She screamed before arching back, the veins in her neck distending. Then she convulsed, pitched forward, and landed hard upon her chin, her neck extended, her face still directed at me. I'd heard a sharp snapping sound. Was it a bone breaking? Was it her neck?

I was breathing again, my heart thumping in my chest. Whatever had happened as I prepared to cast the chain was over; time was now ticking along normally.

The Ordeen seemed to be gazing in my direction, but her eyes were unfocused and glassy, and she certainly wasn't breathing. Was she dead? If so, I couldn't believe how effective the chain had been. I stared in astonishment. I was elated but still wary. I was confronting one of the Old Gods. It had been too easy. Far too easy . . .

I took a step back — just in case it was a trick — and studied her carefully. She was totally immobile, showing not a single flicker of life. Had the contact with silver alloy killed her? Surely not?

Then I spotted something, the first warning of danger to come. Steam seemed to be rising from her body. The air above it was shimmering, too. There was a crackling sound and a sudden acrid stench of burning flesh. I watched as her skin began to scorch, wrinkle, and blacken. She was burning! Flames were leaping back!

Her head gave a jerk. I looked at the powerful lower jaw and saw it widen and lengthen, the head lifting. Still she didn't seem to be breathing, but I could see the side of her throat convulsing even as it charred. I took another step back and readied my staff. Her head had become an orb of fire, and there was a tearing, snapping sound; her jaw suddenly dislocated, and the blackened skull shattered and fell away like shards of broken pottery. But there was something else still there within. Something inside the flames, very much alive and dangerous! Something slowly emerging from the burning, blackening human husk. She was like a snake easing off her old skin. I had to strike now, before it was too late.

I stepped forward quickly, shielding my face with my arm, and lunged with my staff, aiming at the point behind her shoulders where I judged her heart to be. The blade struck something hard—far harder than bone. It jarred my hand painfully; the shock went right up my arm to my shoulder so that I lost my grip on the staff. But my dismay gave way to relief.

It was fortunate that I'd relinquished my hold on the staff. Otherwise I'd have lost my arm—because the next second the staff went up in flames with a loud *whoosh*, consumed by a heat so intense that it disintegrated into white ashes. I backed away as something emerged from the flames on four clawed legs, sloughing off the blackened skin of what had been a human form, shaking itself free of my silver chain.

It was a large lizardlike creature, mottled green and brown and covered with warty protuberances. It had the shape of the salamander, the most potent and dangerous of all the fire elementals, which Seilenos had told me about. But, if so, this was no ordinary example. The Ordeen had now taken on her true form, it seemed—that of a creature that basked in fire and ruled that element.

She scuttled out of the ashes of her previous form, her mouth opening to reveal two rows of sharp, murderous teeth. There was a loud hiss as she breathed out, and a large plume of hot steam erupted from her nostrils straight at me. I stepped to one side, and it just missed me, passing close to my face so that I was forced to close my eyes against the scalding heat.

I had just one remaining weapon—the blade that Grimalkin had given me. With my left hand I reached over my shoulder under my cloak and shirt, tugging it from its sheath. Then I faced the Ordeen and concentrated. Again I felt time slowing. I breathed deeply and steadied my own heart, trying to calm my nerves, and took a slow step toward my enemy.

The Ordeen didn't move, but her salamander eyes, the pupils vertical red slits, regarded me intently, her claws splayed as if she was tensed to spring. I focused on her long body and the place behind the neck where I intended to bury the blade. But would I be able to drive it home? Would it burst into flame like my staff? I had no alternative but to risk it, though I would have to get very close if I was to be successful. Much closer than when I'd used my staff. And intense heat was still radiating from her body.

Her jaws widened slightly, then extended quickly to reveal the ruby red oval of her open throat. That was all the warning I got. This time, rather than scalding steam, a jet of orange-yellow fire speared directly at me.

Again it missed me by inches. The Ordeen suddenly stood up on her hind legs so that she towered above me, her head beginning to sway from side to side.

I concentrated again, locking my eyes on a new target — the pale throat beneath the long jaws. This was softer. More vulnerable. That was the spot to aim for. Almost immediately, the Ordeen stopped moving.

Was that it? Concentrate and time slowed . . . almost stopped? Yes, it had to be. It was a result of focus and concentration.

But asking myself that question and reaching that conclusion almost cost me my life. It had disrupted my intense focus. The Ordeen's lizard head swayed from right to left, and another tongue of flame surged straight at me. Just in time I dropped to my knees, and I felt my hair crackle and singe.

Concentrate! I told myself. *Squeeze time! Make it stop!*

Once more my focus began to do its work and I came to my feet, readied my blade, and took a tentative step toward my enemy. That was it. Focus on the task. Take one step at a time. That was the way. And I remembered what Mam had once told me.

"When you're a man, then it'll be the dark's turn to be afraid, because then you'll be the hunter, not the hunted. That's why I gave you life."

Well, I wasn't a man yet, but suddenly I did feel like the hunter.

I was less than an arm's length from the Ordeen's open jaws now. Too close to escape if another plume of fire erupted. I tensed, then struck her throat, burying the blade to the hilt and releasing the weapon instantly. A wave of despair washed over me as I watched the blade melt, dissolving into globules of falling molten metal.

I staggered back as burning heat radiated at me. Time was moving again, and I could do nothing about it. But I saw that I had hurt her after all. Boiling black blood spouted in an arc from the Ordeen's throat to fall onto the mosaic floor, where it instantly turned to steam, forming a thick mist that obscured my view. Surely I had weakened her at least? The stench of burning was so bad that I retched and choked, my eyes stinging and watering, momentarily blinded.

But when the steam cleared, the Ordeen was still standing. The wound in her throat had healed, and now she fixed her pitiless eyes upon me. I had no weapons left. She came straight at me, faster than I could run. In seconds I would be reduced to ashes.

Then, just when I thought I was finished, as good as dead, it happened. . . .

My ears gave me the first warning. There was a sudden silence. That utter stillness—as when an owl swoops toward its unsuspecting prey. A silence so intense that it hurt. I looked up and saw something plunge down from the balcony above as the Ordeen twisted sideways and upward to meet the airborne threat.

It was Mam. Her transformation was complete, but she

was nothing like I'd expected. There were wings, yes, and outstretched claws, ready to rend and tear her enemy. But they were not the insectile wings of the vaengir. She was more angel than insect, and her wings were feathered, white as freshly fallen snow.

She fell upon the Ordeen, bearing her down onto the marble floor, and the two locked together fiercely. As I rose to my feet, my heart lurched in agony, for Mam's feathers were beginning to singe and burn, and I heard her cry out to me in an agonized voice: "Leave, Tom! Go while you can! I'll hold her here!"

My instinct was to go to Mam's aid, but I had no weapons left, and as I watched them tearing each other apart, blood spraying upward, feathers crackling and burning, I realized there was nothing I could do. If I approached them, I'd be dead in seconds. All that remained now was to obey Mam. And, although it tore at my heart, I snatched up my chain and fled that place. It was the hardest thing I had ever done, the darkest moment I'd ever faced.

CHAPTER XXII
LAST WORDS

CHURNING with emotion, I raced up the steps, only halting to pick up my bag and the lantern. I thought Mab would follow me, but she gave me a nod of farewell.

"I can't go that way because of the barrier, Tom. I'll get out the way your mam opened and see you later."

I said nothing. I didn't trust my

voice. I knew that if I spoke to her, the pain and tears I was holding inside would come cascading out.

I quickly descended the spiral staircase and began to cross the vast dark, empty space, hoping I was heading in the right direction, toward the invisible barrier.

When I finally reached it, I was relieved to see the shadows of Alice, Arkwright, and the Spook beyond it. I quickly stepped through.

"Oh, Tom!" Alice exclaimed, rushing toward me. "You've been so long. We couldn't find another way in, so we came back to wait for you. But we've been here ages. I thought you weren't coming back—that something terrible had happened to you."

She halted suddenly and looked into my eyes. "But something really bad *has* happened, hasn't it?"

I nodded, but the words stuck in my throat.

"Oh, Tom! You're burned," she said, lightly touching my singed hair and a painful burn on my face.

"It's nothing!" I said. "Nothing at all compared to what's just happened. . . ."

"Come on, lad," said the Spook, his voice surprisingly gentle. "Tell us."

"It's Mam. She's fighting the Ordeen. She says both of them will die and it'll bring about the destruction of the Ord. We need to get out just as fast as we can!"

"Is there nothing to be done, Tom? Nothing we can do to help her?" cried Alice.

I shook my head and felt hot, silent tears begin to escape from my eyes. "All we can do now is fulfill her last wish — that we get ourselves to safety before the Ord is destroyed. It'll soon start to collapse back through the portal."

"If we're still here when it does, we'll be dragged into the dark!" Arkwright said, shaking his head grimly.

There was no time to discuss further what had happened. There was only a frantic flight through the dark chambers and corridors of the Ord. Down steps and ramps we ran, descending ever lower toward the cobbled courtyard.

Soon we were uncomfortably hot, but it wasn't just with the exertion. The air itself was growing warmer, the walls beginning to radiate heat. The Ord was preparing to be engulfed once more by the pillar of fire as it retreated through the portal to its true home. Its occupants, denied the chance to surge forth and ravage the world beyond, were sinking back into their dormant state. At one point the glowing orb of a fire elemental made a tentative approach, but the Spook jabbed at it with his staff and it just floated away, fading as it did so.

We'd almost reached the final passage that led to the inner courtyard. We were close, very close, to escaping the Ord when it happened. Another glowing orb came out of the wall behind us. It was large, opaque, and dangerous, and started to drift closer. Two more emerged, so we broke into a run.

I glanced back over my shoulder. They were catching up with us. And now there were more than three. Maybe six or seven.

We reached the narrow entrance to the passage. It was then that Arkwright came to a halt.

"You go on!" he said, readying his staff. "I'll hold them off!"

"No! We'll face them together!" cried the Spook.

"No sense in us all getting killed," Arkwright snapped back stubbornly. "Get the boy to safety. He's what matters, and you know it!"

For a moment the Spook hesitated.

"Go now while you've still a chance!" Arkwright insisted. "I'll follow on just as soon as I can."

The Spook seized me by the shoulder and pushed me into the passageway ahead of him. For a moment I tried to resist, but Alice had grabbed my other arm and was dragging me on.

I managed to glance back once. Arkwright was readying himself with his back to us, his staff held diagonally in a defensive position. A glowing orb was surging toward him. He struck at it with his blade, and that was the last I saw of him.

The Spook, Alice, and I crossed the courtyard and raced down the tunnel to emerge beyond the outer walls of the Ord. We hastened toward Kalambaka as fast as we could, hampered by the soft, clinging mud created by the deluge.

Soon we found we were not the only survivors. A group of witches—including Grimalkin and some members of all three clans, among them Mab and her sisters—was running a little ahead of us. We caught them up—and even my master, I suspect, felt a little relieved to see them.

A sudden roar behind us, like the angry cry of a wounded animal, made us turn and look back. The dark cloud above the Ord had now re-formed and was filling with fire. Zigzags of lightning were flickering down to turn the tips of the twisted towers a glowing orange.

We felt the heat on our backs increasing at an alarming rate and realized we had to retreat further—and quickly. At any moment the fiery artery would connect the cloud to the ground. How wide would it be? Were we still too close and about to be engulfed by fire?

At last, exhausted by our flight, we turned to look back, alerted by the banshee howl of the pillar of fire. Once again it was throbbing and twisting, the Ord within it still visible, the tips of the towers now glowing white hot. I thought of Mam, still within that chamber, holding the

Ordeen in her grip. As we watched, the citadel began to disintegrate and the towers toppled. The Ord was being carried back into the dark, but the transition was destroying it. Within it, the Ordeen would also be defeated and would never again be able to return to our world. But Mam would also die in that inferno. My whole being was racked with sobs at the thought of it.

And then there was Bill Arkwright. Had he held off our pursuers and managed to get clear in time?

Within moments the fire faded and a great wind began to blow at our backs; the air was being sucked in to the place where the Ord had once stood. When that eased, a cold drizzle fell. I closed my eyes, and it was almost like being back in the County. We waited a long time, but there was no sign of Arkwright. It seemed certain that he was dead.

We walked back to Kalambaka in silence. My face was streaming with both rain and tears.

We skirted Kalambaka to the west and headed for Megalo Meteorou, the grandest of the high monasteries. The

Spook thought we should visit the Father Superior there and tell him what had been achieved.

I remembered what Mam had said about women not being welcome in the monasteries, but I said nothing, and Alice ascended the steps together with the Spook and me. She'd already used herbs from her leather pouch to make a soothing ointment, which she'd smeared onto the burn on my face. She had simply employed the methods used by many a County healer, nothing from the dark. It had eased the pain immediately, but John Gregory had shaken his head in disapproval. He didn't trust Alice to do anything for me. I prepared myself for a confrontation. Alice had played her part in saving the monastery, and if she was denied entry, then I too would turn back.

But we all entered unchallenged and were escorted into the presence of the Father Superior. Once more we entered that spartan cell to find the gray-faced, gaunt priest at prayer. We waited patiently, and I remembered my last visit, when Mam had still been alive. At last he looked up and smiled.

"You are welcome," he said. "And I am most grateful to you, for I assume that you were victorious—otherwise none of us would still be alive—"

"Mam died to bring about our victory!" I said. I'd spoken without thinking, and it was as if the words had been uttered by another. I could hear the hurt and bitterness in my voice.

The priest gave me a kind smile. "If it's of any comfort to you at all, I can tell you that your mother was happy to give her life to rid this world of our enemy. We've talked together many times in the past year, and she once confided in me that she expected to die in accomplishing what had to be done. Did she ever tell you that, Thomas?"

I shook my head. This old priest probably knew more about Mam than I did, I thought, the feeling of hurt growing in my chest. Mam knew she was going to die and hadn't told me until the very last moment! Then I took a deep breath; I knew there was something I needed to ask him. Something I desperately needed to know.

"The Ord was destroyed and carried back toward the

dark. Is that where Mam will be now? Trapped in the dark?"

It was a long time before the Father Superior replied. I had a feeling that he was choosing his words carefully. No doubt the news would be bad, I thought.

"I believe in the infinite mercy of God, Thomas. Without that, we are all doomed, because we are all flawed, each and every one of us. We will pray for her. That's all we can do."

I stifled a sob. I just wanted to be alone with my sorrow, but I had to listen while the Spook gave the Father Superior a more detailed account of what had happened.

After that we walked to the *katholicon*, where once more I heard the hymns of the monks soar up to fill the dome. This time the Father Superior told me that they were praying for Mam and for others who had died in the citadel. I tried in my heart to believe that it was all right, that Mam had escaped to the light. But I couldn't be sure. I thought of the crimes she had committed so long ago. Would they hinder her now? Make it harder for her to reach the light? She'd tried so hard to make restitution, and the thought of her facing an eternity in the dark was almost unbearable. It wasn't fair. The world seemed a terrible, cruel place. And very soon I'd have to face the Fiend again. My hope had been that Mam might somehow be able to arm me against him. Now I was alone.

It was the following day before my master and I spoke together in detail about what had happened. Soon we were to set off for the coast, but for now we rested, trying to regain our strength for the long journey ahead. The Spook led me away from the campfire, no doubt in order to be out of earshot of Alice, and we sat down on the ground and talked face-to-face.

I began by telling the Spook how Mam had changed back into her feral form before giving her own life to hold the Ordeen fast. I told him almost everything—but not, of course, about Mam's real identity, nor about the pact I'd made with the Fiend to gain the chance of victory. *That* I could never tell him—it was something I'd have to deal with myself. The Fiend was to come for me the next night.

I felt as if I was drifting further and further away from my master. He had sacrificed some of his principles to come to Greece and take part in the struggle against the Ordeen. But my compromise was greater: I had sacrificed my own soul. Soon it would be possessed by the Fiend, the dark made flesh, and I could think of no way to save myself.

When I'd finished my account, the Spook sighed, then reached into the pocket of his cloak and pulled out two letters. "One is from your mam to me. The other is to you, lad. I've read both. Despite my strong misgivings, they're the reason I changed my mind and traveled to Greece after all, against everything I hold dear."

He handed them both to me, and I began to read my letter.

Dear Tom,

If you are reading this letter, I will already be dead. Do not grieve too long. Think of the joyous times we shared together, particularly when you and your brothers were children and your father was still alive. Then I was truly happy and as close to being human as I ever could be.

I foresaw my death many years ago. We all have choices—I could have stepped to one side, but I knew that by sacrificing my life I could win a great victory for the light. And despite the price paid in human suffering, the Ordeen will now have been destroyed.

You must take the next step and destroy the Fiend. Failing that, at least he must be bound. In this task, Alice Deane will be your ally.

Whatever the outcome, I will always be proud of you. You have more than lived up to my expectations.

All my love,
Mam

I folded the letter and pushed it into my pocket. It was the last thing I would ever receive from Mam, her last words to me. Next I started to read what she'd written to my master. The letter that had made him leave Chipenden and, despite his misgivings, travel with us to Greece.

Dear Mr. Gregory,

I am sorry for any distress that I might have caused you. I do what I do for the best of motives. Although you may not agree with the means that I employ to achieve it, I hope to win a great victory. If I fail, the Ordeen will be able to strike anywhere in the world, and it is most likely that the County will be her first target. She will not forget what I attempted to do and will vent her wrath on the place where my family still dwells.

I will almost certainly die within the Ord, and then my son will need you to train and prepare him to deal once and for all with the Fiend. As for yourself, remain true to your principles, but please, I beg you, make an exception in two cases. The first, of course, is with respect to my son, Thomas. Your strength and guidance will be vital in seeing him safely through the next phase of his life. Now he is in even greater danger.

I beg you also to make an exception for Alice Deane. She is the daughter of the Fiend and a potential

*malevolent witch. She will always walk a narrow
path between the dark and the light. But her strength is
tremendous. If she were ever to forge an alliance with
the dark, Alice would be the most powerful witch ever
to walk this earth. But it is worth taking the risk. She
can be just as strong as a servant of the light. And only
if both Tom and Alice work together will they complete
something that has always been my goal—something that
I have striven for most of my long life. Together they
have the potential to destroy the Fiend and to bring a new
age of light to this world.*

*You can help make this possible. Please journey with
us to my homeland. Your presence is vital to protect my
son and make sure that he returns safely to the County.
Be less than what you are so that you can become more.*

Mrs. Ward

"She was a great woman," said the Spook. "I certainly
don't agree with her methods, lad, but she did what she felt
had to be done. Her homeland will be a far better place

because of what she achieved. Indeed, the County and the whole world will be safer."

The Spook was making allowances for Mam that he had never really made for Alice. But of course he didn't know the full truth. I could never tell him that Mam was Lamia, the mother of the whole brood of witches and hybrids. He wouldn't be able to come to terms with that. It was one more secret that we could never share. One more thing with the potential to drive us apart.

"What about Alice? Will you do what Mam asked?"

The Spook stroked his beard and looked thoughtful. Then he nodded, but his face was strained. "You're still my apprentice, lad. Now that Bill Arkwright's most likely dead, it's my duty to help you all I can and to carry on training you. Aye, I don't dispute that. But the girl worries me. No matter how much care I take and how carefully I watch her, it could all go terribly wrong. I'm of a mind to give it a try, though—at least for the time being. After what your mam's done, how can I refuse her?"

❂ ❂ ❂

Later I thought over what we'd said to each other. As we'd spoken, I'd almost made myself believe that everything would soon be all right and that the Spook, Alice, and I would return safely to Chipenden to continue our former lives there. But how could that be when I had less than one day remaining on this earth?

I was so afraid of what was going to happen to me that, in a moment of weakness, I considered going to my master again and telling him what I faced, hoping against hope that somewhere in his vast store of accumulated knowledge he would find a way to save me. But I knew it was hopeless.

My final chance would be to use the blood jar as Alice had suggested, adding a few drops of my own blood to hers. But then we'd have to stay close to each other for the rest of our lives so that she could benefit from my defense against the Fiend. Something would eventually happen to separate us, and then his fury would be unleashed on Alice. No, I couldn't allow that to happen. I had gotten myself into this situation, and I had to get myself out — or accept the consequences.

CHAPTER XXIII
HIS FEARSOME MAJESTY

THE Spook was sleeping on the other side of the campfire, and Alice lay to my right, her eyes tightly closed. It couldn't have been more than ten minutes to midnight.

I got carefully to my feet, trying to make as little noise as possible, then moved away from the fire and into the dark. I didn't bother to take my chain.

It would be useless in the face of the power that I'd soon confront. In just a few minutes the Fiend would come for my soul. I was afraid, but despite that I knew it was better to face him alone. If Alice or the Spook were nearby, they might try to help me and would suffer as a result, maybe forfeiting their own lives. I couldn't allow that to happen.

I walked for about five minutes, then descended a slope through some stunted trees and scrub to reach a clearing. I sat down on a rock beside a small river. Close to the riverbank it was muddy underfoot, the ground churned up by livestock that had come down to drink. There was no moon and the sky was hazy, obscuring the stars, so it was very dark. Despite the warmth of the night, I began to shiver with fear. It was all going to end now. My life on earth was almost over. But I wasn't going to the light. My fate was to belong to the Fiend. Who knew what torments he'd have in store for me?

I didn't have long to wait. I heard something on the other side of the river. A thudding sound. A hissing, too. Then a splash as something very large entered the water.

At first it sounded like a horse. Certainly some big, heavy animal. But the rhythm of its crossing suggested two legs rather than one. It had to be the Fiend. He was coming for me now. Coming to claim my soul.

I could hear eruptions of steam, the water hissing and spitting as he approached. Then I saw huge cloven hoof-prints appearing in the soft, muddy bank, glowing red in the darkness. He'd crossed the river. With the formation of each print, there was a hiss as the hot feet of the Fiend came into contact with the soggy ground. Then he began to materialize. This was no image of the murdered Matthew Gilbert; this was the Fiend in his true, terrible shape—a shape that caused some people to die on the spot from fear. And he glowed with sinister light, so that every detail of him was visible to my terrified gaze.

The Spook had told me that the Fiend could make himself large or small. Now he had chosen to be big. Almost three times my height, with a chest like a barrel, he towered above me. He was a titan, roughly human in shape—though that similarity only served to make him appear more monstrous.

His feet were the cloven hooves of a goat, and his long tail dangled behind him in the mud. He was naked, but no flesh was on view; his body was covered in long black hair. His face, too, was hairy, but his features were plain to see: the prominent teeth and curved horns of a goat, the malevolent gaze of the eyes with their elongated pupils. He came close, very close, within the reach of my arm, and the stench that came from him was ranker than anything from a barnyard. I could only stare upward into those terrible, compelling eyes. I was transfixed. Helpless.

My knees threatened to give way, and my whole body began to tremble. Was I dying? About to take my last breath?

At that moment, I heard a sound behind me. Footsteps! There was a light, and I saw it reflected in the pupils of the Fiend. Saw his eyes widen in anger. I turned. Someone was standing close behind me, holding a lantern. It was Alice, and she was gripping something in her other hand, too. Something small. Something she was holding before her like a weapon. She pushed it into my left hand.

"Leave him be!" she cried. "He's mine. Tom belongs to me! Get you gone! You can't stay in this place!"

At those words the Fiend let out a terrible bellow of rage. For a moment I thought he might reach down and crush us both. His anger surged toward me with palpable force. I was blown backward off my feet into the mud, and I heard the trees on the slope behind me crack and splinter. Then the wind seemed to reverse direction, and he simply vanished.

There was utter silence. All I could hear was my own breathing, the beating of my heart, and the gurgle of the river.

Then, by the light of the lantern, I saw what I was holding in my left hand.

The blood jar.

I struggled to my feet just a second after Alice, who was already retrieving the lantern from the mud.

"What were you doing out here all alone, Tom?" she demanded. "Did you come here to meet the Fiend?"

I didn't answer, and she came nearer, holding up the

lantern to look closely into my eyes. My heart was beating wildly, my mind in turmoil. I was still trembling at my escape, yet wondering if the Fiend might reappear again at any moment. How could Alice have driven him away like that? How was that possible?

"Something bothering you, Tom, isn't there? Been funny for days, you have. Too quiet . . . and there's something in your eyes. An expression I ain't ever seen before. Know you lost your mam, but is there something else? Something you ain't telling me?"

For a moment I didn't speak. I tried to hold it back, but the urge to share my fears with someone made me blurt it out in a torrent.

"The Fiend visited me in the Ord," I explained. "He showed me the future. That all of us were going to die — you, the Spook, and everyone in Kalambaka and Meteora. All the refugees on the road. He said he would give me a chance. He delayed the Ordeen's awakening for an hour. He also told me where she was to be found. But for that I wouldn't have been able to help Mam. We'd have lost."

For a moment Alice was silent, but I could see the fear in her eyes. "What did he want in return, Tom?" she asked. "What did he want from you?"

"Not what you think, Alice. He didn't ask me to be his ally and to stand at his side. I would have refused him—"

"So what, Tom? Come on. Don't keep me waiting."

"I gave him my soul, Alice. I sacrificed myself. You see, if the Ordeen had won, she'd have been able to use her portal and appear anywhere she chose. And she would have come to the County. So I did my duty—"

"Oh, Tom! Tom! What a fool you've been! Don't you know what this means?"

"I know I'll suffer in some way, Alice. But what else could I have done? I suppose I was hoping that Mam would be able to find some way to save me. But now she's dead, and I've just got to accept what's eventually coming to me."

"It's worse than you can imagine, Tom. Much worse. Don't like to tell you this, but it's best you know the truth. Once you are dead and the Fiend has your soul, you'll be totally in his power. He'll be able to make you feel pain worse than you've ever known. Don't you remember what you once told me about how Morgan tormented your dad's soul?"

I nodded. Morgan was a powerful necromancer, and he'd trapped Dad's soul in limbo for a while. He'd made him think he was burning in Hell, and tricked him into feeling the actual pain of the flames.

"Well, the Fiend could do the same to you, Tom. He could make you pay for fighting against him. Not only that; you'll have given up your life. He'll not have taken it. That means the hobbles will have been nullified, and chance will prevail. He'll no longer face the threat that you might destroy him or send him back through the portal. With you out of the way, he'll be free to grow in power as the dark itself waxes until he finally rules the world. And you'll be in such terrible pain, tormented beyond anything your soul could bear, that you might actually become his ally just to be released from it. We may have defeated the Ordeen, but at a terrible price. The Fiend might have won, Tom. He might have beaten you. But there's something he didn't allow for. . . ."

Alice pointed to the blood jar that I was still holding in my left hand. "You really need this now. You have to keep it with you always. This is what drove him away."

"But can it possibly work? I thought it needed my blood mixed with yours?" I asked.

"I took it without asking you, Tom. Sorry, but it had to be done. When those rocks came down on you, you were unconscious for a long time, so I took a little of your blood. Just three drops—that's all I needed. Your blood and my blood are together in this jar. Keep it on your person, and he can't come anywhere near you!

"So you've one chance! Just one! Forget your principles. None of 'em matter now, do they? You've used the dark wish that Grimalkin gave you, and you've sold your soul. It's the only thing left to do, Tom. Keep the blood jar. If you use it, we've defeated the Ordeen and the Fiend's gained nothing!"

I nodded. She was right. That's all I had left now. A final chance, the means to keep the Fiend away from me. But the Spook's worst fears were coming true. Bit by bit I was being compromised and pulled toward the dark.

"But what about when I die, Alice? Even if it's five or fifty years from now, he'll still be waiting to take my soul. He'll get it in the end."

"Can't get your soul if you destroy him first!"

"But how, Alice? How can I do that?"

"Got to be a way. Your mam gave you life so you could do that. Didn't she ever say how it could be done?"

I shook my head. I wondered if Mam had had any idea at all. If so, she'd never mentioned it. Now she was dead, and it was too late.

"We'll find out how to do it, Tom. Slay him or bind him, one of the two, and then you'll be safe!"

I grasped the blood jar very tightly. It was the only thing keeping the Fiend at bay.

At dawn on the following day, we began our journey west toward the port of Igoumenitsa, where we hoped the *Celeste* still would be waiting. The witches already had left for the coast, and it was now only the Spook, Alice, and me.

Hardly had the journey begun when something happened that lifted my spirits a little. The sound of barking alerted us—and Claw and her pups bounded toward us. And it was me they came to first, my hands that they licked.

"Always knew that dog would be yours one day," Alice said with a smile. "Didn't think you'd have three, though!"

The Spook was less than enthusiastic. "They can travel with us, lad, and we'll get them home to the County, but after that I'm not too sure. They're hunting dogs, and Bill put them to good use. There's no place at Chipenden for them. Those dogs and the boggart certainly wouldn't mix. They'd not survive even one night in the garden. We'd best try and find a good home for them."

I couldn't argue with that. But it was good to have them back for now, and it made my own journey toward the coast a little easier.

We were relieved to find the *Celeste* still waiting at anchor. The captain was happy to see us and, in the absence of

Mam, immediately dealt with me as if I was the one who'd chartered the vessel. These were the instructions Mam had left, he explained.

We waited for several days, just in case there were any more survivors from the party that had sailed to Greece so long ago. A few stragglers turned up, and by the end of that time fifteen witches, including Grimalkin and the Mouldheel sisters, were sheltering in the hold. But there was no Bill Arkwright. It was clear now that he'd sacrificed his life to enable us to escape.

When we sailed for home, I didn't spend the nights on deck in a hammock as before, but in the comfort of a large bed. It was the Spook's idea that I take Mam's cabin.

"Why not, lad?" he said. "It's what she'd have wanted."

So it was that my voyage home was one of relative luxury, and there, at night, listening to the creaking of the timbers and feeling the roll of the ship and the occasional snuffle from the dogs guarding my door, I had plenty of time to think. I went over and over again in my mind all that had happened, and always I returned to the same grim thought: Was Mam trapped in the dark, her soul carried there as the ruin of the Ord passed through the portal? Had that been Bill Arkwright's fate, too?

I kept hoping that I would dream about Mam; each night that was my aim. Suddenly dreaming was more important than waking. It didn't happen for almost two weeks, but finally she appeared to me. And it was a lucid dream, too—I was fully aware that I was dreaming.

We were back in the kitchen at the farm, and she was in her rocking chair, facing me across the hearth. I was sitting on a stool, and I felt happy and contented. It was the Mam of old, not the one who had returned from Greece to make Jack fear she was a changeling; certainly not the one I'd talked to within the Ord, who had changed rapidly into that fearsome, beautiful angel.

She started to speak to me, her voice full of warmth, love, and understanding.

"I always knew that you would be compromised by the dark, son. I knew that you would bargain with the Fiend because it was in you to do so from the very beginning. And you did it not just to help those you love, but for the whole of the County—for the whole world. Don't blame yourself. It's just part of the burden of being who you are.

"Above all, remember this," she continued. "The Fiend has damaged you, but you have also damaged him and hurt the dark badly. Believe, son. Have faith in who you are. *Believe* that you will recover, and it will truly happen. And don't judge yourself too harshly. Some things are meant to be, and you had to fall so that later you may rise and become what you are truly meant to be."

I wanted to walk across and embrace her, but no sooner had I come to my feet than the dream faded and I opened my eyes. I was back in the cabin.

Was it a dream or something more? It was three days later, as we were sailing through the Strait of Gibraltar, that I had my second encounter with Mam. The wind had dropped away to almost nothing, and we were virtually becalmed. That night I fell asleep as soon as my head hit the pillow.

It happened just as I was waking up. I heard something directly in front of me, very close to the bed. A strange noise. Something sharp in the air. A sort of crackling, tearing sound. And for a moment I was scared. Terrified.

It wasn't the feeling of cold I often experienced when something from the dark approached. This was powerful and shocking. It was as if, close to my side, there was a being that had no right to be there. As if something suddenly had torn aside all the rules of the waking world. But just as some cozy dreams quickly can turn into nightmares, this was the reverse. My terror was gone in an instant as something warm touched me.

It didn't touch my skin. It wasn't a warm hand. It was a sensation that passed right through me, upward into my bones, flesh, and nerves. It was warmth and love. Pure love. That's the only way I can describe it. There were no words. No message. But I no longer had any doubt.

It was Mam. She was safe, and she'd come to say goodbye. I felt sure of it, and with that certainty, my pain lessened.

CHAPTER XXIV
IT CAN'T BE TRUE!

Once again we endured a storm in the Bay of Biscay that threatened the ship, but despite a broken mast and tattered sails, we came through it and sailed on toward the cliffs of our homeland, the air growing colder by the hour.

We reached Sunderland Point and set off for Jack's farm. It was my duty

to break the news of Mam's death to the family.

Grimalkin, Mab, and the other surviving witches hurried off to Pendle. With the dogs at our heels, we began the trek to the farm.

We walked on in silence, each of us deep in our own thoughts. As we approached the farm, I suddenly realized that Alice would be expected to keep away for fear of offending Jack and Ellie. Yet she needed to be by my side to gain the protection of the blood jar. If we were separated, the Fiend might attack her in revenge for what she'd done.

"Better if Alice comes with us to the farm," I suggested, thinking quickly. "Jack's bound to take things badly, so Alice could give him some herbs to help him sleep."

The Spook looked at me doubtfully, probably realizing that Jack wouldn't accept Alice's help anyway, but I turned on my heel and hurried to the farm with Alice at my side, leaving him with poor Bill Arkwright's three dogs.

Within minutes, the farm dogs began to bark and Jack came running across the south pasture. He halted about three feet away. He wouldn't necessarily have expected Mam to leave her homeland again and return to the County, so her absence wouldn't have concerned him, but he must have feared the worst from the sad expression on my face.

"What is it? What happened?" he demanded. "Did you win?"

"Yes, Jack, we won," I told him. "We won, but at a terrible price. Mam's dead, Jack. There's no easy way to say it. She's dead."

Jack's eyes widened, not with grief but disbelief. "That's not right, Tom! It can't be true!"

"I know it's hard to take, but it's the truth, Jack. Mam died as she destroyed her enemy. She sacrificed herself and made the world a better place—not just her homeland."

"No! No!" Jack cried as his face began to crumple. I tried to put my arms around him to give him some comfort, but he pushed me away and kept saying, "No! No!" over and over again.

James took the news more calmly. "I sensed that was

going to happen," he told me quietly. "I've been expecting it."

When he gave me a hug, I felt his body trembling, but he was trying to be brave.

Later Jack took to his bed while the rest of us sat around the kitchen table in silence — but for Ellie, who was weeping softly. To be honest, I couldn't wait to get away from the farm. Things felt really bad, and it had reopened the wound of my own grief at losing Mam.

Ellie had made us some chicken soup, and I forced myself to dunk rolls of bread into it to build my strength for the journey. We stayed only a couple of hours, but just before we left, I went up to take my leave of Jack. I knocked lightly on the bedroom door. There was no reply, and after trying twice more, I gradually eased it open. Jack was sitting up, his back against the headboard, his face a mask of grief.

"I've come to say good-bye, Jack," I told him. "I'll be back to see you in a month or so. James is here to help with the farm, so things should be all right."

"All right?" he asked bitterly. "How can things ever be all right again?"

"I'm sorry, Jack. I'm upset as well. The difference is that I've had weeks to get used to it. It still hurts, but the pain's faded a little. It'll be the same for you, too. Just give it time."

"Time? There'll never be enough time. . . ."

I just hung my head. I couldn't think of anything I could say that would make him feel better.

"Bye, Jack," I said. "I'll be back soon, I promise."

Jack just shook his head, but he hadn't finished speaking yet. As I turned to leave, he let out a great choking sob and then spoke slowly, his voice full of hurt and bitterness.

"Things have never been the same since you started working as a spook's apprentice," he said. "And it started to go really wrong the first time you brought that girl, Alice, to the farm. It sickens me to see her here again today. We were happy before. Really happy. You've brought us nothing but misery!"

I went out and closed the door behind me. Jack seemed

to be somehow blaming me for everything. It wasn't the first time, but there was nothing worth saying in my defense. Why waste words when he wouldn't listen anyway? Of course, everything had just been part of Mam's scheme from the beginning, but Jack was never going to understand that. I just had to hope that he would eventually see reason. It wasn't going to be easy, and it would take a long time.

Ellie gave us some bread and cheese for the road, and we took our leave of her and James. She didn't hug me. She seemed a little cold and aloof, but she did manage to give Alice a sad smile.

The Spook was waiting with the dogs in the wood on Hangman's Hill. He had cut me a new staff while we were away.

"Here, lad, this'll have to do for now," he said, holding it out toward me. "We'll have to wait till we get back to Chipenden to get you one with a silver alloy blade, but at least it's rowan wood, and I've sharpened it to a point."

The staff had a good balance to it, and I thanked him.

Then we headed north again. After about an hour I left the Spook's side and fell back so that I could talk to Alice.

"Jack seems to blame me for everything," I told her. "But I can't deny one thing. The moment I became the Spook's apprentice marked the beginning of the end of my family."

Alice squeezed my hand. "Your mam had a plan, and she carried it through, Tom. You should be proud of her. Jack will understand in time. Besides, you're still with the Spook, still his apprentice. Soon we'll be back in Chipenden, living in his house, and I'll be copying his books again. It's not a bad life, Tom, and we still got each other. Ain't that true?"

"It is true, Alice," I said sadly. "We've still got each other."

Alice squeezed my hand again, and we walked on toward Chipenden with lighter hearts.

ONCE again, I've written most of this from memory, just using my notebook when necessary. We're back at Chipenden and into our old routine. I'm continuing to learn my trade while Alice is busy copying books from the Spook's library. The war is going badly, with enemy soldiers pressing north toward the County, looting and burning everything in their path. It's making the Spook very nervous. He's worried about the safety of his books.

Arkwright's dogs, Claw, Blood, and Bone, are being looked after temporarily by a retired shepherd who lives near the Long Ridge. We still need to sort out a permanent home for them, but I visit them occasionally and they're really glad to see me.

I keep the blood jar in my pocket, my defense against a visit from the Fiend. It's a secret I share

only with Alice, who needs it as much as I do and never ventures far from my side. If the Spook knew, he'd dash it against a rock and it would be the end of us. But I know there'll be a reckoning one day. On the day that I die, the Fiend will be waiting for me. Waiting to claim my soul. That's the price I paid for the victory at Meteora. I have only one hope, and that is to destroy him first. I don't know how I'm going to do it, but Mam had faith in me, so I try to believe that it's possible. Somehow I must find a way.

THOMAS J. WARD

The Journal of
THOMAS J. WARD

fire Elementals

Not found in the County—too wet and windy. Too near the sea. But very dangerous in Greece, because it's hot and dry in summer.

Lots of different sizes and shapes. Often take the form of glowing fiery <u>orbs.</u> Some you can see through. Others look solid. Solid ones hotter and more dangerous. Watch out! Indoors these often float close to the ceiling but can move very suddenly. Very fast. Hard to dodge. They cause severe burns. A painful death. Can turn you to ashes almost instantly.

Some bigger than a human head. But can be as small as a fingernail. Little ones try to go up your nose and sizzle your brain. Or sometimes go down the throat into stomach. Always keep your mouth closed when they attack.

At noon, usually found near rocks from which they draw heat and power. Sometimes lay in wait inside ruined buildings.

Other fire elementals are called <u>asteri.</u> Look like a starfish with five fiery radiating arms. Cling to walls and ceilings. Drop onto the heads of unsuspecting victims. Burn them to death in seconds.

The most dangerous fire elemental of all is the salamander. Looks like a big lizard and sleeps in a hot fire. This type can spit fire or scalding steam.

Hard to defend yourself against fire elementals. But Spook's staff has metal alloy blade and can cut them into pieces. But need to have quick reactions.

Water weakens fire elementals. Become dormant. Hibernate until drier. Water also offers a refuge when under attack.

Tappers

Earth elementals that live deep inside cracks in rock. Can cause tunnels to collapse. When in new or unknown tunnels, County miners scared of them. Tappers found in other countries, too.

Try to drive humans away. First the use fear—make scary rhythmical tapping sounds. But if that doesn't work, they bring down rocks to squash intruders.

In an abandoned mine, lots gather over time. Very dangerous. But even lots of them can't make a tunnel collapse unless there's an existing fault line. But if they do find a serious crack, can easily bring the roof down. Either crush or seal victims underground. Perish from lack of air or water.

Sometimes County miners know a section of tunnel is safe. Know tappers can't harm them. So they rap back the walls with their hammers. Sometimes dance in their clogs to tapper's rhythm.

The Ordeen

One of Old Gods, found in Greece. Visits our world every seven years. Other gods who use portals need the help of humans to get to our world. Ordeen doesn't. Her portal is a pillar of fire. So how does she do it? Was something done in the past to help her? Very dangerous if other gods could do the same.

Prayers of monks in Meteora monasteries have kept her confined to southern plain so far. But their power waning. Strength of Ordeen waxing. Danger increasing.

Not a lot known about her. But very bloodthirsty. Her chief worshippers in Greece are <u>maenads</u>. But brings other servants with her from the dark: demons, flying lamias, and fire elementals. Nothing known yet about demons. What type are they? Spook wants to know more so can put in his Bestiary. Her servants slaughter all in their path. Great bloodshed. People die for miles around. Very few survive to record what happens. Knowledge limited. Spook says it's a mercy that County seems far beyond her reach.

Maenads

Maenads usually stay in Greece but one tried to kill me in the County. Very scary and dangerous. Get power from wine and blood. Fly into a frenzy. Fight their enemies with wild fury. Sometimes use blades (one who attacked me in garden did) but have great strength. Can pull enemies apart with just bare hands.

Maenads slowly regressing. Emotion taking over from thought. Eventually lose the power of speech. Become like water witches—more animal than human.

Receive no reward for worship of Ordeen but still gather in great numbers to await her arrival. Once she and her servants have ravaged the land, maenads feast upon dead and dying.

Maenads not witches but do have scryers. Don't use

mirrors. Make sacrificial goat drink lots of wine. Force it down animal's throat. Then split open its belly and study its intestines. See into the future.

Abhuman Spirits

These are fallen human souls. Degenerated and now more like souls of beasts. Sometimes half human and half animal. Why? Not always certain. Could be because trapped in Limbo too long. Or maybe committed some terrible crime when alive.

Can usually persuade spirit to go to the light by asking it to focus upon a happy memory from its lifetime. Not with abhuman, spirits though. Very difficult to achieve because can't remember much of their life on earth. So don't have happy memories. Most can't be helped by a spook. Doomed to exist in torment until end of time. Nevertheless, we should always try to help them.

Sirens

Female water creatures found on Greek coast. Lounge on rocks at water's edge. Lure sailors to their deaths using siren song. Sailors become enchanted. In thrall to dark magic. Try to reach sirens. Sail their boats onto rocks. Or dive into sea and drown. Sirens feed upon flesh of the drowned.

Song makes sirens appear beautiful. But are really hideous. Huge fangs and swollen lips. Spooks have some resistance to their song. Greek sailors press wax into their ears. Can't hear song then magic doesn't work. Sail on to safety.

Lamia Witches

Two types: feral and domestic. Most ferals scuttle on all fours, have sharp claws, and drink the blood of humans. If can't find people, make do with animals, like rats. Can also summon birds to their presence. Pull off their wings so they can't fly and drink their blood slowly.

Homeland —Greece. But often found beyond that nation's boundaries. Some in the County. Worst place in Greece for them is Phindos Mountains. Very dangerous there.

Domestic ones human in appearance but green and yellow scales run the length of their spines.

Lamia witches are slow shape shifters. Those close to people gradually take on human female form. The opposite is also true. Bound in a pit, or somehow cut off from humans, a domestic lamia witch gradually goes back to her feral form.

Some feral lamias, called <u>vaengir</u>, have wings. Can fly short distances attacking victims from the air. Once thought to be rare. Now know that they come through portal with Ordeen.

FROM

THE LAST
APPRENTICE

RISE *of* THE HUNTRESS

·BOOK SEVEN·

The Spook, Alice, and I were crossing the Long Ridge on our way back to Chipenden, with the three wolf-hounds, Claw, Blood, and Bone, barking excitedly at our heels.

The first part of the climb had been pleasant enough. It had rained all afternoon but was now a clear, cloudless late autumn evening with just a slight chilly breeze ruffling our hair: perfect weather for walking. I remember thinking how peaceful it all seemed.

But at the summit, a big shock awaited us. There was dark smoke far to the north beyond the fells. It looked like

1

Caster was burning. Had the war finally reached us? I wondered fearfully.

Years earlier, an alliance of enemy nations had invaded our land far to the south. Since then, despite the best efforts of the combined counties to hold theline, they had been slowly pushing north.

"How can they have advanced so far without our knowing?" the Spook asked, scratching at his beard, clearly agitated. "Surely there'd have been news—some warning, at least?"

"It might just be a raiding party from the sea," I suggested. That was very likely. Enemy boats had come ashore before and attacked settlements along the coast—though this part of the County had been spared so far.

Shaking his head, the Spook set off down the hill at a furious pace. Alice gave me a worried smile, and we hurried along in pursuit. Encumbered by my staff and both our bags, I was struggling to keep up on the slippery, wet grass. But I knew what was bothering my master. He was anxious about his library. Looting and burning had been reported in the south, and he was worried about the safety of his books, a store of knowledge accumulated by generations of spooks.

I was now in the third year of my apprenticeship to the Spook, learning how to deal with ghosts, ghasts, witches, boggarts, and all manner of creatures from the dark. My master gave me lessons most days, but my other source of knowledge was that library. It was certainly very important.

Once we reached level ground, we headed directly toward Chipenden, the hills to the north looming larger with every stride. We'd just forded a small river, picking our way across the stones, the water splashing around our ankles, when Alice pointed ahead.

"Enemy soldiers!" she cried.

In the distance, a group of men was heading east across our path—two dozen or more, the swords at their belts glinting brightly in the light from the setting sun, which was now very low on the horizon. We halted and crouched low on the riverbank, hoping that they hadn't seen us.

I told the dogs to lie down and be quiet; they obeyed instantly.

The soldiers wore gray uniforms and steel helms with broad, vertical nose guards of a type I hadn't seen before. Alice was right. It was a large enemy patrol. Unfortunately, they saw us almost immediately. One of them pointed and barked out an order, and a small group peeled off and began running toward us.

"This way!" cried the Spook, and snatching up his bag to relieve me of the extra weight, he took off, following the river upstream; Alice and I followed with the dogs.

There was a large wood directly ahead. Maybe there was a chance we could lose them there, I thought. But as soon as we reached the tree line, my hopes were dashed. It had been coppiced recently: there were no saplings, no thickets—just well-spaced mature trees. This was no hiding place.

I glanced back. Our pursuers were now spread out in a ragged line. The majority weren't making much headway, but there was one soldier in the lead who was definitely gaining on us. He was brandishing his sword threateningly.

Next thing I knew, the Spook was coming to a halt. He threw down his bag at my feet. "Keep going, lad! I'll deal with him," he commanded, turning back to face the soldier.

I called the dogs to heel and stopped, frowning. I couldn't leave my master like that. I picked up his bag again and readied my staff. If necessary, I would go to his aid and take the dogs with me; they were big, fierce wolfhounds, completely without fear.

I looked back at Alice. She'd stopped, too, and was staring at me with a strange expression on her face. She seemed to be muttering to herself.

The breeze died away very suddenly, and the chill was like a blade of ice cutting into my face. All was suddenly silent, as if every living thing in the wood were holding its breath. Tendrils of mist snaked out of the trees toward us, approaching from all directions. I looked at Alice again. There had been no warning of this change in the weather. It didn't seem natural. Was it dark magic? I wondered. The dogs crouched down on their bellies and whined softly.

Even if it was intended to help us, my master would be angry if Alice used dark magic. She'd spent two years training to be a witch, and he was always wary of her turning back toward the dark.

By now the Spook had taken up a defensive position, his staff held diagonally. The soldier reached him and slashed downward with his sword. My heart was in my mouth, but I needn't have feared. There was a cry of pain—but it came from the soldier, not my master. The sword went spinning into the grass, and then the Spook delivered a hard blow to his assailant's temple to bring him to his knees.

The mist was closing in fast, and for a few moments my master was lost to view. Then I heard him running toward us. Once he reached us, we hurried on, following the river, the fog becoming denser with every stride. We soon left the wood and the river behind and followed a thick hawthorn hedge north for a few hundred yards until the Spook waved us to a halt. We crouched in a ditch, hunkering down with the dogs, holding our breath and listening for danger. At first there were no sounds of pursuit, but then we heard voices to the north and east. They were still searching for us—though the light was beginning to fail, and with each minute that passed it became less likely that we'd be discovered.

But just when we thought we were safe, the voices from the north grew louder, and soon we heard footsteps getting nearer and nearer. It seemed likely that they would blunder straight into our hiding place, and my master and I gripped our staffs, ready to fight for our lives.

The searchers passed no more than a couple of yards to our right—we could just make out the dim shapes of three men. But we were crouched low in the ditch, and they didn't see us. When the footsteps and voices had faded away, the Spook shook his head.

"Don't know how many they've got hunting for us," he whispered, "but they seem determined to find us. Best if we stay here for the rest of the night."

And so we settled down to spend a cold, uncomfortable night in the ditch. I slept fitfully but, as often happens in these situations, fell into a deep slumber only when it was almost time to get up. I was awakened by Alice shaking my shoulder.

I sat up quickly, staring about me. The sun had already risen, and I could see gray clouds racing overhead. The wind was whistling through the hedge, bending and flexing the spindly leafless branches. "Is everything all right?" I asked.

Alice smiled and nodded. "There's nobody less than a mile or so away. Those soldier boys have given up and gone."

Then I heard a noise nearby—a sort of groaning. It was the Spook.

"Sounds like he's having a bad dream," Alice said.

"Perhaps we should wake him up?" I suggested.

"Leave him for a few minutes. It's best if he comes out of it by himself."

But, if anything, his cries and moans grew louder and his body started to shake; he was becoming more and more agitated, so after another minute I shook him gently by the shoulder to wake him.

"Are you all right, Mr Gregory?" I asked. "You seemed to be having some kind of nightmare."

For a moment his eyes were wild, and he looked at me as if I were a stranger or even an enemy. "Aye, it was a nightmare, all right," he said at last. "It was about Bony Lizzie. . . ."

Bony Lizzie was Alice's mother, a powerful witch who was now bound in a pit in the Spook's garden at Chipenden.

"She was sat on a throne," continued my master, "and the Fiend was standing at her side with his hand on her left shoulder. They were in a big hall that I didn't recognize at first. The floor was running red with blood. Prisoners were crying out in terror before being executed—they were cutting off their heads. But it was the hall that really bothered me and set my nerves on edge."

"Where was it?" I asked.

The Spook shook his head. "She was in the great hall at Caster Castle! She was the ruler of the County."

"It was just a nightmare," I said. "Lizzie's safely bound."

9

"Perhaps," said the Spook. "But I don't think I've ever had a dream that was more vivid."

We set off cautiously toward Chipenden. The Spook said nothing about the sudden mist that had arisen the previous night. It was the season for them, after all, and he had been busy preparing to fight the soldier at the time. But I was sure that it had appeared at Alice's bidding. Though who was I to say anything? I was tainted by the dark myself.

We'd only recently returned from Greece after defeating the Ordeen, one of the Old Gods. It had cost us dear. My mam had died to gain our victory, and so had Bill Arkwright, the spook who'd worked north of Caster— that's why we had his dogs with us.

I'd also paid a terrible price. In order to make that victory possible, I'd sold my own soul to the Fiend.

All that prevented him from dragging me off to the dark now was the blood jar given to me by Alice, which I carried in my pocket. The Fiend couldn't approach me while I had it by me. Alice needed to stay close to me to share its protection—otherwise, the Fiend would kill her in revenge for the help she'd given me. Of course, the Spook didn't know about that. If I told him what I'd done, it would be the end of my apprenticeship.

As we climbed the slope toward Chipenden, my master grew more and more anxious. We'd seen pockets of devastation: some burned-out houses, many that were deserted, one with a corpse in a nearby ditch.

"I'd hoped they wouldn't have come so far inland. I dread to think what we'll find, lad," he said grimly.

Normally he would have avoided walking through Chipenden village: most people didn't like being too close to a spook, and he respected the wishes of the locals. But as the gray slate roofs came into view, one glance was enough to tell us that something was terribly wrong.

It was clear that enemy soldiers had passed this way. Many of the roofs were badly damaged, with charred beams exposed to the air. The closer we got, the worse it was. Almost a third of the houses were completely burned out, their blackened stones just shells of what had once been homes to local families. Those that hadn't gone up in flames had broken windows and splintered doors hanging from their hinges, with evidence of looting.

The village seemed completely abandoned, but then we heard the sound of banging. Someone was hammering. Quickly the Spook led us through the cobbled streets toward the sound. We were heading for the main road through the village, where the shops were. We passed the greengrocer's and the baker's, both ransacked, and headed for the butcher's shop, which seemed to be the source of the noise.

The butcher was still there, his red beard glinting in the morning light, but he wasn't carrying out repairs to his premises; he was nailing down the lid of a coffin. There were three other coffins lined up close by, already sealed and ready for burial. One was small and obviously contained a young child. The butcher got to his feet as we entered the yard and came across to shake the Spook's hand. He was the one real contact my master had among the villagers, the only person he ever talked to about things other than spook's business.

"It's terrible, Mr Gregory," the butcher said. "Things can never be the same again."

"I hope it's not . . ." the Spook muttered, glancing down at the coffins.

"Oh, no, thank the Lord for that at least," the butcher told him. "It happened three days ago. I got my own family away to safety just in time. No, these poor folk weren't quick enough. They killed everybody they could find. It was just an enemy patrol, but a very large one. They were out foraging for supplies. There was no need to burn houses and kill people, no cause to murder this family. Why did they do that? They could just have taken what they wanted and left."

The Spook nodded. I knew what his answer was to that, although he didn't spell it out to the butcher. He would have said it was because the Fiend was now loose in the world. He made people more cruel, wars more savage.

"I'm sorry about your house, Mr. Gregory," the butcher continued.

The color drained from the Spook's face. "What?" he demanded.

"Oh, I'm really sorry. Don't you know? I assumed you'd called back there already. We heard the boggart howling and roaring from miles away. There must have been too many for it to deal with. They ransacked your house, taking anything they could carry, then set fire to it."